About the Editor

PETER WILD is the coauthor of *Before the Rain,* and the editor of *Perverted by Language: Fiction Inspired by The Fall* and *The Flash.* His fiction has appeared in numerous journals, e-zines, anthologies, and magazines, including *Dogmatika, 3:AM Magazine, NOÖ Journal, SNReview, Word Riot, Straight from the Fridge, Thieves Jargon, Pindel-dyboz, Pen Pusher, Scarecrow, The Beat, Litro,* and *Dreams That Money Can Buy.* He also runs the literary blog Bookmunch.wordpress.com. He lives in Manchester with his wife and three children.

Please

Please

Fiction Inspired by The Smiths

Edited by Peter Wild

HARPER ● PERENNIAL

NEW YORK ● LONDON ● TORONTO ● SYDNEY ● NEW DELHI ● AUCKLAND

HARPER ● PERENNIAL

Originally published in the United Kingdom in 2009 under the title *Paint a Vulgar Picture* by Serpent's Tail, an imprint of Profile Books Ltd.

HarperCollins books may be purchased for educational, business, or sales promotional use. For information please write: Special Markets Department, HarperCollins Publishers, 10 East 53rd Street, New York, NY 10022.

Designed by Folio at Neuadd Bwll, Llanwrtyd Wells

Library of Congress Cataloging-in-Publication Data is available upon request.

ISBN 978-0-06-166930-9

10 11 12 13 14   OFF/RRD   10 9 8 7 6 5 4 3 2 1

For Weez

Contents

Is It Really So Strange?

An Introduction

OK, yes. I admit it. Part of what drew me, and undoubtedly countless others, to The Smiths was the fact that *they seemed to get it*. They seemed to get how difficult and unfair and just downright unpleasant and nasty it was growing up (in Manchester or anywhere) in the 19-haties. They seemed to get it because they seemed to be living it alongside us; or maybe they had lived it alongside us but now they'd escalated into the realm of gods. Later, much later, when the decade was on the change, The Stone Roses told us they wanted to be adored – The Smiths never had to demand that fealty. They knew they had it. They could see it in the glassy-eyed, occasionally tear-stained mugs of the faithful. *Man but these kids love us*, Johnny Marr might have said once a long time ago.

What was it they had? What was it that made them so special and so singular? Was it the fact that – no matter how far they encroached into the world of *Top of the Pops* – they always felt like a secret? Was it the fact that no matter how many people 'got into them', they always felt like yours and yours alone (because – *ah!* – Morrissey was singing to you, yes, *you*, just you, *dear heart*). It's impossible, really, to count all of the ways in which The Smiths stood out from the crowd. But here goes anyway: if you'd had your heart broken, if you thought you loved someone and she wouldn't give you the time of day, if you had a thing with someone and it didn't work out, if you bumbled, felt crap, thought that the person staring back at you out of the mirror more closely resembled a gargoyle than the person you thought you were – you know – *inside*... if you were a teenager, basically, the argot of The Smiths was the articulation of your every inadequacy. But if they were just a band for teenagers, they would've dated as quickly as the New Kids. Surely? So what else? Well, The Smiths weren't *literature* – although Morrissey's literate sensibility helped elevate the songs to a wholly different level, that much is true – they were a band. And bands live and die on their tunes. It was the beef and the muscle supplied by Morrissey's gang, Marr, Rourke, Joyce (with Gannon loitering in the shadows wielding a bicycle chain, maybe), that gave Morrissey the confidence to be who he was on stage and in between the lines of every song.

The Smiths weren't literature, but they were steeped in literature. Oscar Wilde, Joe Orton, Shelagh Delaney, James Joyce, Alan Sillitoe, Charlotte Brontë, Alan Bennett, Rita Mae Brown, Truman Capote, George Eliot, Dorothy Parker, Sylvia Plath, Marcel Proust, Hubert Selby Jr, Edith Sitwell, Elizabeth Smart... all these and dozens of others have been mentioned by Morrissey over the years. Reader, the man is a reader!

That's all well and good, you might say. But what about *Paint a Vulgar Picture: Fiction inspired by The Smiths*? That doesn't explain the whole idea of fiction inspired by a band, does it? What does that even mean? Fiction *inspired by* whomever... Well, what it means is this: some writers are inspired by a snatch of conversation overheard on a bus (that was certainly true of, say, Joe Orton); others find an image appears in their mind, some hard, frozen picture that itches and urges and requires articulation (I remember reading an interview with Michael Ondaatje years and years ago where he said that *The English Patient* started out as the image of a woman hanging washing on a washing line – the novel unspooled from there); still others frame their inspirations about what if's and what was's and what will never be's. Inspiration strikes in many forms. It can be a tree. It can be a photograph. It can be 'emotion recollected in tranquillity'. The writers in this collection have been inspired, in some way, and to a greater or lesser extent, by the music of The Smiths. Some of them have taken the song title and run with it. Others have been inspired by something conjured up by the lyrics. Still others have found the music or even the very mystique of The Smiths the thing that lights the blue touchpaper of their imaginations.

What fiction inspired by a band doesn't mean: fiction *about* a band. These stories are not stories about The Smiths. This is not – to use a seemingly popular pejorative – fan fiction. Although a great many of the writers in this book would, I think, say they are big, big fans of The Smiths. What fiction inspired by a band means – and apologies if I'm spelling it out in letters fourteen metres high with the paint still wet – is fiction for which music is the starting point. No more, no less. Which isn't to say that The Smiths are not explicitly referenced: John Williams's 'The Boy with the Thorn in His Side' is a sort of memoir about a Smiths fan John knew back in the day; Chris Killen's 'Stretch Out and Wait' revolves around an imagined visit to Morrissey's grave. The presence of The Smiths can be more keenly seen, though, in the many implicit ways writers have chosen to interpret the source material. In her preamble, for instance, Rhonda Carrier says, 'I tried to evoke... an overall Smithsian mood (fatalistic miserablism meets intense yearning).' For James Flint, it's a 'mixture of resignation and optimism'. For some, The Smiths were always funny – dark and strange, yes, but always amusing. For others, The Smiths were dangerous, political, taboo-busting. Charlie Williams says The Smiths hit him like 'a call to arms'.

All of the writers in the book would, I'm sure, agree that The Smiths were important – and not just because they have become, as that once great institution *NME* had it a few years ago, 'the most influential band ever'. In fact, certainly for the fans who were there (man), at the time, the importance of The Smiths is prefigured by the wilderness in which they appeared: the mainstream was trapped in a seemingly endless cycle of bad hair, bad clothes and bad music. Liking The Smiths was, at times, tantamount to sticking a piece of paper on your own back that read: please beat me. Especially if you also (ahem) looked a little bit like Morrissey. Or *tried* to look a little bit like Morrissey. Back then, The Smiths were as divisive as it got. You either loved them, with every trembling fibre of your weak and puny body, or you hated them and all they stood for ('being fey', 'reading books', all that noncey stuff). It's funny, these days, looking around the average Morrissey gig – all the bruisers you get, all the lads, 'avin' it large down the ol' Morrissey gig. Who's getting beaten these days? Certainly not the Morrissey fans. That particular cloud of disaffection seems to have shifted in Emo's direction... Poor Emo.

But we were talking about The Smiths. The most important and emotionally urgent band of my adolescence – a band whose songs stand endless listens, a band that haven't dated, whose best work stands alongside the best work of anyone, who were important and (at the time) neglected and (for a bit) punished just for being a little bit different. Lord love 'em. A band, furthermore, who celebrated books and reading – what was it Morrissey sang? 'There's more to life than books, you know, but not much more' – in a way that no band has before or, to my mind, since. When you think about it, it's amazing that it's taken this long for a book of fiction inspired by that most literary of bands to arrive. Is it really so strange? We don't think so...

Peter Wild
Manchester

Ask

Gina Ochsner

I'm fascinated by the endless possibilities each of our lives represent. Each day is a door full of yeses or noes. Each choice leads to another corridor opening to another series of doors, a labyrinth of more yeses, more noes. I sometimes wonder what would have happened if my father had not asked my mother out on that first date. What would have happened if my husband had not overcome his shyness to ask a girlfriend for my telephone number? What would have happened if I had not overcome my preternatural shyness and not said yes?

One day a girl, utterly unremarkable in every way, sees a boy she recognises from her high school. He's standing in the frozen food aisle at the neighbourhood grocery store. The long muscles in his arms, that little down of fuzz over his lip, and the smell of grass and sweat on his skin indicate that he's going turn into a man any day, a phenomenon he has anxiously awaited – though he doesn't quite know why. The girl loops a plastic shopping basket over an arm and walks toward the boy, who is contemplating a series of frozen burritos.

She touches the point of his elbow and says, 'You don't know me, but you should because you are 100% perfect for me.'

The boy blinks and his face colours slightly. No one has ever told this boy that he was anything but imperfect and the unexpected compliment sounds so foreign in his ears that he stands there as if frozen. He watches the girl round the end of the aisle. He can tell from the way she slouches toward the Entemann's pound cake, and from the day-glo green sweater exhaling the smell of mothballs and unravelling at the cuffs, that she is absolutely ordinary, and for some reason, he likes this about her.

The boy continues to shop at that supermarket, loitering in the frozen food aisle, hoping for another chance encounter. As luck or fate would have it, or more likely because the girl knows the boy is the one for her, she too makes a point of shopping in the frozen food aisle. Before long, they have an established pattern of rendezvous in the freezer section of the store. Sometimes their timing is off, but each of them knows that the other has been there because inside the sliding glass doors of the cut corn, French cut beans, snap green and petite peas, traced in the hoar frost on each of the glass panes, is the figure 100%.

Soon, the boy and girl are in love, each of them sure that the other is 100% right for them. For a time everything is as it should be when you have found the 100% perfect person: the sun warms the street under your feet, and the ordinary cacophony of morning birds cartwheels in tune, the air turns more tolerant and it seems that nothing can go wrong, and if something does, with a wink it is easily dismissed.

But the boy, having slowly become a man, is still youngish in his ways. So too with the girl, who is now by all appearances a woman. They graduate from high school and, after a whole summer of freezer food love, they become restless, wondering whether there aren't more perfect loves out there waiting for them. After an exchange of forwarding addresses, they part, each of them 100% convinced that should their expectations in others fail, they will certainly find one another again someday.

The man travels. Vagabonds. In no time he meets beautiful and interesting women from all over the world. He dates many of them, falls in love with several, and almost marries one. And while he doesn't regret falling in love, none of these women seem 100% perfectly right for him. He suspects that these women know, too, that he isn't the one for them, either. And when he says goodbye to these women, or they to him, he is sad, but not broken hearted. For some reason, he even feels grateful to have loved and been let out of it so easily. As he flies in airplanes, rides on slow boats down winding rivers, climbs mountains of dizzying heights, he begins to wonder whether the idea of 100% perfect isn't little more than an imperfect myth. He begins to wonder whether the perfect girl for him isn't little more than an assortment of all the perfect parts of all the imperfect girls he's met. And then he remembers a girl from his old neighbourhood grocery store. He can recall her only in fragments: her slouching walk, her love of Klondike bars and the smell of her mothball-riddled sweater, the feel of her hands in his, the way her eyes disappeared entirely when she smiled. And in place of her name, he thinks: 100%.

The girl, too, has had her adventures. Her heart bent, bruised, and twice broken. She tells herself these are the risks of modern romance and that love would be simpler if reduced to numbers. She buys many copies of Euclid's *Geometry*, which are no help at all. After another serious heartbreak, she becomes the kind of girl who harbours grudges against those who have hurt her, never considering the harm she herself might have done. Days collide with months. She stores her tears in an old pot she keeps under the stove. Eventually the sharp desire for love encourages a reckless but forgiving myopia. She buys a new pair of glasses and in time the hatch-mark scars of her heart diminish. She calls it healing, and marries the man who doesn't say no.

And then one day she shops in her old neighbourhood, at that very same grocery store she used to visit all those years ago when she was a girl in love. While checking the nutritional value of frozen snow peas she is arrested by the sight of a man. Her hands flutter to the handles of the freezer doors, and her fingers – remembering something from a lifetime ago – trace a figure. The girl squints fiercely at the man. There is something very familiar about him and she scrolls through her mental list of previous lovers: 37%, 50%, 2% – and she's being generous with that figure – and the one she married, 87%, but none of those men match the one standing there at the end of the aisle, carrying a stack of frozen pizzas in his arms. She squints even harder behind her new glasses, but still, she can't recall things with the same clarity she used to have; she doesn't have the same faculties of her youth and her memories are like trampled mud, each new day full of new prints that reshape the old. But where her memory fails, her muscles remember. Her hand jogs the point of his elbow. The pizzas drop and the man falters, stumbles into an open freezer bin of turkeys.

The man blinks, feels his heart quicken. Here's the crazy thing: when he stands and brushes himself off he sees a figure of a number carefully drawn in the condensation of each of the sliding freezer doors: 100% – a number he knows should mean something to him, would solve every puzzle if only he knew what it meant. For now, all he can do is stare at the woman before him. There's that awkward pause, the heavy silence under which entire islands of forgotten languages might shoulder to the surface, but don't.

And then the glimmer passes; the spell is broken. They share a quick laugh. The woman apologises profusely and the man assures her that he likes turkeys and that no harm has been done. As he speaks, the woman relegates the man to her long-established categories: a nice-looking, polite fellow whom she will remember later as possessing an earnestness that suggests a grave belief in second chances. They part then – he more determined to find his 100% perfect girl, she more desperate to make her husband a little more perfect.

And so it goes. And so it goes, the story spilling past clumsy borders. The end becomes another beginning. It's a long walk home. A tug on the woman's sweater leads through foggy recollection, fuzzy intentions. Though she's married – happily so – she's finding it hard to brush away notions of previous lives she might have had with previous loves. She is wearied by her dimmed desires and this package of frozen snow peas, which feels for all the world to her like a heavy bag of stones. Having eaten the warm bread of doughy fairy tales, the moral fibre of which she counted on to buoy her through the hard years, she's finding it difficult to keep her feet planted deep in the ordinary soil of her days. But somehow she knows it's unfair to hold her husband to that standard: 100%.

She arrives home and sees her husband bent over an ancient typewriter, the keys and strikers of which he is realigning for her because he knows his wife loves that beat-up old thing. He is doing it, she realises with a series of blinks behind her glasses, because he loves her. With a final blink she forgets about the man she sent sprawling in the grocery store. She thinks instead about this beautiful perfect gesture made for her for the purest of reasons. In that pot where she had stored her tears, she heats the remaining peas. The salt makes for flavour and she is glad something good at last has come of her foolish sorrow, glad to serve it up and give it away. But even in this she has her faults. As she sets the table for their supper she can't help herself:

'You're not perfect,' she says, but not unkindly. 'Not 100%.'

'I know,' he says.

She peers at the pot and wags her head slowly. 'I'm not 100% either.' She's burned a few of the peas, but they both know that's not what she's talking about.

'I love you anyway,' he says – the perfect and only thing he can say.

And, as she sits there, the green sleeve of her sweater still unreeving, she is schooled in an old lesson she had long ago forgotten: how it is with such simple words love finds us, finds us in spite of our calculations and unswerving devotion to childhood myths. Finds us and splits us wide open along our fault lines. Finds us and asks us to make allowances for those faults and failings, unsmoothed edges, to find beauty in the imperfection and call it love.

This Charming Man

Mike Gayle

Relatively speaking, I was late to the Smiths. Most people had been into them for years by the time I purchased the tape of Hatful of Hollow *from Woolworths in Bearwood in Smethwick back in 1987 at the age of sixteen. A few months later they split up. The two events were not connected. Question is why did I buy* Hatful *over the other album I really wanted at the time (*Whitney Houston *by Whitney Houston)? The answer, of course, is because as undoubtedly great as 'The Greatest Love of All' was, 'This Charming Man' completely knocked the spots off it.*

The launch party for my debut novel *This Charming Man* is being held on the top-floor bar at Soho House. I arrived at just after 7 p.m. with Ashley and, when I gave my name at the reception, the girl behind the desk gave me a little smile of recognition and said, 'So you're *the* Keith Richards.' How am I supposed to answer a question like that? In *my* head I wasn't *the* Keith Richards. I was just plain and simple old Keith Richards (albeit a plain and simple Keith Richards wearing a very expensive black Kenzo suit and a matching shirt that I'd bought from the Bond Street branch of Gucci only three hours earlier). In the end I decide the best thing to do with a question like that is just to smile awkwardly and give the impression that I'm acutely embarrassed, which was easy as that was exactly how I felt.

'This is too weird even for me,' says Ashley, my hot new publishing girlfriend, as we walk hand in hand up the stairs towards the top bar. 'You do realise that you're famous?'

'I'm not famous. I think *notorious* would be the better word. It's not genuine fame. It's more like being flavour of the month.'

'Well, flavour of the month or not, I think you should brace yourself for a few ladies trying it on with you tonight.'

It hadn't actually occurred to me that any of what had happened would make the slightest difference to how women saw me. It hadn't made the slightest difference to the women who frequented The Griffin or The Cross Keys; it had made no difference to any of the women at my local gym; and it certainly hadn't made any difference to the women on the check-out at my local supermarket. But it does make a lot of difference here in the media world – a world that right now I pretty much own. I pause for a moment and ask myself the question we all ask ourselves sometimes: do I have any regrets?

How I got here is a long story. It started on a Monday morning. Just before ten. Standing in front of me were Mr Blake and Ms Fowler, a couple in their late teens, and their sixth-month-old baby girl, Kayla. They were really nice kids and, as usual, we were doing our utmost to make their already miserable lives just that little bit more miserable. They wanted to know when their new bathroom was going to be installed as apparently they'd been promised it would happen four months ago and they had been waiting patiently ever since. I asked them what was wrong with the old bathroom but it would've been quicker to have asked what was right with the old bathroom, to which they could've answered succinctly: nothing. Everything was cracked or leaked, cold water taps had no pressure, the hot water tap on the sink dripped continually and the toilet could only be flushed if Mr Blake took the lid off the toilet cistern and pushed down the ball cock mechanism with his hand. I promised them that I would call up Maintenance again and also flag up their case on the computer screen as being 'Very Important'. Mrs Olsen, who was next in line, provided my morning with a brief moment of light relief. She wanted to know whether it was possible to get someone to change the batteries in her front doorbell again because she couldn't reach the box and still wasn't allowed to stand on a chair in order to do so in case she had a funny turn again. Last time she told me this story, rather than bother Maintenance (who would never have gone anyway) I popped round to her flat myself and changed the batteries for her. As a thank-you for a job well done, she made me a cup of tea with milk that had long since soured and showed me photos of her family.

It was pretty much the same all morning. Hopeless cases followed by more hopeless cases and, all the while, there was me suffering from a constant feeling that I wasn't part of the problem or the solution... I was just there breathing air, shedding skin... wasting space. It occurred to me while I was dealing with my next client, Mrs Anifowose, that what really needed to happen to the housing association in order for us to stop letting people down was for the entire building to be blown up along with everyone in it, including myself. Only then, I concluded as Mrs Anifowose drew her kitchen cockroach infestation story to a close, would the people in power begin to listen. In the meantime, I took down all of Mrs Anifowose's details and promised her that I would do all I could to sort out the problem.

Then the phone behind me rang and everything changed.

I picked up the phone. 'Starlight Housing Association.'

'I'd like to speak to...' The speaker paused. They all do when they say my name. '... Mr Keith Richards.'

It was the bank. It had to be. I'd been well over my overdraft limit for months now and had been expecting this call for some time.

'I'm afraid Keith's not been in for a while,' I said. 'I think he's been a bit ill. Not very well at all. It could be touch and go, so I hear.'

'Really?'

'Yes, really.'

'And you say he's been off for a while?'

'Months.'

'Oh.'

'Well, if that's—'

'—just that Keith sent me his novel and—'

'—what did you say your name was?' I knew who it was. I couldn't believe it. But I knew.

'Christian. Christian Kennedy from JPA.'

'Mr Kennedy. It's me. I'm Keith. Keith Richards. It's me.'

'But—'

'It's a long story.'

Christian laughed. 'Well, I can guarantee that you won't have to worry about *that* any more. Because I've just finished reading *This Charming Man*. And I love it.'

'You love it?'

'Yes, I love it. Every single word of it.'

'You love every single word of it?'

'All of them.'

'This isn't making any sense to me.'

'I'm telling you that I think your book is the best thing I have read all year. It's funny. It's got pace. It works on all kinds of different levels. In short, it's going to be a hit.' He paused. 'Here's the plan. You come to the office. I'll take you for a drink. Have you been to the Groucho?'

'No.'

'Excellent. I'll take you there, then. We'll have a few drinks, sign the necessary paperwork and then talk over the changes that need to be made to the manuscript before we can send it out to publishers.'

'I thought you said it was perfect?'

'It is.'

'So what about the tweaks?'

'Just making the perfect even more perfect.'

There was a long silence.

'Also we need to talk about film rights.'

'Film rights?'

'To *This Charming Man*. The film department is looking at the manuscript as we speak. I've told them that I think it's an absolute winner so, fingers crossed, we could possibly be looking at an option from a producer or a studio by the middle of next week. Have you thought about casting yet?'

'For the film? Are you joking?'

Christian laughed. 'OK, we may be getting a little ahead of ourselves here. But, even so, I was thinking it would make a great little Brit flick in the hands of those guys that made *How Soon Is Now*.'

'Working Title.'

'Yeah. Those guys. I was thinking maybe someone cool like Ewan McGregor as the hero Danny, then maybe Minnie Driver as the love interest Kate and Jonny Lee Miller as the best friend Adam.'

'You're kidding.'

Christian laughed. It sounded sinister. 'One thing you should know about me, Keith, is this: I never kid around about anything.' He laughed again. It was even more sinister than before. 'So, do you want to sign on the dotted line?'

I wanted to say now. Right now. I will sign anything you say right now. But I knew I couldn't. Because I knew I had a problem. A big problem. A huge problem. I needed to check things over with my girlfriend.

Becky threw down my manuscript on the bed. 'There's no way you can publish this.'

'So, it's as bad as I think it is?'

Becky nodded. 'You didn't even do it very well. Jason in the book is quite clearly Tim. At one point you describe him as being "the tightest man in Britain".'

I couldn't help but laugh. 'But Tim *is* the tightest man in Britain.'

'But it doesn't stop there. You go on about the fact that he's got a bad breath problem and how his girlfriend always bosses him about.'

'Which is all true.'

'But it's really unflattering.'

'But he knows that I'm his mate, doesn't he?'

'Let's move on to your character "Leon",' said Becky without looking at me. 'It's Jakey, isn't it? Do you think that Jakey will mind you referring to him as "an ugly bird magnet" or pointing out that Sarah, his girlfriend, is so ugly she 'makes small children cry".'

'It was meant to be funny.'

'Well, let's not stop there when we have so much farther to go. Next up your character "Mike", who is quite clearly Graham. In the book you describe him as being so dull "that even his parents cross the road to avoid speaking to him…" Then there's "Marco", who you cunningly made half Italian in the book so that people wouldn't realise it's Alan, who is half Portuguese.' Becky shook her head in disbelief. 'You even gave him a job in computing. Alan works in computing!' This time it was my turn to shake my head in disbelief. I couldn't quite believe that I had been so crass as to do this to my friends. At the time it made sense to use them as templates but now it didn't seem quite so clever. 'You describe Alan as being on a seafood diet – "He sees food and he has to eat it." Not only is that the oldest joke in the book but you're telling the world that Alan has a weight problem.'

'This is terrible,' I said, wincing. 'You're right. I've made a huge mistake.'

'Yes you have,' replied Becky, 'but before I get to the worst bit you do manage to redeem yourself with the character "Kate", who works as a dentist in Manchester. You describe her as being "too beautiful for words", and point out that the hero "Danny" who works for the Heartlands Housing Association doesn't deserve to have such a wonderful girlfriend.' Becky paused. 'Saying all of that, I was surprised to hear that "Danny" had a crush on "Christina", a barmaid in his local pub.'

'That bit's completely made up,' I replied quickly. 'There is no Christina.'

'I know,' said Becky. 'You wouldn't be in one piece if I thought there was.'

'Well, there isn't, OK?'

'OK,' she replied. 'But now I'm getting to the worst bit. Your book's big finale—'

'—I know what you're going to say.'

'Well, if you know what *I'm* going to say didn't you think for a moment what Phil and Liam – or should I say "Adam" and "Jason"? – would say when *they* read it? And, of course, let's not forget the really important person in this triangle: "Stephanie", aka Steph, aka Liam's fiancé.'

'I know,' I replied, not looking at her.

'You keep saying "I know", Keith, but if you really *did* know then you wouldn't have done this, would you? It's not going to take a genius for Liam to work out who's who. And when he *does* he's going to know that Phil had an affair with his girlfriend when we all went to Amsterdam for your thirtieth.'

'But that was made up,' I lied.

'Don't lie,' said Becky. 'It's so obviously *not* made up. It all makes perfect sense now. Phil was in a funny mood all that weekend and Steph wasn't herself at all and, ever since, they've barely said two words to each other. Which is weird because they used to talk all the time.'

Becky was right. It *was* all true. We'd all gone to Amsterdam to celebrate my birthday and stayed in a posh hotel not far from the station. Most of the weekend had been taken up with eating out, seeing the sights, visiting museums and going out in the evening. As far as I was concerned all that had happened was we'd all had a great time – yes, Phil had been a bit moody but I'd barely seen him speak to Steph that weekend, let alone anyone else. The evening after we got back, Phil and I went for a drink at the Cross Keys on our own. I could tell he wasn't himself and, as his dad had been quite ill of late, I thought he might want to talk about that. So, I asked him straight out whether he was OK. He said no and so I asked, 'Is it your dad?' and he said quietly: 'No. The problem is I slept with Steph.' It turned out that, unbeknown to any of us, Phil and Steph had had some sort of flirting thing going on between them and, in Amsterdam, things had gone too far. On the Saturday afternoon, Phil had claimed that he was feeling tired and so had gone back to the hotel. Steph, meanwhile, had told Sarah and Becky that she wanted to do some shopping on her own. With their cover stories straight, they met up in Phil's room where it all happened. Phil was really upset when he told me. He added he regretted it more than anything he'd ever done, especially as he loved not only Liam but all of us like brothers. He asked me what he should do. Whether he should come clean or keep it to himself. 'What's done is done,' I said. 'Just make sure it doesn't happen again.'

'It wasn't really an affair,' I said, trying to explain to Becky. 'It was more of a fling and—'

'—Do you really think that is going to make the slightest difference to Liam?' snapped Becky. 'Or, for that matter, Phil? If you publish this book, it's all guaranteed to kick off like it does in the book. There's no way that Liam will ever talk to either you or Phil again. And, once it's all out there, Phil will be so angry with you, I'm not sure he'll ever forgive you. You were the only person he told about what happened with him and Steph.'

I found myself about to utter the words 'I know', but managed to stop myself before the words left my lips.

'What were you thinking?' asked Becky. 'I know how much you care about your mates. I don't understand why you'd do something like this.'

'I don't know either,' I replied. 'The best I can come up with was that I wasn't really thinking at all. I was sort of on autopilot. When Christian rejected *Bengali in Platforms*, he said it was because he didn't believe in the characters. I think I must have taken that comment to heart. All the novels I started after that were terrible. Which was why I never finished them. I could see what he was saying. I really *was* terrible with character. So then, when Amsterdam happened, I just got this idea in my head to use it as the basis for a story. I never thought I'd get any farther than a few chapters but, when it started to flow, I just knew that I finally had the right story...' I paused and thought for a moment. 'I believed in all the characters and the situations they were in... because I suppose it was about us… well… me… and my mates and the things that were going on in our lives.'

'But that's because they *were* things that were going on in your life.' She paused and handed me back the manuscript. 'There's no way you can let your agent sell this book. You'll just have to call him up and tell him that he won't be able to send the manuscript out for a while because you've got to make a few changes.'

'I can't do that,' I replied.

'Why not?'

'Because he loves the book as it is. He wants me to make some changes but they'll be his changes not mine. I know what he's like.'

'Don't you understand what's at stake here?' asked Becky.

'I know, but…'

'There you go with that "I know" stuff again. There's no point in knowing anything at all if you're not going to do anything with the information.'

There was a long pause.

'Do you think I'm going to go to hell for this?'

Becky rubbed her eyes and stretched out her arms. 'Probably.'

'I'll call Christian first thing in the morning and tell him I need to make some changes.'

'No,' said Christian. 'Absolutely not. Every writer's first novel is based on their friends. It's just a fact of life. You'll move on and develop your craft in Book Two.'

'What if they read it?'

'They'll be flattered.'

'But the portrayals aren't exactly flattering for some of them.'

Christian sighed. 'This happens all the time. I had one of my authors base his whole novel on his relationship with his ex-girlfriend. It wasn't a flattering portrayal at all. He used real events with an added twist here and there but it was all pretty much as it happened. Do you know what happened to my author?'

'No,' I replied.

'Nothing,' said Christian. 'Nothing happened to him. His ex whined for a while about how she was going to take legal advice and then it all went quiet until last week I received her manuscript in the post. She's written a novel about her side of the story and I've got quite a few people interested in it – but, just to put your mind at ease, with my hand on my heart, I have never heard of anything like this going to court. So. You'll be fine.'

'It's not just the legal thing, though. The thing is I could upset quite a few people if this did get published… So I was thinking… How about I take back the manuscript and I change a few things?'

'Like what?'

'Well, mainly I'd have to change the big revelation that breaks up the friends.'

'It's essential to the plot.'

'Couldn't I make it… I don't know… that maybe "Danny" has been secretly seeing "Adam's" sister?'

'It'll lack emotional punch then.'

'Well, what if Adam turns out to be gay?'

'The gay thing has been done to death.'

'Well, what if it turns out that "Danny's" girlfriend "Kate" had an affair with "Adam"?'

'Look, I can see where you're going with this. But I have to say, I'm not liking any of what I'm hearing. The book's great. You'll just have to trust me.'

'What about if you tell the publishers to give me a couple of weeks to soften what I say about some of my other friends – I mean, I'll definitely have to take the stuff out about the character "Leon" being an ugly bird magnet. The fact is, Jakey – who he's based on – is one of my best mates in the world.'

'The thing is, Keith, if you start letting people mess around with your art like this, I can't see your career going very far.'

'OK,' I replied. 'Maybe I'll leave that. But I'll have to change the stuff about Marco being fat because my mate Alan will never forgive me.'

'Look,' said Christian. 'I can tell you're getting cold feet about this, so let me put it on the line for you. I think this book is great as it is. It has bestseller written all over it. If you start arsing around with it, I guarantee it won't be half as good as it is now. And the fact of the matter is I only represent books that I think are the best. I don't want to put any pressure on you because, you know what? I've only spoken to you a few times and I already like you a lot. But, at the end of the day, the choice is yours about whether you tell me to go ahead with this deal or not. At the same time, it's my choice about whether I represent this book or not. And, yeah, maybe there'll be another agent out there somewhere who'll take your book on once it's been butchered and sanitised but I guarantee you they won't be as good as me because I am the best there is.'

'I don't know what to say,' I replied.

'Just trust me, Keith. That's what the agent–client relationship is all about. Trust. So what's it going to be? Have we got a deal or have we got a deal?'

'It's a deal,' I replied.

'Good. Then that's all I need to know.'

It's all been a bit of a blur since then. I'd never dreamed in a million years of earning the kind of money that Cooper and Lawton were offering for my book. (Briefly, the realistic plan for the rest of my life had been something along the lines of: try not to get sacked from housing job, move in with Becky one day, get married, have children, Becky goes out to work while I raise family, drift into middle age, lose hair, become fat, return to work, continue soul-destroying career in housing, move up a staggering two grades on career ladder, get divorced because Becky's finally given up on me, be made redundant at fifty-five, fall into deep depression, sit around in underpants on sofa and wait to die.) So, no matter how I went over it in my head, I always came to the same conclusion: I'd be a fool to give up on all this just because I'd insulted a few mates.

The next few months went by incredibly quickly. I handed in my notice at the housing office the Monday after I signed the contract with

Cooper and Lawton, much to the consternation of my boss. No one could believe that I was actually leaving for good and my boss actually told me that there would always be a job waiting there for me if I wanted it. I was very polite and told him that if I ever found myself working in housing again it would be because I had died and was being eternally punished for all the wrongs I'd committed during my life.

It was difficult to know what to tell my friends about my news. On the one hand, without them I wouldn't have been in the fortunate position I was in now; on the other hand, once they read it I knew there would be big trouble. In the end, I decided to tell them all the Friday that I signed the contract. We were all in the Griffin and I just sort of stood up and announced: 'I've got a book deal and it's so good I can pack in my job and write full time.' To say they were stunned would be something of an understatement. I don't think any of them thought that I would ever make it as a writer because I hadn't even believed it myself. Once they'd got over the initial shock, however, I spent the whole evening drinking congratulatory pints, after which I took them for a celebratory meal at the Star of the Punjab in Kentish Town, which I paid for with my already overextended overdraft. Of course, they spent most of the evening making jokes at my expense, mostly along the lines of recounting stories about me to sell to the tabloids if I ever became really famous. But it was all good humoured. They really did wish me well. At the end of the night they all demanded their own free, signed copy of the book when it came out. On hearing this, I just laughed a lot and no doubt looked shifty and promised them that they'd get their copies in good time. Tim said he wanted five signed copies because, if I got famous, they'd make half-decent Christmas presents; Jakey informed me that he only ever read factual books about gangsters and/or serial killers but promised me he'd get his girlfriend Sarah to read it and tell him if it was any good; Graham said he would read my book on holiday with his parents but he strongly doubted whether his mum would want to read it because she was more into Barbara Taylor Bradford; Alan announced proudly that he hadn't read a book since *To Kill a Mockingbird* had been foisted on him at school and wasn't about to make an exception for me, but he did concede that if they made it into a film he'd probably get it when it came out on video; Liam assured me he'd read it even though it was written by me and if he liked it he'd write a glowing review on amazon.co.uk for me; and finally Phil revealed that he'd put it on his "to read" list ahead of *Bridget Jones's Diary* but well behind the complete works of Kurt Vonnegut. Phil made out like he was joking, which he was to a degree, but I could tell there was more to it than that. I think of all of us, myself included, he was the most surprised at my success. And, while he'd been very successful in his career so far, I couldn't help but feel that he wished more than anything that what was happening to me was happening to him. I tried to talk to him a few times about it but he never took the bait. I think he knew I knew how he felt and even that was too much.

I was told by my editor at Cooper and Lawton that, although they loved the book, it still needed some work, so I spent the next few weeks carefully addressing each of the one hundred and thirty-seven queries that he had about the plot, characters and structure. I ended up working on it most nights, emailing him one revised chapter of the book at a time (which, after a few days, he would return to me with further 'queries'). A number of times I tried as subtly as possible to tone down/ further disguise some of the more unpleasant things I'd said about my friends, only to have him catch every single one of them by circling them in the manuscript with a red pen. To make matters worse, he told me that the character of Adam (aka Phil) needed a darker streak to be more three-dimensional, so I did just that. Did I feel bad doing this? Absolutely. Did I do it? Yes, I did. Honestly, Machiavelli had nothing on me.

In the meantime, the book just kept getting bigger and bigger. About a month or so after signing the deal, I received a call from Christian. By this point I was receiving calls from Christian or his assistant on a daily basis. I got a sense that there was always something new to know. On this particular day, however, there really *was* something new to know.

'Hi, Rob,' said a female voice. 'It's Javine here, Christian's assistant. He's just on another call at the moment but he'll be with you in a moment.'

I had to admire Christian's skill in reminding the world just how important he was. I loved the fact that, moments earlier, I had been minding my own business, sitting on the sofa, watching daytime TV – and now, seconds later, I'm holding for someone who hasn't even called me. It was amazing.

'Hi, Rob,' said Christian, eventually. 'Sorry for keeping you on hold, mate.'

'No problems,' I replied.

'How are you today?'

'Good, thanks,' I replied. 'How about yourself?'

'Me? I'm always great. But today I'm even better. Are you ready for some more good news?'

My heart skipped a beat. I wasn't sure I could take any more good news. 'What's going on?'

'I bet you thought things had gone quiet on the film front.'

'Well…' I began. 'I just reasoned that you had it under control.'

'That's good because I did. Brace yourself for the best news you're going to hear for the rest of this week… We've sold the film rights to *This Charming Man* to a major studio.'

'A major studio?' I repeated needlessly.

'A major *Hollywood* studio,' expanded Christian. 'Sony, Miramax, Paramount and Universal were all bidding for it but then, out of the blue, we were offered a killer deal from Globalcom. Have you heard of them?'

'I think so,' I replied, and then, for my benefit, Christian reeled off a long list of films that I'd definitely heard of featuring everyone from Benicio Del Toro to Jude Law and Jennifer Lopez to Nicole Kidman. I was speechless.

'Anyway,' continued Christian. 'It's like this: they love *This Charming Man*. They're seeing it as a kind of a new generation Brat Pack romantic comedy. They want to relocate the action from London to San Francisco, and they've already attached Ben Affleck for the lead and Kate Beckinsale for the love interest.'

'Ben Affleck?' I echoed.

'You know,' said Christian. 'The *Good Will Hunting* guy.'

'And Kate Beckinsale?' I echoed again.

'The girl in *Pearl Harbor*.'

'I know who she is, Christian,' I said impatiently. 'It's all just too surreal. Up to a few months ago, my mate's nickname for me was The Man with No Ambition. I worked in a mind-numbingly tedious job in a housing department in north Haringey. The nearest I'd ever got to having anything to do with Hollywood was the Odeon Leicester Square. And now you're talking about real Hollywood stars being in the film version of a book that came out of my head. It just doesn't make sense. You're telling me that Ben Affleck – a man who has appeared on the front covers of thousands of magazines – knows who I am. And, on top of that, Kate Beckinsale – a woman who appeared in one of the most expensive films ever made in Hollywood and, let's not forget, the daughter of the late, great Richard "Lennie Godber" Beckinsale – also knows who I am.'

'That's absolutely what I'm telling you,' said Christian. 'I'm telling you, my friend, that you have absolutely hit the big time.'

Just in case I was under any impression that I hadn't hit the big time, two days later there was an article about me on the front page of the *Daily Telegraph* under the headline: 'Housing officer earns millions in book deal'. The article began by describing me as a 'lowly thirty-something officer clerk' with a 'secret passion for writing' who had been 'discovered' by 'twenty-eight-year-old wunderkind agent Christian Kennedy, from the world-renowned literary agency JPM'. It continued by stating that there has been a 'ferocious bidding war' between several publishers resulting in a 'very significant six-figure deal'. The article also featured several fictional quotes from me saying that I was 'over the moon' with how things had gone and that 'never in my wildest dreams did I ever imagine that *This Charming Man* would be this huge'. The article then went on to reveal that, through a combination of the film deal (if it were to go into production), the book deal, US publication rights and foreign translations, I would be earning £5.5m from my debut novel. A phone call through to Christian that morning (following several hours' worth of phone calls from stunned parents, relatives and friends) revealed that the article was in fact all down to him. He'd provided the quotes and massaged the figures, name-dropped 'Ben' and 'Kate' and given the newspapers exactly what they wanted to hear. Thanks to Christian, I then spent the next three days being interviewed by the *Evening Standard*, the *Daily Mail*, the Radio Four programme *Front Row*, the *Guardian*, *The Times*, the *Sunday Times*, the ITV programme *This Morning*, *Newsweek* and the *New York* sodding *Times*.

So, as I stand here, surrounded by all these well-wishers, I think about my big question: do I have any regrets about everything I've done to get here? The friendships I've betrayed, the loyal girlfriend I left behind and my general lack of integrity? And the answer is: of course not. Because I can get another book out of it. Or at least a short story. Maybe even a short story like this short story. After all, life is art. Art is life. And everybody's got to make a living somehow.

Heaven Knows I'm Miserable Now

Kate Pullinger

For me, the iconic Smiths song is 'Heaven Knows I'm Miserable Now', which is, at the very least, one of the very best song titles ever. The character in my story keeps recurring in all the short stories I've been writing lately; his life is on the edge of becoming miserable, but somehow he resists despair and rises up again. This story is, to my somewhat biased view, funny in the way that The Smiths' music is funny – dark, strange, but deeply amusing.

I didn't mean to become a laughing stock. I made a virtual birthday card for a woman I work with, nothing more than that. Not because I fancy her or anything, I'm a happily married man! Though I do fancy her, to tell you the truth. It's a work thing, you know how it goes, she is kind and clever and good looking and when I'm with her I'm funnier and sharper and a little bit more alive. And it was a simple enough gesture, really – give your colleague at work a birthday card, nothing sinister about that. But things got out of hand. Things always seem to get out of hand. 'A laughing stock' – what in God's name does that mean? I should know, because that's what I became.

In my job I don't spend that much time on the computer but I do use it for work email, timekeeping, logging complaints, that kind of thing. And YouTube videos do the rounds, like in any office – that pop band dancing on the treadmills, the baby whose fart sends a mushroom cloud of talcum powder up into the air. That was where I got the idea. I had all the right bits of technology at home; I kept our computer up to date with the latest software and hardware because I want my boy to be an active user of technology, it might help him out when it comes time – perish the thought – for him to find his own way in the world. I'd never been that big a Smiths fan – my father wouldn't let me listen to pop music when I was a kid, so my passion for the stuff came along a while after the Smiths had departed the scene, if a band like that can ever be said to have done such a thing. But there was one song I'd always liked, and I thought it would be funny to make a video of myself lip-synching to it.

For some unknown reason – unknown to me, at any rate – I decided it would be a good idea to perform the song naked. A man singing along to the Smiths is one thing, but a naked man singing along to the Smiths – that would be funny! I wore a skinny necktie and a pork-pie hat that I had purchased especially for the video on one of my trips through the West End of London. I positioned the camera in a place where I was sure I'd be filmed only from the waist up and I planned to jump into the air a couple of times, rock-star stylee of course, as I thought that might make the video even more amusing.

Downloading the track and setting up the webcam took longer than I expected – I wanted to be done before my boy got home from school – so when it came time to record my performance there was only long enough for one take. So I recorded it, and then I uploaded it, and I wrote a short and, I thought, carefree and light-hearted birthday greeting email to my work colleague, containing the link to her birthday treat. I pressed 'send' and thought nothing more of it. Finished buttoning my shirt as the boy came through the front door.

That night my boy woke up with some kind of stomach bug; he came into our bedroom to tell us he was going to throw up and then he did throw up, right there in the middle of the carpet. He continued to be sick for a couple of hours and afterwards I sat with him in his room and stroked his forehead until he finally went back to sleep. I called in sick the next day so that I could stay home with him; this was the arrangement my wife and I had made years before as her job is both much more lucrative and substantially more important and interesting than mine. I didn't mind, to tell you the truth; staying home with the boy was kind of like a mini-break for me.

I work in the secure psychiatric unit of a large teaching hospital here in south London; I work part time, mornings only. My job title includes the word 'administrator', but really I'm a kind of glorified orderly. I have had a certain amount of trouble in my own life with mental health, mostly when I was a teenager, and mostly because of my father, but I won't get into that now; the people in the secure psychiatric ward put paid to any real doubts I've ever had about my own sanity. Most of them are stark raving lunatics. On my first day at work when I went into the men's toilet the sink was missing; the night before one of the patients had accidentally torn it from the wall when he used it as a launch pad in an attempt at suicide-by-hanging; he'd almost drowned instead when his not inconsiderable weight brought down the sink and flooded the bathroom.

This craziness, and the trauma and drugs that accompany its treatment, means that here in the hospital among the staff there is a hardy camaraderie which translates into a lot of joking and a certain amount of drink-fuelled high-jinks in the pub after work. At least, that's what I am told; I tend not to socialise much, actually not at all, with my colleagues, mainly because of my duties at home with the boy. At the end of the day, I'm not really a very sociable person, a bit shy even. But at work we all get on famously, or so I thought. My favourite colleague was always very kind to me, sweet and good natured, even though she was a high-up consultant and I was a low-down orderly.

My boy took two days to recover from his night of throwing up, and then it was the weekend, and I had enough seniority by this stage to not have to work on weekends, which was just as well as my wife often had to work right through both days. So by the time I went back to work on Monday I'd forgotten all about my light-hearted and carefree birthday email.

That morning when I arrived I said hello to the man who does the night shift. Ordinarily he is very cordial and he almost always asks after my wife and my child. But this time he got straight to the point: 'You're lucky she's not going to sue, mate!'

'Who?' There was no one called Sue in our unit.

'Sue you, of course, you great naked wally. Litigation. Whatever possessed you?'

Of course, I remembered the video then. But how did the night-shift man know about it? It was between me and my colleague.

'The object of your affection thought it was hilarious – you are lucky she has a good sense of humour, mate. She took it upon herself to spread the news. It's not the song I would have chosen, of course.'

'Nor I,' said one of the junior doctors, who had just arrived in the office – clearly they'd been discussing it endlessly. 'But it does have a sort of poignancy to it, I'll admit.' Suddenly the room was full of other people, more of my work colleagues, laughing and talking among themselves, as if they were the audience and I was up on the stage and they were waiting for me to start my performance.

I cleared my throat, and the crowd fell silent. 'Where is she?' I asked.

'You're lucky, she's got the day off,' someone said.

'Today's her actual birthday, you pillock, not last week,' added another voice.

And then they revealed the full truth to me: I had become an overnight sensation. My favourite colleague had forwarded my video to her colleague, who had forwarded it to the whole hospital. The NHS employs people from all over the world these days and they had all forwarded my video to their friends and family who, in turn, had forwarded it to everyone they knew. My birthday greeting video went around the globe and back again, several times. Turned out the entire world – at least, millions of people with access to the Internet – was laughing at me.

What could I do? I couldn't quit my job; I love my job and it suits me and my life perfectly. Without this job I'd be even more of an idiot than I already am. I could apologise, I would apologise to my colleague, of course, but I couldn't apologise to the entire world: I'd have to keep apologising for a very long time. I could front it out and claim the video had nothing to do with me, but then, perhaps, I'd look even more foolish. I could say I'd actually meant to send it to my wife, but that would remind everyone that I have a wife, and I wouldn't want anyone to have the bright idea of forwarding the video to her as well as the rest of the world. Assuming, of course, that she hadn't already seen it. Assuming that she hadn't already been forwarded my famous naked lip-synching video.

I could not think of anything to say. Luckily for me, one of the ward alarms went off, and everyone rushed away. I sat back down at my desk and wondered whether it was possible to die from humiliation.

But no, I didn't die. I got on with the day and was almost offended to discover that my video was, in fact, pretty much old news as far as my colleagues were concerned. They were bored by me and my video already.

After lunch I made my way home, as always, on the bus. I walked over to my boy's school in order to pick him up – these days he usually makes his way home by himself, but I wanted to see him, wanted to be distracted by him. Once we got home we played football on the PlayStation together for about twice as long as he was allowed, ordinarily. Then I cooked a big tea, and ate with him, then cooked and ate again once my wife got home at nine. She clearly did not know about the video; unlike the rest of the world, she hadn't been forwarded that particular email. Our household remained peaceful and calm; I didn't have to explain why the video had seemed like a good idea at the time. I should have felt relieved, but I was still too embarrassed to feel much of anything. Embarrassed, but full of dread as well: what would happen when my favourite colleague returned to work the next day? I had a bath and went to bed, but none of this was of much use to me.

I was at my desk when the consultant, the birthday girl herself, came into the office. I kept typing, although what I wrote was complete monkey. I heard her stop and I could tell she was looking at me, but I could not look at her, could not take my eyes away from the computer screen. After a few very long minutes, she said, 'Hi.'

I stopped typing. It took all of the fortitude I possessed not to lower my head on to the keyboard and sob. 'Hello,' I replied. I forced myself to turn around and look at her.

She was smiling. She looked genuinely friendly.

'You don't have to be mad to work here,' she said, after a pause.

I finished the ward motto for her: 'You have to be bloody crazy.'

She put her hand on my shoulder and gave it a squeeze. 'It's a good song,' she said.

'It is,' I replied, 'it is indeed.'

Bigmouth Strikes Again

Nic Kelman

'Bigmouth Strikes Again' appealed to me because of the repressed anger it expresses. With the introduction of Joan of Arc, it then reminded me in some ways of a female version of Thoreau's quote: 'The mass of men lead lives of quiet desperation', which is a theme I find I often return to in my work, so this story was born...

Mexican Flaming Heart Bush (*Sanctimonium rubor aeger Mexicana*) 13+ Yrs. Recognisable bifurcated trunk, superior flower density and colour saturation. Stolen from 135 Hitchcock Ln. Sat. night. $5,000 reward for information leading to its return.

The men had arrived early that morning. Pushing their barrows and driving the mini-digger through the bottom corner of the herb garden, they had destroyed much of the coriander and other parsleys. Julia sighed as she pushed at the earth with a pale, bare toe. She could see the leaves, the stems, their green like confetti, scattered through the loam. She even thought she might be able to smell the deaths of the little plants, but she couldn't be sure. There was a fine breeze and her coffee was strong.

She regretted now asking to be called so late. She should have been up and about and out here when they came. She knew she had been over everything with them already, that they probably knew what they were doing and where they were supposed to do it. But still. She pushed at the earth with her toe one more time, the red nail turning up an intact Riccio Verde Scuro. She bent, picked up the leafy herb and pushed it into her dressing-gown pocket, the head now adorning the red silk of her kimono, a green pom-pom. Martina could clean it and add it to her salad for lunch.

With her eyes, Julia followed the trail the men had left across the grass. It joined up with the slate paving stones and disappeared through a gap in the tall wall of privet that separated the herb garden from the orientalist Koi pond. She should put some clothes on and supervise them. She knew from experience they couldn't be trusted. Left to their own devices, they would take none of the necessary precautions.

She watched them eat. They had brought their own lunches, of course, but she found they always worked better if she gave them lunch. It didn't matter whether they were painters or bricklayers or electricians. A few beers and some of Martina's cooking and coffee and they always worked better in the afternoon. They felt like they owed you something then, not the other way around.

They ate so quickly, pushing enormous forkfuls of food into their mouths, mopping up the marinara sauce with bread. Julia looked at their hands, at their fingers, as they ate. The dirt there didn't seem to bother them. Still, it was only soil. Soil was clean, wasn't it? She didn't know.

'Thank you, Mrs. Barnes,' said Jorge, raising his beer to her. The other men said nothing. They had never even really looked at her, she realised. When she needed to convey something, she always spoke to Jorge. Then he would talk to them and they would talk among themselves in Spanish. Sometimes they laughed. She wondered now whether Jorge ever said something she had not or left out something she had.

'You're welcome,' Julia said, smiling politely. They were well on their way now; it seemed impossible they could do something wrong at this point. Sure enough, this morning, when she had come out here in her gardening clothes – jeans, sweatshirt, sneakers – they had begun to dig the holes for the bushes on exactly the wrong side of the pond. But they had the location of the three holes correct now and she had watched them add the bags of Japanese fertiliser, the Dutch topsoil and the live Mississippi mudworms. Now all they had to do was drop the bushes into place, the two Dwarf Ylang-Ylang flanking the Pua Keni Keni, and they would be done.

'Phone call for you, Mrs Barnes.' Martina's voice from the other side of the hedge.

'Who is it?'

'Charlie.'

'OK – I'll be right there – thank you.' Julia looked around at the group of men. They had finished their food and were just taking the last sips of their beers. 'Jorge, the Pua goes in the middle, right?'

'Yes, Mrs Barnes, of course.'

'OK. Good. Well – thank you, I'll send the cheque over to the nursery tomorrow.'

'OK, Mrs Barnes, thank you.'

Julia smiled at him, and turned to smile at the other men, but they avoided her eyes. She walked as far as the gap in the hedge and then turned back, suddenly remembering. 'Oh, and don't worry about the plates, you can just leave them there. Martina or someone will come out and get them.'

Jorge smiled at her and waved 'OK' but one of the men, looking down at his beer bottle, said something in Spanish and everyone laughed. She smiled again, uncertain, then made her way back to the house.

'But, Charles, you promised.' She cursed herself when she heard her tone, winced, her face tightening up as she damned herself in silence. She knew the last thing he would respond to was a plea. Just like

Robert. She listened to his response, to his excuses – the latest girl, the invitation from her family, St Moritz. It was all nonsense, she knew. Not a fabrication, but nonsense nonetheless. She nodded quietly, not caring that he could not see her. The acquiescence was not intended for him. She put the cordless down on the empty kitchen counter. 'We could have all gone together,' she said to the back of the phone, its screen still displaying Charlie's number on the caller ID.

'*Scusi, signora?*' said Martina, looking up from the deep-freezer. Around her black hair, her dark eyes, the frosty air rose, drifted, white.

'Nothing,' said Julia, 'It's nothing.'

Creeping Jew's Gold (*Serpere aurum Iudaicus*) detached from conservatory wall at 13 Bridge Road Sat. night. Unique specimen – recessive variegated blood-blue leaves and stem. VERY RARE. $11,000 reward for information leading to its return.

Julia stared in disbelief at the far side of the orientalist Koi pond. The Pua Keni Keni was on the right-hand side, the two Dwarf Ylang-Ylangs next to each other on the left. It seemed impossible, she had been so clear. How could they not have understood what she wanted? It was so simple. She could hear Robert now, 'You always have to watch them... Always... They just don't care about their work.' She sighed. At least she hadn't delivered the cheque to the nursery yet. She walked slowly back to the house and in through the kitchen door. The phone was ringing.

'Hello? Robert! What a nice surprise! You found a minute then... Oh, right. OK. Yes. No, he said he had decided to go with Lynn's family to St Moritz. No, I told you Sarah said she wasn't coming either this year – something about Teach for America. Well, we could go to the American Hotel – it'll be like our first year here, it'll be fun. Oh. I see. But don't you think it would be nice to see each other? Yes, of course I understand – I always have, haven't I? Yes. Yes, of course, but— Yes, Robert. I love you too.' She put the phone down gently, hesitating for a moment before actually placing it in its cradle, as if it were this action of hers that would end the conversation.

Through the kitchen windows she caught sight of Charlie's garden shed. It had been there for nearly twenty years, but had stood unused now for at least a dozen. During Charlie's sixth birthday party (or was it seventh? or ninth?) he had announced he wanted to help Julia in her garden. Julia and her friends, in the absence of any men, had been amused by the proclamation and one of them had suggested Charlie needed his own gardening shed to be 'effective'. They had all laughed, but Charlie had clung to the idea. He brought it up with such persistence that, in spite of Robert's disapproval, Julia had eventually bought a small shed for him, placing it within sight of the kitchen so someone could keep an eye on him as he came and went. Looking at it now she noticed it was slightly open and must have been for some time – between the frame and the door the grass was quite long.

Stopping by the garage for some trimming shears, she walked to the shed and pulled at the door, yanking at the wood until it opened past the overgrown grass around its base. She crouched and trimmed the grass by hand, down to the level of the rest of the lawn. When she was satisfied, she stood and, after surveying her work, looked inside. Dust drifted, moved by a breeze Julia could not feel. The small tools were still hung at the back on tiny hooks without any sharp points or edges and on the shelves to the left and right all the gnomes were intact but one. It had turned out Charlie was not as interested in gardening as he was in the small gnomes he had seen in other people's gardens on the way to school. 'I don't understand,' he had said, 'our garden is so much bigger – why don't we have gnomes?' Robert, relieved, began to bring gnomes home with him whenever he returned from a trip, but only on the condition Charlie keep them in his shed when he was not playing with them.

Julia stepped inside and straightened one or two, her hands coming away covered in dust. She looked down at the one that had fallen and shattered on the ground and crouched and picked up the pieces one by one, placing all but the two largest in her pockets. As she left, she paused for one last look. Certain the little men were now all in order, she closed the door and threw the latch.

When she returned to see the kitchen, there was a note from Martina on the fridge, on the whiteboard with the little clay model of Capri at the top. 'No worry, signora – I take cheque for you to nursery.' There was a happy face drawn underneath the message, its eyes in the European style – not just two dots, but horseshoe lids and pupils like semicolons. Julia sighed. She would deal with the nursery later, or perhaps tomorrow. For now, she had to be certain Martina and Ceylon had put everything out correctly for her guests. She looked at the clock. A couple of hours before everyone arrived. She felt she should eat something, but she wasn't hungry.

'But Julia, sweet-thing, how could you not *know*?' Lawrence, president of the East Hampton Garden Club, pressed a caviar-laden toast-point into his mouth. 'Beluga?'

'Oscetra,' replied Julia. 'I don't know – I don't know how... no one told me...'

'But we've all been talking about it!' He sipped his champagne. 'This is lovely, by the way... lovely.'

'Thank you.'

'No one told you what?' Henrietta had drifted over, Miriam in tow. Behind them, Martina replaced an almost empty tray of hors d'oeuvres.

'About the missing plants.'

'*Stolen* plants, sweet-thing.'

'But Julia,' said Miriam, 'we've all been talking about it.' She looked up at Julia as she did at everyone, her fat little face pursed into a perpetual 'oh'.

'Apparently,' said Julia, looking for Ceylon to tell her to refill Susan's glass. Ceylon really wasn't working out. She'd hired the girl only out of pity when Francis St John across the estuary had gone bankrupt.

'It's been in the papers as well, you know,' said Henrietta. Lawrence had told Julia Henrietta had been quite insulted the social committee had chosen Julia to host the annual holiday party.

'I'm sure,' said Julia, smiling, although she couldn't say why. Henrietta made her nervous. Her husband was an unknown number of years younger than her and no one was quite sure where or how they had met. His accent was vaguely European but could also have been African or Oceanic by way of Germany. Furthermore, the divorce settlement which supported them both was equally mysterious in its size. 'I've been busy with the house, getting everything ready for Christmas.'

'Yes, I saw your new Ylangs and the Pua – interesting decision with the placement. Asymmetry is so important for that true oriental feel…' Henrietta smiled at her. Lawrence coughed. Miriam, oblivious, looked about for another canapé, lost.

Martina took a third tray of glasses to the kitchen while Ceylon moved about the room picking up one napkin at a time, placing each one on a pile off to one side before returning for another. Julia and Lawrence sat on the comfortable couch, sunken into each other. Julia's glass was still full, Lawrence's still empty. With one eye, Julia watched Ceylon through the champagne, moving the glass back and forth as Ceylon drifted here and there, tiny bubbles rising from her arms, her hair, her shoulders. 'I just don't want to be one of those women,' she said, 'I can't. You know? I'm not Henrietta. I can't do that. I can't pretend to be happy with a ski instructor.'

'A masseur. And I don't think she's pretending… I wouldn't be.'

'You know what I mean.'

'Yes, sorry, sweet-thing, I do, I do – I'm sorry – I shouldn't make light – I know exactly what you mean.'

'I know Charles and Sarah will come back. I know they will – I did, my brothers did – they're just at that age – I know that. But what I know in my head doesn't make it any easier… And I don't know what to make of Robert. He's not having an affair, I know that much.'

'You never have known, even when you married him. Especially when you married him. He'll come back too. You'll see, I think.'

'It's not that. I'm not worried about that, that's not what I mean – I know he'll come back. I'm worried that when he does, I won't be here any more – Ceylon, for God's sake, now take them to the laundry room!'

Ceylon glanced at her, startled, as if she'd been hit. She looked down at the pile of linens that had been her focus of attention for the last couple of minutes, scooped them up into her arms quickly but with much care, as if a crying baby were hidden among their folds, and scurried out of the room. Behind her she left a trail of napkins, crumpled white leaves, collapsed snow birds, fallen from a winter sky.

Chinaman's Hat (*Petasus orientalis*). Stolen from greenhouse at 1804 Tuckahoe Ln. World's largest recorded example. Perfectly symmetrical striations. Irreplaceable and unmistakable. Reward for information leading to its recovery available upon request.

The town hall was packed. Julia had never, in fact, seen it quite so full. The meetings about the illegally large residence, the uproar over the splinter group of beachfront property owners attempting to incorporate their own town for insurance purposes, even the great summer parking permit debate, had not generated such interest and attendance. From their places on the panel on the stage, East Hampton's two police officers were attempting to calm everyone down, but it wasn't working. The mayor's last comment – that they were only plants and could easily be replaced once people's insurance came through – had not gone down well. Lawrence stood next to her, screaming, 'We'll replace you! Maybe we'll replace you!' Other people's comments were less intelligible.

As she looked around, she noticed Henrietta was the only other person beside herself who wasn't shouting at the stage or talking to the people next to her. She seemed to be text-messaging someone, but Julia couldn't be certain and she found herself wondering vaguely whether her own cell phone could do that. She looked back at Lawrence, his face red from the yelling. Poor Lawrence. Unable to uproot his Maori Plums, the thief had taken cuttings from the most established trees. Now the pride of Lawrence's garden looked crippled, the hard, gnarled wood lopsided and leaking sap. Lawrence was unsure whether they would recover and was already saying he might replace the copse with some Albanian Figs. Julia knew it was just talk. Lawrence had raised those plums from cuttings he had brought back from New Zealand and, just as she knew he would be able to nurse them through this trauma, she also knew that every time he looked at them he would see the branches that were now missing, not the branches that were still there.

'Listen, this is pointless – I'm going to head home, OK?' Julia tried to say over the general din. The police had sat back down and the mayor, playing patient principal, was tapping a pencil on the table, waiting for the room to quiet of its own accord. Lawrence, now shouting 'This isn't about that! This isn't about that, you fool!', didn't seem to hear her, so she simply turned and walked out into the cold evening air. The way it stung her face felt pleasant after the stuffy heat of the hall; when she breathed now, she could feel it. She walked down the main street to where she knew Harold was waiting with the car, but before she got there, she turned and walked back the way she had just come.

Past the town hall was a small bar. When Robert had first bought the house, it had a Genovese Cream Ale sign in its one small window. Now there was a menu offering broccoli rabe and pizza with Jerusalem artichokes. Inside, Julia found it empty but for the mother of the current owner, whom Julia had seen down front, near the stage, just minutes before. The old woman could barely see over the bar, but she stood back there waiting for her son to return, or perhaps for the employees to turn up for the first shift. Julia felt a little guilty asking her for a drink, but then again, what she had in mind wasn't very complicated.

'Champagne, please, Mrs Taleggio.'

The woman seemed surprised that Julia knew her name, which made sense really since they had never met. Julia didn't even really know her son either, just that Antonio Taleggio had bought the bar from its original owner, Bill O'Hare.

The old woman placed the glass of champagne in front of her. 'Seventeen dollars, please.'

'Thank you,' said Julia, handing her a twenty. She didn't wait for her change, but instead, wanting to avoid sitting at the bar with the old woman so near, wanting to avoid feeling the polite necessity of talking to her, she made her way to a booth near the back. Once she had taken off her coat, sat down and settled in, the old woman slowly, laboriously, made her way to the end of the bar, exerted tremendous effort in lifting the bar trap high enough to make her way underneath, and shuffled slowly over to her.

When she was very close to Julia she said at last, 'The tables are for eating. Are you eating?'

Julia looked at her for a moment. Even though she looked directly into her eyes, the old woman didn't seem to see her. It was as if she were blind, which, of course, she couldn't be. There was no hint of humour in her question.

'No, no I'm not.'

'Then I'm sorry, but you will have to drink at the bar.'

Julia looked at her again for a moment. Again, there was no trace of humour. She sighed and picked up her coat. 'Never mind,' she said, standing, 'never mind.'

She looked back just for a second as she left. The old woman sat in the booth, looking at the ceiling, her hands around the glass of champagne.

As Harold pulled out of the parking lot, Lawrence's Bundeswagon pulled up next to them. Julia lowered her window as Lawrence lowered his. The Bundeswagon was packed. Julia could see Miriam in the back seat along with three other members of the Garden Club. Henrietta sat in the front passenger seat, clutching several thermoses.

'Sweet-thing!' cried Lawrence. 'We're vigilantes! We've decided we're going to drive around all night and catch this bastard in the act! Kind of a neighbourhood watch sort of thing. Do you want to come? I'm sure we can make room!' Miriam squirmed slightly at this comment, but said nothing. Lawrence's breath clouded out into the space between them, smelling both slightly sweet and slightly sour.

'No, thank you, Lawrence. I'm actually quiet tired. I think I'm just going to have Harold take me home and go to bed...'

'Are you sure? We have mulled wine and Miriam brought some of her girl's Christmas cake – it's very good!'

'No, really, I just need to get to bed. Thank you, though. And good luck being vigilantes – it does sound like fun.'

'Fun-schmun, we'll see how much he likes having *his* plums pruned!'

Julia smiled. 'Goodnight, Lawrence...'

'Goodnight, sweet-thing!' He tore off down Millbrook Road, narrowly missing the town's single police car, which swerved to get out of his way.

As Harold carefully turned out on to the road in the other direction, Julia raised her window, the thick glass of the Bentley blocking out the cold, if not the night.

Gleaming African Broadback (*Dorsum robustus fulgere Africanus*). Entire tree missing from 181 Church Road. Barkless Ebony, extremely rare, many hundreds of years old, several carvings on trunk of ancient and primitive origin.

When she woke, Julia wondered why it was of her own accord. Then she remembered, she had given everyone the day off, there would be no one waking her this morning with her cappuccino and croissant and Belgian hazelnut praline spread. It irritated her that she hadn't been woken by the phone, that no one had yet called her to wish her a Merry Christmas – especially Charlie, who was seven hours ahead. At least both Robert and Sarah were an hour behind. Strange they could be in the same time zone and yet so far away from each other.

She got out of bed, slipping her feet into her slippers, and looking at the phone console on her nightstand. Nothing. No blinking red light. She hadn't slept through anything. The clock surprised her, though; it was only 7.10 a.m. She usually asked Martina to wake her at seven, so she had expected to sleep much longer today. She sighed and stood and shrugged into her bathrobe.

Downstairs, in the kitchen, it took her some time to find the coffee and, even then, the milk she steamed remained flat. There didn't seem to be any croissants. She sat at the table in the kitchen where Martina and Harold – and more recently Ceylon – took their meals. It was actually a nice, comfortable space, less austere than the real dining room or even the TV room where she remembered eating when Charlie and Sarah were younger. Through the window she could see the herb garden, all trace of the damage left by Jorge's men now long gone. When the phone rang, she hit the table with her thigh as she got up, spilling coffee.

'Hello? No. Thank you. I said no.' She hung up and cursed as she looked back at the table, the coffee dripping down on to the heated slate floor. She realised, as she crouched and wiped it up with a paper towel, that this was the first time she had cleaned this particular floor since they'd had the house. At least she knew where the trash was.

The television only made her depressed. Carol services and preachers and Christmas cartoons from twenty years ago. 'When did they stop making Christmas cartoons?' she wondered. She walked about the house aimlessly, picking up objects almost at random. Was it strange she could remember where every single one had come from and when? Here was the Wade porcelain boar Robert had bought on their honeymoon in Barcelona, assured by the woman who sold it to them that in Catalonia it was good luck for newlyweds. They found out later it was, in fact, a fertility symbol. And here the Lalique crystal bowl with the orchid flower rim, a gift from Charles when he was in college, Christmas his sophomore year. That the money for the present had come from her hadn't mattered as much as the fact that he had remembered her favourite orchid and then sought out a piece incorporating it. She realised now she had never asked whether this had been intentional; now, on this morning, she wondered whether it might have been nothing more than coincidence. And there, up there, the tetratych of Versailles Sarah had bought for her on her junior year in France, each panel a season, each border gilded. The vases, the books, the teapots and the masks. So many gifts over so many years. Perhaps I should start a museum? She laughed to herself.

Standing, she ate some salad from a Tupperware bowl she had found in the refrigerator. As she forked the arugula and endive into her mouth, she looked down at the table where she and Robert (or perhaps just she) kept the family photos in a variety of frames. These moments she remembered less or, perhaps, had been taught to remember less by the photographs themselves. As she looked at the image she knew had been taken of Charles on his second birthday – confused, a little terrified, a little happy, astride a handmade rocking horse, his eyes focused on something off-camera – she could not recall that specific instant or what he had been looking at. Rather, she remembered the photograph. If she thought of the rocking horse, still intact as a matter of fact, stored in the basement against the possibility of grandchildren arriving before woodworm, if she thought of the rocking horse, she could remember other moments, other times she had seen Charles riding it, but not the one in the photo. The same went for Sarah, fresh faced, in skiing gear at Whistler, at the bottom of a lift. She remembered skiing with Sarah that year, remembered buying her that hat with her favourite cartoon character emblazoned on its front, but not the moment the picture was taken. There was Robert in black tie at a Met fund-raiser, her brother in the Atacama crouching over three small mummies, the colour of their headdresses still vibrant in spite of their dry, grey, almost petrified flesh, both moments a mystery, although she remembered laughing at someone's jokes at that dinner, remembered touching those same mummies. There she was herself even, in a blue pashmina, ten years ago, sitting like a little girl, legs dangling over the edge of a pier, the flash catching her unawares in the dark, looking into the water. She remembered it had been lit by the moon, remembered the way the moon had shimmered out over the surface of the water, leading somewhere, but she couldn't remember what she had seen there or even why she had been looking.

All at once, she had to be in her garden.

The day was crisp and the air clear. Listening to the MP3 player Charlie had given her for Christmas the year before, Julia walked from one zone to another with no particular agenda, snapping off dead limbs and pulling up winter weeds when she saw them. The orchard seemed to be wintering well, the few wasted apples and pears a deep, deep brown in the sun, like underwater egg sacs hanging from the brittle, leafless coral of the trees. The vegetable garden looked almost barren, belying none of the roots that slept below the soil, and she stopped here to tie up a broken trellis or two, mending the joints where the rope had rotted through, reknotting what was left now it was no longer hidden behind tomatoes' tentacles. Passing the bottom of the path that wound up to the front door, Julia paused and looked along its length. As they should be, the beds of Indonesian Crystal Slipper that lined it remained hidden beneath the winter grass, buried deep in the hard, cold ground. She squinted as she tried to imagine what they would look like in the spring, when the rows and rows of tiny white bells would once again hang silently in the air, but she couldn't quite picture it. Even though she knew the bulbs were there, unlike anyone else who might look at the path, even though she had seen them flower in the past, the knowledge didn't help. It had always been a weakness of hers, imagining how sections of the garden might look in bloom. Charlie had once bought her a landscape design computer program to help her, but it remained in its shrinkwrapped plastic on the shelf above her computer. And yet now, as she looked, she thought she saw not a flower, but the outline of a flower, some distance away, close to the house. She squinted harder and realised it was not her imagination, but that one of the bulbs really was blooming in the dead of winter. Still, it seemed off somehow, different. She walked up the path, along the invisible rows of flowers, remembering planting them for her and Robert's fifth wedding anniversary, the same year he'd bought the house. As she'd supervised the two girls from the nursery, he had snuck up behind her, wrapped his arms around her waist, and whispered in her ear, 'What do you think, Cinders? Is it perfect?' She bent to look at the flower and could see now what was different about it. Completely lacking in pigment, its petals were transparent. It was almost as if it wasn't there at all, which, of course, it shouldn't be, not now. She plucked the oddity, wondering whether there might be a steam pipe running beneath where she stood. As she slipped it into her pocket, she tried to remember her answer. She knew what she must have said because she knew what she had been expected to say, but that wasn't the same as remembering.

She rounded the corner of the hedge enclosing the orientalist pond and looked with a certain melancholy at the misplaced bushes. She reached out to the Pua Keni Keni and stroked the topside of its furry leaves. It would be spectacular in just a few months. Who could say, perhaps the mistake, the asymmetry, would be beautiful in its own way. Her nails were a wreck now she noticed, full of soil, one cracked. Against the surface of the leaf, with its delicate spotting, they appeared all the more wild. Julia wondered whether the nail salon she went to in Sag Harbor would be open today. She would go if they were. After all, why not?

As she walked back to the house, she noticed the birds overhead. Not that it was ever noisy, but the neighbourhood seemed especially silent today and the birds' cries and calls had caught her attention. The geese were migrating again and flocked across her land, honking as they went. What could they possibly be saying to each other? she wondered. Do geese really have so much to talk about? As she reached the house, she saw a tiny black bird flying by itself, too far away to identify, puffed up against the cold and the wind, football shaped. If you watched birds fly, she realised, none of them really flapped their wings. This one just beat against the enormity of the sky in little frantic bursts, a jellyfish, a black heart pulsing through the air.

Inside, when she reached for the phone, she saw the red light blinking. She had three new messages. With a sigh, she checked each one. Sure enough she had missed all of them. Each message was the same, more or less – sorry they'd missed her, hoping she was having a nice day, they were going out but they'd try back later, and so on. She turned the delicate pages of the phone book slowly as she looked for the number of the salon, and she paused between each digit as she dialled the number. But when, in her broken Korean–American English, the woman told her they were open, she was still pleasantly surprised.

It felt strange to be behind a steering wheel and she sat for a moment, her hands on the hub, trying to remember the last time she had driven. But, like the moments in the photographs, it was gone. She remembered driving Charles to the doctor late one night, remembered picking Sarah up from a date or two, but these incidents were a long, long time ago, and she felt certain she must have driven herself somewhere in the interval between then and now. As she started the car at last, a single goose flew overhead, honking as furiously as any of the flocks. The engine drowned out its voice.

Then, crossing the wooden bridge over the railroad tracks, as the rubber wheels thumpity-thumped, she passed Jorge walking along the side of the road. He was with what Julia could only assume was his family. Immediately behind him walked a plump woman about his age followed in turn, single-file, by six children of varying ages – the youngest just old enough to walk on her own, the oldest about Charles's age. Dressed in cheap parkas and baseball caps and sneakers and jeans and synthetic scarves and ski gloves and mittens, they were all talking to each other, their words becoming fog before their lips, obscuring their mouths. She slowed down and watched them recede in the rear-view mirror, growing smaller and smaller and smaller. It occurred to her to stop, to ask where they were going, to give them a lift – especially when she thought she could just make out Jorge waving to her – but she decided not to. Instead, she accelerated, drove on, wondered where they were going and how long it might take them to get there.

St. Matthew's Crimson Razor Edge (*Novacula acies coccineus Matteum*). Missing from 838 Glen Pond Drive. Please return. No charges will be pressed.

The air is cold, still. Robert is at last inside now, warm, asleep, but Julia is outside in the night, the light of the stars and the moon reaching down like so many icicles. She does not know why she woke at 3 a.m., why she put on her robe and her slippers and came out here only to think how cold it is, how the cold always lasts so much longer than she expects, how she should be inside. She stands and she does not move and she wraps her arms around herself and she looks up and she looks around and she shivers. There is a scraping sound coming from beyond the privet hedge, she realises, coming from the orientalist Koi pond, the sound of something large tunnelling into frozen winter soil.

Julia moves quietly through her garden, knowing just where to tread to make no sound, even wearing her clumsy comfy slippers. She slips through the trimmed-away archway and behind an evergreen. The sound is coming from somewhere near the new bushes and she makes her way from tree to tree, quietly, until finally she is behind one that affords a clear view. When she peeks out, she sees Jorge crouched down in the dirt, a trowel in hand, digging at the base of the Pua Keni Keni. She slips from tree to tree again, as if this were something she did all the time, creeping around at night in the wild. She takes to it in such a way that when Jorge notices her at last, she is standing almost on top of him, looking down at him, in silence.

He looks up at her, looks down at the earth, up at her again. He puts the trowel down on the ground and shrugs, pursing his lips. Then he sits cross-legged on the frozen ground and waits for her to yell, to cry out, to run. But Julia just looks at him, at the moon falling in a band across his black hair, at the blackness that is his dark eyes at night, at his wide nose with its sharp ridge, almost like a beak, at his sweatshirt and jeans and work boots.

Then, without a word, she crouches down before him and begins to scratch at the soil with her bare hands, slowly at first, then more quickly, then frantically, pulling clumps of frozen soil from the ground, throwing them behind her, hearing some land with a plosh in the pond, hearing some hiss through the pine needles of the evergreens, she is digging, scooping, tearing up the earth. Jorge merely watches at first, stunned, then reaches quietly for his trowel and digs himself, carefully avoiding Julia's hands as they fly at the soil, her hair in her face, kneeling in her silk pyjamas. Soon the work is done and they both cease, although Julia does not look up. If Jorge had to say, he would guess she was looking at the roots now exposed before them in the ground, lying over the earth like a net. But it is difficult for him to decide exactly what she is looking at, her hair hides so much of her face. He bends and pulls gently at the base of the bush. It lifts free from the ground and he shakes out some earth as he watches Julia, again unsure whether she will do something more. He opens his mouth, closes it again, takes a step back, opens it once more, then turns and burrows away into the loam of the night.

And in the morning, when she wakes, Robert beside her, when she comes down from her room, when she takes her cappuccino from Martina, Martina gasps, drops the mug. It shatters on the slate and the foam and the coffee leap out with more violence than seems possible to either of them.

'My God,' says Martina, holding Julia's wrists. 'My God,' she says, looking into Julia's eyes. 'Please, signora – please,' she says. 'Tell me – what have you done to your hands?'

Shoplifters of the World Unite

James Flint

*There was something I always really liked about the mixture of
resignation and optimism in this song. It seemed right for a story
about a kid hunting down a thieving animal in order to secure
himself a small portion of love. There's a sort of economy of theft
at work in both.*

Them aardvarks are tricky critters. Old fellas, we always call 'em,
cuz they sneak in and around the houses and the compounds
stealin stuff like wise old ghosts, but you never see 'em. Some
say the guys who steal the goats' food and the chickens' eggs aren't
aardvarks at all but are the old bad river spirits, that the aardvarks
couldn't do it cuz no one ever sees 'em. But that's not true, cuz last year
I saw one and more 'an that I captured him so now I know for sure.

I was fully thirteen at the time, I know cuz when Aloysius came
and said he'd seen an ol' fella scuttling down along the river bed, it was
the exact same day as my birthday. I thought he was just tryin to get
attention cuz that's what Aloysius did, he was a real ole liar, and that's
why no way was I gonna start believin him.

The ole fella had eyes bright as a cheetah's, he said, and a back broad as a turtle's, and a thick black stumpy tail that bashed side to side when he was runnin.

I said he should go take a drink of water from the donga pool, if he spected me to believe a word of that, which would be a crazy thing to do cuz the donga pool is down below the village in the elephant rocks and is full of cess and skeets.

But then again Simon Old Old once told me that he'd seen an aardvark once and what Aloysius said, well, in truth it weren't that different. Simon Old Old had been living in the village longer 'an anyone, and he'd seen everthin there was to see. He never xaggerated nor lied about it neither, unlike Aloysius. And unlike my own damn dad, you might as well know, who would never admit that there was nothin he didn't know nor hadn't seen, nor anything that you thought of 'at he hadn't thought of first.

Anyhow, Aloysius was saying he'd seen the fella down in the river bed, right where there are all those 'oles and burrows, and he went on and on about it, tellin everyone how he was special cuz he'd seen by daytime what was only supposed to come creepin out and go softly softly hauntin by the magic of the moon, and all in all spoilin what was supposed to be my damn birthday. So next day on the way back from school I went round the way of the widow's goat yard and wound a good fine strand of wire off the bottom of her fence, right out of sight where she wouldn't see it nor the goats wouldn't see it neither.

The wire was all kinked up and rusted, but after I'd got it between my feet and rubbed round a useful bit of rock it came up straight and fair old shiny. When I'd got it as good as it was gonna get, I looped one end into a loop just 'bout the right size to fit round my thumb. By threading the end through that little 'ole what I got was a sort o' lasso. And the first half of my plan was done right there.

The second half was simple as pumpkin soup. I went and got myself a good bit of stick from the wood stack round the back of our shack, good meaning straight and true with no boles nor branches sticking up off it. And then round the middle of this I wound the wire, three, four and then five times, so it was fixed on good and strong.

To test it – cuz nothin that's gonna work is no good without testin – I looped the loop over the big old camel thorn that grows by the water tank and swung on it all swing-like til I was sure 'at it would hold. Then I had my trap. A good trap an all. Straight away I unhooked it off the tree and hauled it over to the mud bank. Movin as quiet and sly as I could I set it outside the biggest burrowdown, the same one what as had the freshest droppins. Round the 'ole went the loop, pressed down in the mud at the bottom so the ole guy wouldn't see it, and then with the wire all snakin away down the slope and the stick laying quiet at the end all was set, and nothin suspicious about it nor nothin.

And then I left it and went and had dinner like it was a normal everyday kind of a day, which in most respe'ts it was.

Next day was Saturday an I was up before anyone on account of not being able to sleep. All night long I'd been staring up at the tin on the roof, wondering if the ole fella had got caught in my snare, the only thing keeping me from going down the river bed in the dark being that I'd most likely make lots of noise and frighten him off. But with first light I was up and out and down there like someone had buried a box of bucks and I'd just dreamt a dream of exactly where they'd hid it.

But I saw pretty quick my snare hadn't worked. The old guy must've been in and out because it'd been knocked out aways from where I'd put it. It hadn't caught nothin, and it didn't catch nothin the next night neither, even though I reset it better 'an before. When I put it back for the third time I'd already pretty much decided that my plan wasn't gonna work and that Aloysius had been lying all along, just like I'd thought. But then I stopped by there on Monday on my way off to school, and the snare was snapped down out of sight and the stick was dragged all the way right up to the 'ole.

The old guy was caught! I dropped my books and hopped around and ran down to the mudbank where straight away I grabbed that stick and started hauling on it, thinking I'd just fetch up that old aardvark right away and get a proper look at 'im.

Well, if I thought that I was crazy all right. I pulled on that stick and I pulled and I pulled, but every tug I gave that old guy tugged back twice as hard. If that 'ole of his had been any deeper he'd've dragged me clean down in it, stick or none. That's how hard he was pullin.

I pulled and I pulled. I pulled till my arms and my shoulders hurt like crazy. I pulled till my feet had dug craters in the mud. But the plain truth was I weren't big enough to pull that old fella out by myself. He was too strong for me, I had to give him that. I needed some help if I was ever gonna get to look that aardvark in his face, that's one thing that was for sure.

I ran back to our shack just as Dad was coming in to get his breakfast. The moment he saw me, there was just one question in his mind.

—What you doin here, boy? Why ain't you at school?

—I ain't at school, I said, filled to bustin with how proud he was about to be of me, cuz last night I snared that old guy aardvark what's been stealin all our eggs. But he's dragged the snare down into the bottom of his 'ole, and you gotta come and help me pull him out!

He clearly wasn't listenin to me one little bit.

—I gotta do nothin of the sort, he said. All you've got to do is get your arse to school before I whop it.

—But Dad! I caught an aardvark. And no one in the village 'cept Simon Old Old has ever even seen one.

—School. Now.

—But what could be a better lesson that seeing an animal what no one else has ever seen?

—Don't test my temper, boy.

He nearly had me then – he was lookin at me all sideways like he did when he was gonna raise his arm and biff me. But he hadn't said anything when I'd said that truth 'bout Simon Old Old, and that's where I saw my chance.

—But you've never seen an aardvark either, have you, Dad? And now I've got one wrapped around a wire and all's we've got to do is pull 'im out. And then you'll be the first guy in the village not just to see an aardvark, but to catch 'im an' all.

He waited for a moment and in that moment anything could've happened. But instead of biffin me he sniffed.

—Alright, then. I'll come take a look. But just for a few minutes. After that you get back to class.

—Thanks, Dad, I said, and we started off down the path that led down to the riverbank, me in front, him behind. I know my dad pretty well, see, and I know just how he thinks.

By the time we got to the mudbank he was more excited than even me, I reckon. He looked at the wire and he looked at the 'ole and he looked at the stick and he sniffed.

—That my firewood?

—I'm gonna put it back soon as we're done.

—Well, make sure you do. And where'd this piece o' wire come from?

—I found it out back by the water tank.

—You found a good piece of wire like that just lyin around?

—It was all kinked up and rusted. I put in a lot of time just gettin it polished up and straightened out.

He looked at me like he knew I was lyin, but he was gonna let it pass.

—Could be a fox or a jackal, just as easy, he said, lookin at the 'ole.

I didn't say nothin. I knew that he'd know what it was just as soon as he gave a heave on that wire.

The minute he did it pulled tight like it was wrapped round an iron stake buried deep in the ground. He hadn't counted on that, I could tell that alright. He'd forgotten about me not being at school and all that. All that he was thinking about now was that 'ole, and whatever was stuck down there in it.

He crouched down and had a sniff at the opening, like an old dog. The burrow curved down hard and deep, with the wire vanishin over the lip, not three feet in. You couldn't see nothin. I knew cuz I'd looked.

—He's in there alright, he said, right and low.

—Yes, Dad.

He got up then and brushed the dirt from his knees, then settin his feet either side of the 'ole he started to pull. He pulled, damn it he pulled, he pulled so the lines stood out on his neck like roots round a tree and sweat made a patch like blood on his shirt, even though it wasn't even properly hot yet. He pulled, and he pulled, and the wire pulled back, and then the stick slipped from his hands and he flipped down the bank and landed on his back in the dust.

I daredn't even let out a smile, though I never wanted to let out a gut-rippin laugh half so damn much.

—What's so funny, boy?

—Nothin. Nothin's funny.

—So you gonna stand there like a halfwit, or are you gonna come over and lend me a hand?

I did what he said and helped haul him up to his feet. I don't think I'd ever tried to do that before. His hand felt right strange in mine, and he didn't half weigh some – nearly tipped me over right there. But I got him up and back at the stick now we took one end apiece and started haulin on that just as hard as we could. When that made no bones we turned around and put our shoulders to it, straining away like two ole bulls at a yoke. But push nor pull as much as we could, we couldn't shift that fella, not one single inch.

After a bit we gave up and went and sat on a grey log out in the middle of the dried-up creek bed and rested. While we got our breath, we both stared at the 'ole.

Dad brought up the hem of his shirt and wiped the sweat off his forehead.

—He don't want to come out, does he?

—It's lookin that way, I said, doing the same with the arm of my T-shirt, cuz the hem wouldn't reach.

—Well, we're not gonna get him out like this, Dad said, after a minute of ponderin. I think we'd best go get the truck.

The truck! Now why hadn't I thought of that? But then that's what dads are for, ain't it? For bringing out the heavy guns when the time is right.

—Run and tell your uncle to bring the Toyota down here, Dad said. And an axe. Best tell him to bring an axe. He stopped and ran his hand across his hair. And while you're at it stop by the house and pick up a flask of water.

The Toyota! The Hi-Lux Diesel 4×4! It was the coolest vehicle in the village. Actually that was an easy game to win, cuz the only other vehicle in the village was Simon Old Old's tractor, which had long since lost its wheels and just sat in the sand now driving the water pump or the big ole wooden thresher that we get out when it's harvest time. Uncle has it cuz he's a doctor and he needs it to go pick up supplies like bandages and needles and medicines and stuff. It's not his really, it's the government's, but he gets to use it when he wants as long as he doesn't make too much noise about it. Uncle studied at a university across the border and he's the only doctor in the whole three valleys, so people come from all over to his clinic. When I haven't got school or work I help him out, and we talk a lot about how I'm going to go study to become a doctor too then come back and work with him right here.

Sometimes there's a whole posse of people queuing up outside waitin to be cured, but today we was lucky cuz Uncle was all alone in his office. I spied him through the window, sitting there fillin in some of the forms that needed fillin. It was a job I knew he hated cuz he always told me so, sayin however many forms he did there were always more where they came from.

I raced into the room an stood there pantin.

—What's up with you? he said, peerin down at me over them brown ole glasses he has to wear for readin.

—Me and Dad we's caught an aardvark and we need you to bring the Hi-Lux so as we can pull the fella out.

Uncle looked at me like I'd gone completely crazy.

—Now just slow down a moment, take a breath, and tell me all of that again, he said.

I did as he tol' me, jus slowed right down and went through it like a slow-brain. When he understood what was goin on he sniffed like

Dad sniffs when he's thinkin – I guess they're brothers and that's what brothers do – and then he got up and fetched his medi-bag sayin that he'd best come along just in case any one got hurt.

—What about your forms? I said.

—What? he said, and looked at them like he'd never even seen em before. Oh, they'll still be here when I come back, he said.

We got in the truck and got it goin and we were on the way when I remembered that we needed an axe and water, so we detoured by our shack to pick em up. By the time we got back to the creek Dad had unwound my original fixin from the stick, and had looped it into a big ole loop of triple thickness. I jumped out and signed to Uncle to back up the truck. When it was close enough we hooked Dad's loop on the tow hook. It fitted just so.

—Now we'll get you, aardvark, I said, but quietly, just to myself, so'd I didn't draw down a jinx. Then Dad and me stepped back and Uncle put the Toyota in gear and started haulin away.

Nothin happened. That ole aardvark was so stuck down in his 'ole that even the Hi-Lux couldn't pull him free.

—No way, Dad, no way! I said. It's no wonder we couldn't shift him when we were pullin on the stick.

—Give it some more! shouted Dad, so Uncle revved the engine. But all that happened was the front wheels started spinnin in the dirt. By now the sun was right overhead and suddenly it all seemed a little crazy, us standin in the bakin heat down in this dry ole river bed, next to a Toyota spittin dirt on account of a wire goin straight down into a 'ole.

Uncle slacked off on the power and the wheels stopped and the cloud of dust and sand slowly blew away.

—He ain't budgin, said my dad.

—I don't believe it, shouted Uncle, leanin out the window. He's gotta budge. That snare'll tear him clean in two if he don't.

—Try 4WD, Dad said. If that don't do it, we'll call it quits and leave him be.

—Oh no, I said, but Dad told me to hush and do what I was told.

—You gotta be prepared not to get everything you want in life, he said, like that wasn't a lesson I had to learn close on every day.

Meanwhile Uncle stopped the engine, pulled the lever for 4WD, and started it up again. Then he really went for it. JNGG JNGG, went the engine as it started straining, and this time the wheels bit hard into the dirt and didn't spin.

I counted five seconds passing then another five, and I was just trying to wrap my head around how this was the craziest thing I'd ever seen, an aardvark facing down a Hi-Lux Twin Cam switched to 4WD, when, WAP! The truck scooted forward like a springbok what had caught its tail on fire, and something hard and brown and mean got spat out from the burrow, flew through the air, and landed mashing and squealing in the middle of the river bed.

Quick as anything Dad fetched up the axe, ran down to it, and clunked the ole fella right on the cap of his head. Crick, crack, the bones went snap, and that was him done, very dead.

Uncle switched off the engine and jumped out the cab and everything was suddenly all quiet and still.

We all stood around, getting our first proper look at an aardvark big as this. Or any aardvark, if truth be told. It was a special moment, as we were the first three guys since Simon Old Old to see one up this close and the first guys ever to catch one.

So this was him, the secret aardvark, the ole fella who sneaks about by night and steals eggs and flour and who no one ever sees. Overall he wasn't half as big as I thought he'd be. Still, he was a tough one, though. My wire noose was wrapped around his neck alright, but despite me and Dad and the Toyota Twin-Cam haulin on him half the mornin it hadn't even cut his hide, it was that damn powerful. His arms and legs were real thick, like a honey badger's, and I reckon he'd got bigger claws than any leopard, which makes sense when you think about it, cuz no leopard ever had to dig out a termite mound, hard as old concrete. I reckon they could could tear you right open, if they got close enough, and they were all he had to hold on with down at the bottom of that 'ole. Must've been some sight, to see him clamped on in there for all he was worth. I reckon he must've been frightened near to all hell. Poor little critter.

When we'd looked our fill Dad and Uncle picked him up and slung him in the back of the truck. Then we drove back to our shack where we skinned him and Mum cooked up some of his meat for our dinner, though not before we'd spent a good while roundin up the widow's goats, which had somehow snuck out of their pound.

The meat was pretty chewy and tasted pretty strong, so I can't say it was the best stew I ever ate. After dinner Dad and me sliced up what was left and hung it up to dry and it made much better eatin that way. It took about a week and all that time I was king at school, on account of what had happened. Aloysius was pretty angry to begin with, said it was his aardvark and that I'd stole it from him because he'd seen it first. I asked him did he want to fight me for it and that stopped him complainin because he knew damn well he couldn't take me on. But later when the meat was ready I took some strips round his house and gave em to him along with one of the aardvark's paws. After that we were friends again, and we took the rest of the meat and gave it out at school, and we had no trouble with any one for ages after that, cuz not even the older kids had tasted aardvark before and there was no denyin it was strange and magic stuff.

Girl Afraid

Rhonda Carrier

Being on the cusp of something. Wanting everything to change yet fearing the future and who one might be, or not be. The fear of doing something and simultaneously of not doing it. The fear of one's appetites and dreams because one has a strong suspicion that reality won't ever live up to them... These are the sentiments The Smiths aroused, or met, in me in my teens, and although this project has made me realise just how many utterly brilliant titles Moz and Co. came up with, and not just brilliant songs, it's 'Girl Afraid' that seems to encapsulate them most fully for me. Above all, I suppose what I tried to evoke in this story was an overall Smithsian mood (fatalistic miserablism meets intense yearning), and that's why I chose an adolescent girl fumbling with her nascent sexuality, her self-expression and, through those, her place in the world.

Flying out of Manchester, picking at the chipped purple glitter of her nail polish, she tries not to think of anything. In her lap, the little machine whirrs. With a mechanical motion, barely glancing down, she opens it and flips over the tape. The song starts where it left off, minus about five seconds; she nods, allows herself a smile, of recognition but of something else too, something she can't define. It's as if the song is speaking directly to her, as if someone out there – she raises her eyes and probes the darkness outside the window – knows her. Cares. As if the answer is out there somewhere, in the velvet blackness, even if she's not sure what her question might be.

She knows each song by heart; she's listened to nothing but this for the last six weeks. And the in-between bits too, where John Peel introduces the bands in his voice that reminds her of honey and tar mixed together. A random night on Radio One, as she'd twiddled with the dials while rain smudged the streets beyond her window into something formless, otherworldly. A random night, a random hour, the random decision to hit the Record button, and yet somehow it had become the soundtrack to her life. A dozen or so songs of which she never grew bored. Each one speaking to her, of her life. How could she stop listening?

Prefab Sprout now: a voice, a bit like Morrissey's, now she comes to think of it, singing about words being like trains, a way of getting past things that 'have no name'. She wonders about that for a moment, about the name of the group, what it means, and about nameless things. Like the feeling she has, almost all the time now. The strange dread, a dread without object, a fear of something she can't put her finger on. They tell her she's good at English, have predicted an A at O-level, an A-level, perhaps even uni. But if she has this talent, how come she can't put this feeling into words?

Reclining on a lounger by the pool, she turns over the cassette. After one day in the sun, her legs have scorched; she's hoping they'll turn brown before the week is out, that she'll have at least one thing to show for the holiday. Unfurling them in front of her, she throws her arms up over her head, closes her eyes, abandons herself to the beat of the sun on her body. She feels both sleepy and alert, as if something is waiting for her. She doesn't know what, but it both excites and frightens her. She opens her eyes and glances about her, but there's no one there.

Mum, Dad and Damian are down on the beach, pinking like prawns. If she cranes her neck a little she can just about see them from the terrace where she lies. Damian, ten, is building a sandcastle with a girl of about the same age. They are laughing, flashing white teeth in the sun. She shields her eyes, feels a headache coming on. She doesn't know why she can't be with them, why there's suddenly this funny sour taste in her mouth, this feeling of her chest filling, or her lungs seizing up, or something, whenever she watches them. They look so ordinary, just like everybody else, with their Woolworths towels and too-tight Speedoes and pale skin slathered with grease like turkeys basted for the oven. *Ordinary* – the word makes her shudder despite the noon heat. She turns up the volume on her Walkman, tries to drown it out, erase it from her head. She closes her eyes again.

At the bar, Damian perched on a stool beside her, she lets her long legs dangle and glances about her as she slurps her iced Tango through a straw. Mum and Dad have sent them down ahead, told them not to stray from the bar, not to talk to strangers. She's not sure about the waiter who keeps looking at her as he passes, with lowered eyelids and smoky blue-grey eyes. Does he count as a stranger? Is he one of the forbidden? Not that she could speak to him, if she tried: every time he glances in her direction, she feels dizzy, has to steady herself against the bar with her hand. The fear returns. Or did it ever really go away?

Throat burning it's so dry, she remembers how it was in Affleck's Palace that time, as she browsed for clothes that would express – she didn't know in what way – how she felt inside. Different. Marked. Cursed, perhaps. And suddenly she'd clocked him, riffling through the rails but eyes on her. She'd pretended not to know, and he'd finally stopped her at the door, asked her whether she wanted a coffee. She'd looked into eyes full of a kind of desperate hope and wanted to say 'yes', but 'no' came out instead. And she'd stood there with her bags – inside, a frayed beige suede jacket, a mohair tank top, ankle boots – and wondered when life would begin. She takes another sip of the garish orange liquid, shakes her head. The evening ahead unspools in her mind's eye like a slow-motion film, long hours between her and the moment she can lie on her bed again, looking out into the night, watching the waves glint like little knives beneath the moon, listening to her tape, over and over.

By the pool again, The Associates, Scritti Politti, The Psychedelic Furs in her ears, she's trying to lose herself to the stark red light that floods her eyelids when she closes them, to let it flood her entirely, as if she has slipped into a bath of blood: warm, enfolding blood. But here's that feeling again, of a presence, an imminence. She's imagining things again. A shadow falls across her. She peels open her eyes and he's there, a halo of sun around his head, a tray crowded with empty glasses held aloft on his hand. He's gazing down at her, but with the sun behind him she can't read his expression.

He looks around them, but on this little terrace, partitioned off by a bank of foliage, they can't be seen. Slowly, as if sleepwalking, he bends to place the tray on the table by her lounger and comes to squat beside her. He's so close, she can smell the vestiges of cheap aftershave on his collar, overlaid by sweat, can see an area of his scalp where the hair is growing sparse. He must be as old as her dad, maybe even older. And yet between her legs she's grown wet for him. Her desire shocks her.

He gestures for her to take off her headphones, and she realises that for a moment the rush of blood in her ears has drowned out the music, the music that has become part of her this last month and more, the cadence of her body, the thud of her heart and the flow of her.

He takes the headphones, adjusts them slightly and places them over his own ears, cocks his head on one side. A bemused smile ripples across his features; his eyes, fast on hers, are questioning. She doesn't know what this question is either, can only guess.

'The Cocteau Twins,' she tells him, straining to hear the tinny music above the poolside noise. Not that she needs to hear; she knows the playing order by heart. He's watching her lips now, observing her from beneath those hooded lids, but she knows that he doesn't understand what she said, that it doesn't matter what she said. That there was more than one question in his eyes. He looks up and around as if waking from sleep, and then he reaches out and runs his fine smooth fingers over her bare arm in the same movement as he rises up and away from her, already reaching back to the table for his tray, scanning the poolside again. Before she can say anything, he's going, melting away like a beguiling dream that won't let you keep hold, and her racing heart is drowning out the music from the headphones cast aside on the canvas of the lounger.

And she wants to curl up right there and not get up again. But she's not so lost that she didn't clock, as he moved away from her, the name on the little brass badge on his chest.

At the bar again, on her way back from the loo to the restaurant, she breathes in, swallows the anxiety that's lodged in her throat like a fur ball, and thrusts the square of folded paper towards the man polishing the glasses.

'For Javier,' she says, not even sure whether she's saying it the right way, feeling as if her legs are going to give way beneath her, unable to look him in the face as she speaks. Then she turns and, without daring to look around to see whether he's even on duty tonight, walks back to the restaurant, keeping her pace steady, fighting the urge to break into a run.

At the table, Dad is signing the room tab as Mum stubs out her cigarette and stands up, dressed to the nines for dinner in this terrible restaurant with its tepid all-you-can-eat buffet and lousy pianist. Her mother: standing there with that blue eyeshadow, hair so set she might as well still have her rollers in. She stares, wondering how ordinariness can suddenly look so strange, how what is most familiar can become, in a heartbeat, so alien. She feels a sudden stab of pity for Damian; she, at least, will be able to leave in a year's time. Jangly guitars start up in her head. A year: she can bear that, surely? She turns and heads for the lift.

Damian slips quickly into sleep, exhausted by the pool and the beach.

She's never felt so awake in her life. Opening the balcony door, she steps out into the darkness, looks out over the sea, blue and calm by day but threatening by night, oily-looking and fathomless. She makes to put on her headphones but then remembers. Sitting down, she watches a couple walking on the sand below her. For a moment they stand looking out at the swell, hand in hand. Then they head to the end of the beach, clamber over some rocks and disappear.

She glances towards the door, checks her watch. The bar stays open until late, and there's no telling when he might finish. She's amazed she even had the guts to do it, and she has no idea what she will say or do if he does show up. But something inside her has broken, some kind of bind or restraint. She's still frightened as hell, but she'll be more frightened if she just lets life carry her along like a leaf on the water.

Though her watch tells her it's past two, she's still not sleepy. She steps inside, takes a blanket from her bed, looking at Damian's face in slumber, so untainted, so unmarked by life. She tries to remember when it started, chewing at her guts every morning when she awoke, like a rodent. Bubbling up inside her. But she can't. Or had it always been there, part of her, part of being alive? She heads back out onto the balcony, sits down again.

He's not coming. She knows that now. She doesn't know why – perhaps he wasn't working tonight, or perhaps he had other plans he couldn't get out of. Perhaps – who knows? – he has a family to go home to. Or perhaps he, too, was afraid. She'll never know. For a moment she lets the fear wash over her, submits to it: the fear of failure, of being unloved, of never amounting to anything. But then she thinks she's not sure that it really matters anyway, that he didn't come. He wanted her, she saw that in his eyes, felt it in the way his fingers twitched as they met her arm, as if electricity had passed between them.

On the table before her lies her notebook, open, the cheap, chewed Biro finally still beside it. Words have filled the ruled lines across the pages, exploded out of them, running down the margins, filling all available space like an army of insects marching across the white space. She doesn't really know where they came from, the words, only that they erupted from her as she stared out over the waves, over the beach with its idling couples, with its teenagers swigging from beer bottles on the boardwalk. Had almost vomited out of her as she sat looking at the string of nightclubs with their glittering strings of lights and flickering neon, luring people in like flies to overripe fruit. The yearning inside her she'd felt at the poolside, the yearning to be part of all this, to be part of *something*: that was what had fuelled her as she wrote, letting the words stream out of her like an exorcism, not caring what they meant, not trying to shape or force them, knowing only that they provided relief. The kind of relief that only the razor blade had afforded her, on those days when it seemed that the rain outside her window would never stop, that the grey streets of Withington must finally yield, must be worn away.

Flying into Manchester, her notebook spread in front of her, the sublime, floating guitars untangling her as they always do, she looks out at the lights, at the rain washing away the city's grime, purging it of its sins. Her eyes move back to the pages, her fingers reach again for her pen. She's found her means of escape.

Back to the Old House

Graham Rae

The following sad tale is actually a quartet of true stories from four real people rolled into one; no names, no pack drill. The relationship between the short story and the song title it is named after needs no explanation.

Aye yer right pal, getting dumped eftir goin oot wi a lassie fir five years is a fuckin sair yin right enough. Gettin the bullet oor the phone, tae; fuck that fir a game ay sodjers. Jist get anither beer ben ye n try n firget aboot it the night. Ah ken whit it's like tae get dumped by a lassie yer right intae myself. Iviry man dis. Kin tear the fuckin guts right ootay ye n nae mistake.

Emotion's a funny thing awthegither. The way ah look it it, it's kinnay like drugs, or onythin else thit ye kin lose it on – some kin take it, some cannae. Some fowk jist cannae handle thir fuckin emotions it aw n they end up gettin bent oot ay shape fir the rest ay thir days oor yin specific person when whit they should be daein is getting up n dustin themselves off n jist movin right along.

Tell ye a classic fuckin example ay whit ah'm talking aboot, n yin thit'll pit yer ain problems intae perspective. Happened a few year ago, jist eftir ah left the skill. Ah got a YTS – Youth Training Scheme, mind ay them, the late eighties, Christ, ah'm showin ma age – doon whit used tae be the Magnet N Southerns warehouse years ago doon Etna Road alongside this laddie ah used tae be it the skill wi, same form class n ivirythin. Ah wis workin in the actual mill itsel, whereas he startit off in the office n eventually got shoved oot beside whaur ah wis.

N if thir wis ivir a laddie less suitit tae a mill job than young John then ah've yit tae meet him. He wis yin ay they right quiet, shy, sensitive boys, ye ken the type. Now ah minded ay John fae the skill. Eywis playin the fuckin class clown tae try n get attention, bit ye could tell underneath it he wis a right shy wee bugger. Dinnae think ah ivir saw him talk tae a lassie in the four year we wir in the same form class.

Because he wis so shy, it wis a big surprise when he came intae the work n startit goin on aboot this lassie fae oor year it the skill, Mary Carr. Seemed the wee man wis right fuckin intae her in a big way, hud been fir a fair while. Bear that in mind ah only funt oot a lot ay this story later on, when he laid it on me eftir she fucked his heid up. He telt me because he nivir hud too many neeburs outside ay work n ahwis yin ay the only boys in the mill he spoke tae on a regular basis. He kent thit he could trust me no tae knock a rise oot ay him, because ah kent he wis awfy thin skinned.

Wee John wis right intae this fuckin Mary lassie, stars in the eyes, the lot. Couldnae see it masel, she jist seemed like an average bird tae me, bit beauty is in the eye ay the beholder n aw that, eh? She wis a bit ay a slapper, if the truth be telt. A couple ay ma pals hud a poke it her it the skill, bit ah didnae hae the hert tae tell the wee man. True fuckin love n aw that shite, ken? Ah sometimes wonder if ah'd telt him the score aboot her then whither it woulday made ony difference, bit probably no. Ye ken whit some fowk are like when it comes tae somebody thir right intae, they only hear whit they want tae hear, n even then they sometimes dinnae hear it right.

Bit that's the way John wis wi this Mary lassie. If ye said black aboot her he'd say white, the sun shone oot ay her fuckin erse, aw that rubbish. Perr bugger. It wis embarrassin the way he went on aboot her.

Ye wid ay thought she wis Mother fuckin Teresa instead ay jist anither Fawkirk lassie tae hear him go on. He wis giein her poetry, floors, aw this fuckin romantic nonsense, totally smitten, n she wis jist eggin him on.

Some lassies are jist like that, though. They'll play wi a guy's heid n get him tae dae cartwheels fir them, jist tae see how far they can push him, then jist move ontae somebidy else when they've hud a guid laugh it thir expense. Only thing is, some ay these lassies dinnae ken thir playin wi fire, or jist dinnae care, n they kin drive some guys off the deep end if thir no careful.

Eftir him tellin me whit she wis sayin n daein fir a couple ay weeks ah sussed oot her game. Ah jist kept ma fuckin mooth shut, though. The way ah saw it, John wid go through aw this crap, make a bit ay an erse ay himself n learn a bit fae it. Ye live n learn n resolve no tae make such a fuckin mess ay it the nixt time, haud yer emotions back a bit, we aw go through it. Ah thought, well, it least wee John wis gettin the guts tae approach wimmin, ken? It's aw aboot confidence buildin, as ye'll no doubt appreciate yersel.

So ah listened tae him goin on aboot her fir aboot a month or so. He fuckin took her through tae Edinburgh, bought her her dinner, records, aw that stuff. Which wisnae easy on a YTS wage, believe you me. He nivir got a ride ootay her, mind you – when ah say he telt me ivirythin, ah mean ivirythin. It wis a wee bit embarrassin tae hear the wee man go on. He'd nivir hud sex afore n thought his luck wis well in there. He got as far as her bedroom, sittin on her bed n spoutin aw this fuckin embarrassin personal shite while she jist sat n listened, nae doot gettin a fuckin buzz ootay it. Some boys jist dinnae ken who tae keep thir mooths shut in front ay, especially inexperienced yins like John.

Ah made a couple ay wee enquiries n funt oot thit this Mary wis goin oot wi anither boy apart fae John n she wis obviously jist toyin wi him, fuckin stringin him along fir the hell ay it. They'll huv tae bury her in a fuckin Y-shaped coffin. John widnae believe it when ah telt him aboot the ither boy she wis gaun oot wi. It probably wisnae ma place tae tell him, bit ah jist felt really rotten fir him. He said ah wis jist jealous. Me, jealous ay him! Ah wis goin oot wi a bird it the time, whit the fuck hud ah tae be jealous aboot?

Bit John wis that far gone. He wis fuckin obsessed wi this wee cow n she wis jist toyin wi him the way a cat might wi a moose, only wi less fuckin mercy. He wis headin fir a serious crash n aw thit ah could dae wis jist stand on the sidelines n watch his life turn intae a fuckin car crash.

Aboot six weeks eftir John hud first startit sniffin aboot this Mary he came in in a helluva fuckin state, heid totally wastit, wanderin aboot the mill like a heidless chicken fir the entire day. Telt me thit Mary didnae want tae see him onymair. Ah felt right sorry fir him so ah took him oot tae the pub eftir work tae get a couple ay beers doon his neck n gie him a bit ay a fuckin pep talk, lit him git things off ay his chist.

Well, it turns oot John hus been intae this Mary fir three years – three fuckin *years* – n it wis on account ay she wis apparently the only lassie it the skill thit wid talk tae him much. So he fixated on her, nivir haein the guts thit ony normal young laddie might huv hud tae ask her oot n aw that. N his fuckin feelins jist built up inside. Because this Mary lassie spoke tae him – probably jist fuckin flirtin wi him the way she flirtit wi half the other fuckin boys in oor year – she wis his dream lassie. Or it least yin he could talk tae, n it that point they wur probably yin n the same tae him.

So he bumps intae her eftir he'd left the skill n she gies him a ticket fir an eighteenth birthday pairty she's haein. He gets wrecked it the pairty n makes a fool ay himself n sends her a box ay chocolates tae her hoose tae make up fir it, n she starts writin him letters n phonin him. He goes roond tae her hoose a couple ay times tae visit her, takes her oot n aboot, n things as far is he kin see ur goin jist hunky fuckin dory.

So John is sittin it hame yin time listenin tae this band The Smiths – who're a band ah've nivir been able tae stand, by the way, that Morrissey's jist a whinin-faced cunt – jist thinkin aboot Mary n the fact thit she's goin away tae university soon, switherin whither tae tell her how he feels aboot her n how long he's felt this way, when he gets the idea fae the lyrics tae this song called 'Back to the Old House' – ah'll remember that title till ma dyin day – jist tae dae it n the hell wi the fuckin consequences.

She'd huv hud tae be fuckin blind not tae be able tae read him it that point. Ah telt ye he wis a naive wee punter. She obviously felt fuck all for him, bit he nivir hud the experience base it that point tae read the signs. But he gits the guts – n this dis take a hellay a lot ay guts fir a shy laddie like him – tae go roond n tell this lassie how long he's been intae her.

Baaaaaad move.

Onybidy who kent anything it aw aboot wimmin wid ken thit tellin her somethin like that wid jist freak her oot big style n hae her runnin a fuckin mile in the ither direction. Which is whit happened wi this Mary tae a certain extent, bit she liked him bein that much intae her a wee bit tae. Typical fuckin female ego shite. 'Oh, John, you're not obsessed with me, are you?' she asks him, n he says she hud a look on her fuckin face thit said she thought this wid huv been cool, bit it least he hud the guid sense tae say no. So he walked ootay the hoose, heid understandably spinnin, n ootay her life.

Well, ah tried tae set his heid straight, bit he wis in a right bloody state. Telt me she'd telt him he should see a fuckin psychiatrist, n ah wid agree – ye'd huv tae be mental tae fall fir a wee hoor like that sae badly. Ah telt him, 'John, the hell wi it, son, jist forget it, she's no fuckin worth it, she disnae deserve ye, move on n firget her, there's plenty mair fish in the sea.' Aw the usual shite, ken whit ah mean?

N he seemed tae be listenin tae me. He stopped talkin aboot her n seemed a lot happier it his job. The boy's jist hud a dose ay cold hard female reality, ah thinks tae masel, he'll be aw the better fir it. He'll no git taken sae bad the nixt time, or mibbe the perr bugger'll get somebody who'll treat him a bit fuckin better. Bit it least he seemed tae be gettin oor this fuckin lassie n her twistit fuckin evil wee mind games.

So he didnae mention her fir two or three months n ah starts tae forget aboot her awthegither. Then yin Monday morning he comes in n his heid is fuckin wastit again. Tells me he'd met Mary fir the first time in months on the train comin back fae Edinburgh on the Setirday night n thit she'd telt him he wis a fuckin looney n tae stop fuckin writin tae her cos she wis nivir gonnae reply again.

Ah didnae even ken he'd still been writin tae her, n tae tell ye the truth it pissed me off a bit. Ah hate it when ye gie fowk advice thit they've asked ye fir n then they go oot n dae the exact opposite eftir agreein wi ye. So ah jist telt him straight he wis bein a fuckin idiot n tae get a grip ay himself n leave the lassie alane, thit we'd been through aw this shite afore. Ah wis a bit sharp wi him, but sometimes ye've jist got tae be tae get yer fuckin point across.

Ah thought it yin point the boy wis gonnae start fuckin greetin bit he jist nodded n agreed wi me, sayin thit he kent he wis daein stupid stuff bit he couldnae help himsel sometimes. Ah jist says 'Look, forget her, leave it, end ay fuckin story, ah dinnae want tae hear nae mair aboot it, right?' So we both goes back tae work n ah wis really hopin that would be the end ay it. It wis gettin a bit fuckin weird fir me, tae tell ye the truth. Ah'd nivir seen onybidy as hung up on somebidy else as John wis on this fuckin bitch. Ah nivir saw him fir a couple ay days aboot the work, n ah thought he wis off sick or somethin. Then yin ay the mill boys tells me thit he'd heard fae the office manager thit John hud gone n fuckin topped himsel. Deid. A fuckin... paracetamol overdose. End ay... story. So that wis that. John McAllister, ma workmate n neebur, deid it sivinteen. It wis totally fuckin unbelievable, ah jist couldnae take it in, fuckin sivinteen, Jesus...

Ah went roond tae his hoose that night tae see if it wis true, really true, fir masel. Ah hud tae. It wis John's maw thit answered the door, een rid fae greetin n a bit spaced oot fae the tranquillisers the doctor hud gied her tae calm her doon. Ah'd met her afore, so ah went in n sat n talked tae her. She kept askin me why this hud happened, her n John's faither couldnae understand it it aw. She hud nae idea why he'd done it, he'd nivir left a note, n ah hud tae explain tae her aboot Mary an aw the fuckin hassle he'd went through wi her. She wis completely taken by surprise. John hudnae even mentioned Mary tae her or his dad.

Ah left that hoose that night jist feelin totally numb. Ah jist couldnae fuckin take it aw in! Why did the silly wee bastirt no talk tae me, tell me whit wis goin on in his fuckin heid instead ay takin aw they fuckin pills? We could've worked it oot thegither, but naw, he hud tae go n fuckin top himsel, ae? Whoivir said thit suicide makes murderers ootay yer pals wis right. Fir fuckin months ah kept goin oor the things he'd said tae me in the weeks afore he died, tryin tae find clues is tae whaur his heid wis it. Nearly drove masel fuckin mental, bit in the end the only yin responsible fir John's suicide wis himsel. He wis the yin thit poured the fuckin painkillers doon his neck, n thir's naebidy in the world worth fuckin killin yersel oor. Pity that Mary hudnae sussed oot she wis messin aboot wi a time bomb until eftir she'd lit his fuse, eh? Onybidy who treats ye like she treated John disnae deserve the shite off yer shoes, n ah'm shair ye'd agree.

Ah saw her yin time eftir that, in the Cross Keys up the toon. She wis wi some fuckin guy n ah went up tae her n asked her if she kent aboot John. She said she did n thit he wis a nutter who should ay been locked away years ago. Ah jist shook ma heid in disbelief. Ah've nivir hit a woman in ma life bit ah wis sair fuckin temptit that night, ah kin tell ye. Bit causin a fuckin scene widnae huv solved anything n ah jist left the pub.

Bit time rolls on, n it wis twinty year ago this August thit John died. Ah wis thinkin aboot him eftir ah opened the *Falkirk Herald* n saw Mary in the weddin pages. She wis standin there oh-so-pure-n-fuckin-white glued tae the airm ay some guy ah didnae recognise. Ah thought it wis lucky the photay wis in black n white otherwise ye'd huv been able tae make oot John's fuckin bloodstains on her hands. Ah wis fuckin ragin n ah spat on it, ripped it oot ay the paper n chucked it in the fuckin bucket whaur it belonged.

The way ah see it, she disnae hae ony right tae happiness eftir tearin oot John's hert like that. Ah could understand her gettin freaked oot by him, but she might it least huv been a bit mair understandin, ken?

Bit she's still alive n John is still deid n that, ma man, is life. The whole thing wis a total fuckin nightmare fae start tae finish, n it's jist a pity thit John nivir got the chance tae learn the rules ay the game.

Ye ken it's funny, bit ah kin see history kinnay repeatin itsel in a sense. Ah ken this young lassie who has this quiet young guy thit seems a bit obsessed by her. He's sent her a couple ay bouquets ay floors, n even went tae the lengths ay paintin the words ay some auld love song on the pavement outside her hoose in the middle ay the fuckin night. Pretty mental stuff, eh? Bit like ah says, some boys jist dinnae ken how tae express themsels ony ither way. The sad thing is they build up a mental picture ay the lassie thit she could nivir live uptae, even if they did go oot thegither. So they hit the groond wi a bump…

… or mibbe a fuckin overdose. Ah hope this laddie's got a wee bit mair sense thin John hud, bit if no ah hope ah'm in the pub the night he comes in fir a drink n a talk.

So ah suppose the bottom line ay it aw is that shit happens, bit it hurts like hell at the time. A bit like ma parched fuckin throat here! Your bell, ma man.

Ah propose a toast: tae John McAllister, rest his soul, n tae the insanity ay true love…

… Cheers.

Stop Me If You Think You've Heard This One Before

Willy Vlautin

I didn't find out about The Smiths until long after they'd broken up. I was sitting in a car with my cousin who'd just moved back to town and he played me 'The Queen is Dead' and I couldn't believe I'd missed them. I became a huge fan right away. My life was a million miles away from The Smiths. I had barely left my hometown, and most of the friends I had would have thought I was a real freak for liking The Smiths. But man were they good. I always imagined Morrissey as a dramatic disgruntled co-worker. 'Stop Me If You Think You've Heard This One Before' is a straight-up country song title, but everybody ends up in a country song at some point. Morrissey's lyrics seemed to live in the drama of one, and for a while he could write about it better than anybody. So the story I wrote is my 'Stop Me If You Think You've Heard This One Before'. This is my country song story.

For years I just floated along. I wasn't much. I'm not saying I'm anything today, but back then it bothered me more than it does now. Now I'm all right with where I am. Now I know that just getting along is OK, that it's better than a lot of things.

I grew up in the same house that I was born in. My mom and me lived there. My dad left us when I was eight. He moved out of state with a woman nobody knew or even knew existed.

Growing up I wasn't much of a student or an athlete. I barely got through high school, and I tried at it. I stayed up a lot of nights studying, toiling over it. So when I got out I didn't even think about college.

I'm not extraordinarily gifted in any particular way, and I'm not saying that for any reason except that it's true. I have never been obsessed with working on cars or slaving over a computer or trying to make a trunk full of cash. Plus I've always had trouble speaking in front of people, a lot of times I can barely eat in front of them. And I can get lazy. I can watch TV for days. I can let dishes stack in the sink for a week. I feel bad about all of it. About everything I just mentioned.

I guess when I was younger, deep down I wanted to amount to something, have some sorta normal life like everyone else. Own a house. Have a kid that likes me and a girl that stays with me.

For six years after high school I worked at a chemical warehouse and loaded trucks and answered phones. The chemicals we sold were to mines located all over the northern part of the state. I'd load 48-foot trailers with chemicals used for leaching gold out of the mountains. I couldn't smell, my sense of smell was ruined because of the chemicals, and my hands were scarred. But it was a job and, for a guy like me, with my education and experience, I guess that I felt like I was lucky I had it and I worked pretty hard at keeping it.

So the story starts here. It starts out of the blue. It starts after a year-long dry streak. I met a girl at a bar called the Swiss Chalet.

She was young and had black hair and was small. Not much bigger than the size of a jockey. But she was good looking. It was the summer and she wore summer dresses. The dresses you see poor women from the South wear in old movies. They were thin, almost see-through, and she had a body. Jesus, it was something else. And then on top of that she flirted. She was an expert flirt. She would talk to me and look at me and laugh with me, the whole time giving me that eye. She had an eye worse than a broke hooker.

After a while I began taking her home to my room and she would spend the night there. And the nights, I got to admit they were something. I'd never been with a woman like that. It was like something out of a skin flick, like something you'd read in the letter section of a porno mag.

But then the night would end and morning would hit and everything changed and I should have known it right then. I should have realised it and run as fast as I could, but of course I didn't. Of course I just got myself in deeper. It all went like this.

She got up before me. Her job started earlier. And she'd always make a big production of it. Like she was a real saint just for getting out of bed. She'd wake me, every time, and say a few things like, 'Why don't you get better coffee? Where did you put my underwear? Your neighbours are too loud. You should talk to them. You shouldn't let them take advantage of you like that.' And then she'd get dressed and leave. I didn't know her phone number. I didn't know where she lived. It wasn't like that, you know? We weren't like that.

Then one morning the woman woke me up and told me I slept too much. I told her I didn't have to be to work until ten, that I liked to sleep in and she just shook her head and said it didn't matter.

'A man shouldn't sleep all day if he's going to amount to anything,' she said.

She was in the kitchen making coffee in a black G-string saying all this. She had a tattoo of a cobra on her back. I got to admit that had something to do with it. Her standing there like that in my kitchen. After that I tried to get up early with her, but it was hard.

Maybe a month went by and she got out of the shower and stood there wet and naked, drying her hair. I was at the kitchen table half asleep when she told me the bars we went to were too smoky, that the smoke hurt her eyes, that the smoke ruined her clothes and made her hair smell.

'Smell this goddam shirt,' she said, and threw it at me. 'It's the worst-smelling thing in the entire world. I'm sick of it. I'm seriously sick of it.'

So after that when I saw her, when we'd decide to meet up, we stayed in at my place. We'd watch movies and watch TV and make margaritas or daiquiris and then afterwards she'd try to rape me. And this went on, this went on for some time and I didn't mind it. I didn't mind not spending all my money at bars. Bars are a waste of time the farther you get away from them. They really are. And I like movies. I could watch movies all day long if I had to.

A couple months go by and she comes to my place one night and I offer her a whisky and ginger ale but this time she says she doesn't want to drink any more. She's had enough. She tells me she's a blackout drunk. She says she's the type of drunk who ends up in the bed of a man whose name she can't remember. She says this happens all the time. Not every time, she says, but enough times.

'And listen. I'm tired of it. It's worthless. You're gonna ruin your life if you keep doing it. I'm bad, I am and I admit it, but you're worse and you won't admit it. That's a bigger problem. That means you're an alcoholic. You're gonna get cirrhosis of the liver. My uncle had it. It isn't pretty and it hurts like hell. He could take it, but it would kill you.'

'Look,' I tell her. 'I don't black out. I don't wake up not knowing where I am and who I'm with.'

'I've seen you guzzle down the beer. Anyway, you don't know what it's like for me. If you knew you'd stop just 'cause of that. You'd stop because I'm a blackout drunk. You'd stop 'cause I was an army brat. I went to fifteen different schools by the time I was thirteen!'

Then she falls on my couch and curls up in a ball and begins to cry her guts out. She cries until she passes out in exhaustion.

Maybe a month or so later we're in a mall shopping for a birthday present for my niece. There were a load of people there and I don't like crowds. I hate malls and I hate shopping. So my nerves were already going when she suddenly stops and says, 'I'm not a slut if that is what you think. Is that what you think of me? Is that what you think of our relationship?'

Then she begins to cry frantically in the middle of all those people and stores. We're standing outside of Sears. I begin to panic. What the hell's going on? What did I say? Did I say something that was making her feel this way? Was there a way, without even knowing it, that I had caused this?

She said nothing more after that. I tried to talk to her but she wouldn't. She just closed her mouth like a mute and ran off. I searched around the mall, then looked around the parking lot, but I couldn't find her and finally I just gave up and went home.

I didn't see her for two weeks, and it made me lonely as hell. For the first time in a long time I got really down. I swear to God I didn't understand what I'd done and I felt horrible about it. I was a wreck and Jesus, that's when I realised how deep I was in. Maybe I was really falling for her. She was a serious handful, I knew that, but maybe that's just women. I didn't have much experience. Maybe that's just the way they are. Maybe love worked like that, and maybe it was me that was too stupid to realise that that was what was happening.

I guess maybe a month goes by, and one evening at the Swiss Chalet I see her and she's drunk and flirts with me like she's never met me. She talks with me and holds my hand and gives me that eye. She gives me that eye like she was gonna take off her clothes right there and pull me underneath a table. We each shove down five or six drinks then go back to my room and stay up all night in the sack. Afterwards, near dawn, I feel better. She's got an imbalance or some sort of mental issue, but hell it's hard to be alone once you've had a taste of it the other way. It really is. Plus as they say, love ain't easy. So I decide right then and there that I was gonna give it a serious try.

'I hate this town,' she says some time later. She'd moved her things into my apartment. She stayed at my place almost every night. She became my room-mate without me ever asking her to. But honestly, truthfully, it was all right with me. I'd never moved in with a woman before. My mother, who lived in Bakersfield, was excited about it. She hadn't met her, but me living with a woman. It was a good start, my mother said.

'I hate this town because it made me say all those mean things to you at the mall. It's this goddam redneck town that's made me a blackout drunk and made me sleep around. It's lucky I don't have some horrible disease. It's lucky I haven't been murdered. I swear Reno is the worst town on the entire planet, and it's done it to you as well. It's trying to make a bum out of you. It's the reason you work at a chemical company and pollute our environment. It's the reason your place is so horrible.'

'What the hell are you talking about?'

'I'm talking about the environment. I can't believe you work there.'

'You leave me out of this.'

'All I'm saying is this town is ruining you. It really is. It's ruining us both.'

A week later in the middle of the night she wakes me and says she would spend the rest of her life with me. She had never woken me before. In the darkness she said she would marry me and have my children. That's why I sleep with you, she said, because I want you for the rest of my life. You're the one. I don't sleep around any more. I'm not like I was. Do you feel the same? Do you feel the same way about me? Her voice was soft with uncertainty. She lay naked next to me. It was snowing outside and three days before Christmas. I told her of course I felt the same way. But Jesus, I didn't know what the hell I felt. I just knew I had to get up and work that next morning and I didn't want her to get upset.

Maybe a month goes by and she left a card on my truck while I was at work. She wedges it between the windshield wiper and the windshield. Inside the card was a key to a motel room, the name of the motel, and directions. She said she would be waiting there after I was done with work. So I went to the motel and she was naked on the bed waiting. I opened the door and she attacked me. She had handcuffs and talked like a degenerate nymphomaniac. When we were done I held her and we watched TV and I fell asleep.

She woke me up an hour or so later and said, 'If you truly love me we'll move to a real city and not stay in this shithole. Look, don't I give you everything? Don't I give you my entire soul? I'm not a slut. If that's why you think I brought you here then you're as bad as the rest.' Then she started crying. A full-blown crying blowout. She began to hyperventilate and then finally curled in a ball and fell asleep. I didn't know what the hell to do. So I went down and bought a six-pack and the newspaper and went back to the room and sat in the bathtub. But the thought began creeping in. Maybe she was right. Maybe I was a failure. Maybe it was the town that made me so. Maybe she was right and this was my big chance to change, to prove myself, to take a chance and become someone of substance, someone with some sort of character.

I was lucky and my company has offices in Portland, Oregon, where we had decided to move. They hired me on graveyard shift loading trailers. It wasn't as good a job as I had, but it was a start. It was something. We took her things from a storage unit then loaded as much of mine as my truck would hold and left town.

With my savings we rented a small apartment, an apartment the size of the one I had just left, but these things happen, I say to her. I only have so much money, I say. It won't always be this way, I tell her. I give her my credit card to decorate. I go to work the second day I'm in that city. I drive my truck forty-five minutes each way and I load trailers for nine hours a day. And our lives go on.

Maybe two months later she throws a plate against the wall. She's doing the dishes. She can't find a job. There are no jobs in this city, she tells me. How can there be so many goddam people here and no jobs? What kind of city is this?

Another month goes by and I come home one evening and she says there was a break-in, that our neighbour stood in the bedroom and watched her sleep.

'You know I sleep naked,' she says. 'He's a fucking pervert. I know he's a pervert.'

'Are you sure it was him?' I ask her.

'I'm not lying. What's wrong with you? Why don't you believe me?'

'I'm just asking,' I say. 'I'm gonna go over there and talk with him. I'll kill him if I have too. But are you sure? Are you certain? 'Cause if you are I'll get my shotgun and blow his fucking brains out across his living room.'

'Maybe I was just having a nightmare,' she says suddenly, and begins to cry. 'Don't kill him. Jesus, I don't want that, just don't leave me here alone at night. I'm dying here alone at night. This city is just as bad if you're gone every night. It's boring out here. I don't have a car, 'cause you take it every night and we live out in the fucking suburbs. I don't know why we have to live all the way out here. Why the hell do we live all the way out here? It really isn't a city out here. It isn't the city at all.'

I tried to transfer to day shift, but day shift is what everyone wants and I'm low man on the pole. So after a couple months I quit. I get a new job as a forklift driver and I work days and because of that our life falls along like everyone else. She makes me dinner, we see movies and shop downtown. And she finally gets a job at a pizza parlour. She's happier. And me? I'm more relieved than anything. Maybe things will change, I tell myself. Maybe we're turning the corner.

Then a month later she comes home and says the owner of the pizza place, a fifty-five-year-old man with four kids, made passes, that he had touched her, that the other workers didn't like her, that the other workers were jealous of her, that they were all a bunch of morons who tried to stab her in the back, who said horrible things about her when she left the room.

I didn't say anything and then she says she's tired of being broke all the time. She's tired of the grind. Tired of the goddam grind. 'Why don't we have any money?' she says. 'Why don't you make more money?' It went on and on and on and on and on. It was ugly, that night was ugly, too ugly to really talk about and in the end I just felt bad about being broke, about being a forklift driver, about never making any money, about being a low-wage stupid son of a bitch.

Since I didn't have any friends in the town and had no kids or any other obligations, I took on extra shifts. I worked Saturdays when they needed me and I got a job in the warehouse next door and worked two nights a week on swing.

It was the dead of winter by that point. She stopped going to her job at the pizza parlour. She didn't quit, didn't get fired, just stopped going. She said the winters in Portland were too much. The rain brought her down. She wasn't used to the rain.

'All it does here is rain. And, look, you say we can't afford cable. But you're gone all the time and I'm stuck all the way out here.'

'You said you were tired of being broke.'

'Well, why can't you get a job where you make more money and don't have to work so much? You can't expect me to just sit around and wait for you all day and goddam night.'

It was springtime when she said she would kill herself if we had to live in that apartment in the suburbs any longer. She got a knife and threatened to stab herself. She took a vial of pills in front of me and I had to make her puke them up. I told her I'd find us a new place, a nice place in town. I called my brother and borrowed $1,000 and I rented us a house in a nice neighbourhood in the city. But this time there was no easy stretch, there was no calm time, there were no good times.

'I've given you my body. I've given my life to you. But you won't marry me. What am I to you, a hooker?' she said while crying her guts out. She stood there naked. We had been in bed together. We were right in the middle of it when she started.

I didn't know what to do. I was stuck. It was past anything I knew anything about. But I tell you this. I couldn't marry her. My guts hurt when I thought about it. But then I couldn't leave either. I guess I loved her and what if she really did try to kill herself? What if she wasn't just talking? Then what? So in the end I just stayed.

I began to lose myself. I began to dream of disappearing, of vanishing from the city, from the state, from the world. I began having hour-long daydreams about being an old man, about sitting in a chair knowing it was almost all over. I tried to tell her these things. I tried to let her know that I might be starting to crack.

'If you leave me,' she says, 'I will kill myself. If you leave me, I'll die. I'm not joking,' she says to me. 'Look at what you've done to my life and now you want to leave me. You want to ruin me and then cast me aside like a dirty diaper.'

So I quit talking to her. I mean I'd say hey to her and talk about anything she wanted to, but I guess I quit telling her much of anything I was thinking. I began closing down. I also began drinking again, mostly after work. I began sitting down the block from our place and drinking forty-ounce beers. I'd drink at least one before I had to set foot in that house.

One evening as summer ended she put her hand through a window and sat on our bed and bled.

'It's your fault,' she said in a crying fit. 'It's your fault because you don't love me any more. You don't want me any more. I know. I give my heart and soul to you, but you give me nothing. Where does that leave me? You tell me.'

I tried to say things to get her to calm down. I tried to say what was right, but I would have said anything at that point. I was worn out and she could tell. She could tell I didn't mean anything I said.

Finally one night just before Thanksgiving I told her I was leaving. I broke down. I started crying. I told her if she killed herself then that was her decision. I told her I was finished. I was on empty, I told her. I was all cashed in. I told her she could have everything I owned. I gave her my truck and most of my money. I paid rent for two months and ran. The next morning while she lay in bed crying, I packed my things and left. I stayed in a motel, gave my two weeks' notice, finished that and took the bus back to my home town, the town I was in when I met her.

By then I was flat broke and uncertain of everything. I had to borrow money from my mother. I rented a room in a small boarding house and begged back my old job at the chemical company. I rode a thrift shop Free Spirit 10 speed bike to work there every morning.

Within six months the girl married a man who owns a bar in the city where we had lived. Where she still lives. He owns a bar down the street from our house. This I hear months later from people who knew her.

I remember riding along the road to work as cars and tractor-trailers rushed past me, their frozen air trying to knock me from the bike. I remember riding and thinking to myself that I didn't feel lost any more. Even though I was just where I was. Same job, same town, same routine. And this time I didn't even have a car and was thousands of dollars in debt to my mother, my brother, and three separate credit cards. But the strange thing is I didn't beat myself up all night any more. I didn't lie there wondering why I didn't have more guts, why I wasn't a better student, why I wasn't more of a businessman, or a forward-thinker, or an entrepreneur or a business visionary. All that had changed.

More than anything I just felt lucky. Even when it was snowing and I was trying to pedal my bike through the ice and slush. Or when I had to pull a double shift or when I woke up lonely in an empty bed knowing that it might always be this way, that the woman might have been my only shot, that she might be the only one willing to take a chance on me. Even then, with no end of it in sight, I just felt luck around me like it was some sort of belt.

I Won't Share You

David Gaffney

'I Won't Share You' has always been one of my favourite late Smiths songs. I love its simplicity, its yearning melancholy, the way it points towards later elegiac solo Morrissey songs like 'Hold On To Your Friends'. It begins on the chord behind the home chord then winds around and around itself, starting in the middle and ending in the middle, never going home; more of an extended middle-eight than a complete song. This song that never goes home made me think of sharing and the fragility of the connecting threads between us, and how in reality we can never go home. I used Noël Coward's lyrics because I sensed a deep link between his style and Morrissey's – the loneliness, the separateness, the sparsity of language, the dark humour.

There was a spot of soft earth at the top of the hill overlooking the caravan site and it looked just right so I leaned the spade against a tree, unfolded the blanket in which I'd wrapped it, and laid it out on the grass. I looked at it for a time, lying there, precious-looking. I won't share you. No, I won't share you.

The hill was bleak, dusty, a place where nothing grew apart from stumpy skeletal trees. A breeze ruffled my hair, pleasant after the big-fisted heat of the town and the caravan site. Everything felt different high up on the hill. I kneeled for a few moments, closed my eyes, said a few things in my head, then opened my eyes again, half expecting it to have gone. There it lay, still and pale. I stood and lifted the spade. Burying seemed the correct thing. We couldn't be together, it was better like this. No one to worry us.

> No one to hurry us
> To this dream we found.
> We'll gaze at the sky and try to guess what it's all about.

I placed it in the shallow hole. Shallow. Newspaper reporters make a noise about holes being shallow, as if deeper holes made everything OK, and I think I know why that is. They think it's permanent, they think it will last. But nothing lasts. Used to think everything would last. But why should it?

This can't last. This misery can't last. I must remember that and try to control myself. Nothing lasts really. Neither happiness nor despair. Not even life lasts very long.

It all started only a week ago. I had been paddling in the sea with Felicity and Jamie when I noticed it; a faint indentation, the thickness of a hair, running around my upper arm. I thought it was nothing, dismissed it, but the next day Jamie and I were building a sand palace for Felicity's Barbie and I was putting the finishing touches to the low wall around the moat when Jamie said, 'Dad, what's that funny line on your arm?'

What had been a line no thicker than a whisker was now a shallow groove running round the whole circumference of my arm, just below the shoulder. I squeezed my fingertips into the hollow. It was like a deep wrinkle. Maybe that's what it was; a wrinkle. I stretched my arm to see whether the furrow would disappear. It didn't.

I continued to build the palace for Felicity's doll. The Barbie came with a purple horse and this meant stables and an exercise field, as well as the ten-roomed building she had specified, so we had a lot of construction work to do. I decided to ignore the blemish on my arm. When you notice something odd about your body the idea becomes all-enveloping – like when I was a kid and obsessed that my ears were monstrous flaps, and slept with a heavy book on the side of my face.

I splashed water on to the sand, scooped up a handful, and poured it on to the palace walls to make smooth concrete whirls. Jamie and I set about moulding the runny sand into shapely turrets and balustrades while Felicity marked out the horse's field. Then Georgina came over with ice creams.

'Mum, has your arm got a line on it like Dad's?' Jamie said.

'I don't know, darling. I don't think so.'

'See?' Jamie poked my arm, showing the groove to Georgina.

'That's funny,' she said. 'Maybe it's how Daddy's been sleeping. Have you been leaning on something?'

I brushed sand from the wrinkle. 'I don't think so. It must have always been there.'

She, like me, pressed her fingers into the wrinkle then followed it round my arm like a needle in the groove of a record. 'Does it hurt?' she said.

'No.'

'Has it been bleeding?'

'No.'

'Have you fallen, or cut yourself or bumped into something?'

'No.'

'It's almost like there was something tied around your arm and then it's been taken away and left a wound. But you say it doesn't hurt?'

'No. It's not sore. But I think I'll put my shirt back on – this sun is scorching.'

On the way back we passed Hooch sitting outside her caravan scratching numbers into her ledger. Hooch was the odd-job woman and had the caravan next to ours. She looked after everything –

changing gas bottles, fitting light bulbs, unblocking drains, and organising engineers for the more technical problems. She was a skinny, unclean woman with long straight black hair, a severe fringe and lipstick of a dark red colour which made her teeth glow margarine yellow. But you seldom saw them because she never, ever smiled. She had few callers and there wasn't a man. The solitary nature of her job seemed to give her pleasure. In the evening she sat outside her caravan filling in a ledger. We knew what she was writing about because we heard her talking about it on her mobile phone: the flickering light in number 46, the leaky shower tray in number 49, the smell of gas in number 94.

Hooch had slung a hammock between her caravan and an adjacent tree, and when she'd finished writing in her ledger she clambered into it to read her book. Always a biography, and always of a sporting figure. We used to sit outside our caravan a few yards away from her, drinking cheap wine and looking at the stars. She was a restful presence and some kind of companionable relationship between us developed which was hard to describe. When she wasn't there we felt somehow incomplete.

Hooch listened to one CD over and over again – an album of Noël Coward songs, louche, loungey tunes from another era, with desperate, yearning, lonely words. A soft piano tinkled over a ukulele rhythm:

Speak low, Johnny,
Tip toe, Johnny,
Go slow, Johnny,
Go slow.

'Hiya, Hooch,' I called out. She lifted her head from *Tennis Ace, The story of Chris Evett*, and pointed her ferocious little eyes at me. Her hair looked greasy and held the tracks of her comb.

'Hummph,' said Hooch.

'Hooch, our fridge door won't close properly and I was wondering whether—'

Hooch held up her hand to stop me, then reached under the table from where she produced a polythene bag with a plastic device inside. 'Use this to click around the door,' she said. 'I knew about that problem.'

'So you had that ready for us?'

'Yes,' said Hooch.

'In case we asked?'

'Yes.'

'But what if we had just struggled on and didn't ask?'

'It's up to you,' she said. 'I don't interfere, I just help when I am asked.'

I looked at her for a moment. There were times when she seemed half buried in some sediment of despair.

'But you knew about— oh, never mind,' I said. 'Enjoy your book, Hooch.'

From her stereo Noel Coward cooed that all he needed was

a room with a view and you,
and no one to give advice.

When I woke up the next morning the first thing I did was feel my arm. I sat upright in shock. It was definitely worse than yesterday. My finger went in deep, up to the first knuckle. I lifted it to see whether there was any effect on my movements, but there didn't seem to be.

I made a cup of tea and sat on the step of the caravan. Six thirty. People were assembling for that day's trip. A melon farm? Or was it a pearl factory? I lifted the arm above my head. No problem. I went over to the terrace table and tried to lift the parasol holder, which was anchored by a heavy container of water. I could just about shift it, the strength in my arm didn't seem to be affected. While holding the parasol aloft I caught a glimpse of Hooch at her window, washing a glass at the sink. She was looking at me and frowning more than usual. If it weren't for her thick fringe I imagined I would have seen deep furrows in her brow like dark canals.

When Georgina appeared I told her I was worried. *The situation with my arm*, I called it, and she laughed.

'The situation,' she said back at me.

I told her that I definitely hadn't had it since I was a kid, that it was something new. Again she asked about pain, and infection, and cuts and accidents, and again I told her no.

'Well,' she said, 'I think it's nothing to worry about but maybe you should go to the campsite health centre and see what they say.'

I stopped at Hooch's hammock. Her bare feet were hanging over the end. Hairs grew from her big toes.

'Do you know anything about the campsite doctor, Hooch?'

She looked up and swept her eyes from my heels to my scalp, instantly bored by the query.

'What's up, like? You got a cold or summat?'

I smiled. 'I need to see the local sawbones. You're not in charge of our physical health as well as our gas bottles, are you, Hooch?'

Her expression didn't change. 'No,' she said. 'Just repairs to the caravans, like.'

'I know,' I said.

Her face under the stiff line of her fringe showed no flicker of emotion. 'People think they're funny, like,' she said. 'Dead funny. You know what? Nobody's funny nowadays, that's the truth. You need a doctor, like? Uh?'

'I could do with seeing one today.'

From her stereo Noel Coward pleaded

Please be kind.
When you're lonely-if you're lonely
Call me – call me – anyhow.
If you want me – need me – love me
Tell me,
Tell me,
Tell me now!

'The doctor's surgery is from nine till eleven, thereabouts,' Hooch said. 'He'll see you and he'll give it to you straight. But you have to have your green slip.'

'Oh, I've got the green slip.'

I thought I saw the flicker of a smile before her face resumed its default position of an aggrieved grimace.

Now I was kneeling next to the hole. Now I was getting rid of it, I felt much, much better. It had felt for a time back then as if someone, somewhere, was disassembling me, disaggregating me, taking me apart, fleck by bitter fleck, as if they wanted to shatter me into a thousand and three spores, toss me out of the window, into the shrieking storm. It was as if they needed a cutting from me to stick in the ground, a whole new me to spurt out, to break me up, seed me all over, in every fold of earth, every pleat of skin, in Hooch's greasy hair, in the angry heat of some dead dog yard. To put me in places where people don't go, places they've forgotten, places they never knew they came from that they go back to in the end.

One more look, one more touch, before the dirt. This is the time. My time. The drive. The dreams inside. I had to hide it. Cover it. Cover it with dirt. We call it dirt, but is it dirty? What is on dirt that is dirty? Can dirt be cleaned? Can something be taken away from dirt to make it clean again and, if so, what would be left? Am I what is left when dirt is taken from dirt?

I wondered about leaving the lid off. But it looked so fragile, so needful, yearning for its blanket of dust. Happy under soil. Safe and warm and tired. I wished I could join it. Maybe that's what it wanted.

as happy and contented as birds upon a tree.
High above the mountains and the sea.

I touched it again. One last time. Like placing my hand on the skin of some mummified saint. It felt warm, which was impossible, and soft too. Was that a pulse? A trembling, a tingle? Was there a tiny blush of pink in the fingertips? It still seemed part of me. It was me.

I began to scrape the dirt over the top.

There'll come a time in the future when I shan't mind about this any more.

Later that night we had gone to the campsite bar. It was kids karaoke and Jamie wanted to do Eminem and we'd said he could as long as he did the radio edit with the gaps for the swearing.

Earlier in the shower I had a really good look at my arm. There was a groove all the way round, a definite groove. It seemed even deeper than before at the beach. I could insert the tip of my thumb right inside and trail it round the whole circumference.

'Ladies and gentlemen, Jamie Crowther.'

Little Jamie, hair gelled up, hollered the words to 'Stan' while the Dido track warbled away, and we watched, utterly rapt. Georgina gripped my knee. 'Look at him. I can't believe he's ours.'

'I know,' I said, and squeezed her hand, grinning like an idiot.

The doctor was a young Spanish man with excellent English who listened carefully and nodded seriously as I described the opening that had appeared from nowhere on my arm.

'Have you been OK otherwise?'

'Fit as a fiddle,' I said.

'OK, let's have a look.' He moved me over to the examination couch. I sat on the edge and removed my shirt and the doctor looked at the strange aperture, inserting his fingers just as I had and checking to see how far round it went. 'Just move your arm a little for me,' he murmured, and I worked my shoulder up and down. The split opened and closed like the sucking lips of a horrible shellfish.

'You can put your shirt back on,' he said. 'And sit back down over there.' I did as he asked and he looked at me and tapped his pen on his pad of paper. 'You say it appeared yesterday?' he said.

'Yes.'

'Well, it looks to me like it's always been there. It looks like it's healed perfectly, but that at one time it was some kind of wound. Maybe from tying something tightly around it. Have you had anything tied tightly around it? Some sort of ligature?'

'No.'

'Can you use your arm? Can you lift and stretch?'

'It feels fine.'

'Do you use any drugs. Anything like that?'

'Not really.' The fact was I smoked spliffs most weeks – most days if I was honest – but I didn't see how that was relevant. 'The odd glass of wine.' Bottle more like.

He looked to the side for a beat. 'Any mental health problems – depression, anxiety?'

'No more than anyone else. We all get down from time to time.'

'That's true. Well,' he said, putting down his pen. 'If you can use the arm and you're in no pain and there's no sign of infection I don't think there's much we can do. Just keep an eye on it and come back if it gets any worse.'

Georgina and Jamie and Felicity were waiting for me when I got back. I had promised that we would drive into the local town where there was a market and fairground rides.

'Everything OK?' said Georgina, flapping her arm like a chicken.

'He said to keep an eye on it.'

'Let's do that, then.'

As we packed up the car I saw Hooch looking at us out of her caravan window as she watered a plant. She raised her eyebrows in a peculiar way.

I wandered around the market, making a conscious effort not to check my arm. My hand wandered up there once or twice, but I corrected it. The problem would seem worse if I kept checking all the time. I vowed to leave it alone for a whole day then check in the morning.

The market was crawling with tourists in combat shorts and lumpy off-road sandals. I could never see the attraction of markets. We have markets at home and they are colourful and exciting too, but we never go to them. The stalls were stocked with oddly shaped cheeses, glossy vegetables, olives, and big ugly dried fish. Jamie and Felicity liked a stall that sold dogs, rats and live chickens and we spent a long time hanging about there. After a few hours I had completely forgotten about the situation with my arm. Jamie bought a miniature kite and Felicity a wooden parrot which flapped its wings when you pulled a lever.

When we got back to the car she gave me it and I yanked on the lever. 'Squawk squawk, hello Felicity, where's Jamie?' I said. But operating the toy parrot made me aware that the arm felt quite a bit different now to how it had the day before. It felt much longer than the other arm, like it was heavier. I returned the parrot to Felicity and went behind the car, where I pretended to check something in the boot. I lifted up my shirtsleeve. When I saw what had happened I said, 'Oh,' as if I had been struck. I trembled. I felt faint. The opening had grown much larger, to such an extent that it wasn't a wrinkle or an opening any more. It was as if a huge chunk of flesh had been gouged out of my upper arm, as though it had been turned on a lathe the way you make the indents in table legs. The space was now the width of three fingers and the piece connecting my arm to my shoulder the thickness of a broom handle.

'Georgina, come here a minute.' She got out of the passenger seat and came over to where I was sitting on the lip of the car boot. 'Look at it now.' I gazed up at her imploringly. I must have looked like a sick puppy.

She looked at the arm and I saw panic flash across her face. But then she calmed herself. 'Is it hurting?' she said.

'No.'

'And you can still use it?

'Yes. Look.' I lifted the arm and touched her hair. I sensed her flinch a little as if she were afraid, as if my arm were some kind of monster.

'What's wrong?' I smiled at her. 'I don't think you can catch it.' For the first time Georgina looked worried, and for some reason, this made me feel a little better, as if I had passed some of my fear on to her.

'Maybe you should, sort of, have it up in a sling? Maybe you should rest it and then the flesh will, I don't know, *grow back?*' She looked at me for a long time. 'Oh, Roger,' she said finally. 'What have you been doing?'

'Doing?' I said. 'What could I have been doing that would cause this?'

'Mum,' said Felicity from the back seat. 'Can we go back now? It's Little Mr and Mrs Universe tonight and me and Jamie have entered. Come *on.*'

'Will you be able to drive?' Georgina asked me.

'Yes,' I said. 'It *feels* fine. Just the idea is a bit weird, that's all.'

Everything bad safely hidden away under the earth. I patted the dirt down, stamped it flat with my boots, then looked about me for some kind of marker – stones, or a stick for a cross. But why? A lump of meat. We talk of minds, of souls, but it's just a ball of nerves. Fingers remembering movements, like a pattern of piano keys, or a lover's curves, or changing gear in a car, or throwing a cricket ball. Recalling electronic pulses. I could hear the breeze strumming the telegraph wires, a low hum, making the wires sing. But do we bury these wires? Do we dress in dark suits and shiny shoes to accompany them to the scrapyard, do we sing when they are dismantled, do we cry when the poles are burned or shudder when the connectors are melted for tin? No. We do things, we stop doing them. End of. Nothing has ever really happened if you don't tell anyone about it and no one writes it down. Life tends to come and go. And that's OK, as long as you know.

I found a rusted Coke can and tore it open. Its shiny, inner skin. Twisted it into an antic shape, distressed and hopeful at the same time, twin aluminium arms curling up towards the starless sky. I placed it on the spot. Despite the marker, I knew no one would find it. I'll know where it is, I'll know that it's mine, and in some strange way it will always be with me.

That sounds a paradise few could fail to choose.
With fingers entwined we'll find relief from the preachers.

I set off down the hill to the campsite. The lights from the caravans below glowed soft yellow. Seagulls called – wild, haunting – and music boomed from the clubhouse. A plane was taking off from the airport on the other side of the island, a steep trajectory over the mountains and out towards the sea, tilting gracefully like a gull, its lights winking in the dusk.

But I can look back and say quite peacefully and cheerfully how silly I was. No, no, I don't want that time to come hither.

Hooch was sitting outside talking into her mobile when we got back, with her ledger open in front of her. She stopped talking and switched off the phone as we walked past and looked at us with no expression.

'The fridge is fine with that clip holding it shut,' Georgina said to her. 'Thank you.'

'That's what it's for,' said Hooch.

Georgina stopped at her table and said, 'Do you ever miss home, Hooch? It must be a long season.'

'Five and a half months. It's what I do. It's very cold at home. Scotland is very cold. I like to be outside, like.'

'Did you do the same sort of work in Scotland?'

'No.'

'What did you used to do?'

'I was a social worker.'

Georgina nodded and followed the rest of us into our caravan.

'She's a miserable bitch,' she whispered to me.

'What's a social worker?' said Felicity.

'It's like a life coach for poor people,' I said.

We heard her turn her CD player on, Coward's words drifting over again, as if she were using the songs to communicate something to us.

And when you're so blue,
Wet through

And thoroughly woe-begone,
Why must the show go on?

I was carrying a tray of drinks back from the bar when I noticed that the arm with the situation was hanging down much longer than the other one. We sat in silence and watched the Little Mr and Miss Universe competition. Jamie had dressed himself up as Tarzan, Felicity was a fairy, and after the competition they danced on the stage to the latest summer disco hits, which involved regimented dance routines known by every kid. Georgina and I watched the gyrating children and hummed along to the cheesy pop. We drank a carafe of cheap red wine and I said I wanted some more and she said, yes, so we drank more. If I were honest I wanted to be drunk so I would be sure to get to sleep. I didn't want to lie there worrying about my arm.

Hooch was outside in her hammock, drinking a glass of something amber coloured and reading the life of George Best by the light of the caravan. She was smoking a cigarette. Coward sang out from the machine:

Go slow, Johnny,
Maybe she'll come to her senses
If you'll give her a chance.
People's feelings are sensitive plants.

I mumbled, 'Evening, Hooch,' and a grunt came back.
Inside the caravan I wrapped a towel around the affected area and went to bed. I had a vague idea that the newly exposed flesh might need protecting or that maybe the warmth would encourage it to grow back. I fell asleep and dreamt of diseased bodies and hideous limbless creatures.

The next day I sat up in bed and immediately unwrapped the towel. My arm flopped out and dangled down. It seemed to hang much lower than it had yesterday. I looked at my shoulder and saw that it was now attached by only a sliver of flesh, no thicker than a pencil. I was afraid to let this fragile-looking thread take the weight so I held the arm with my other arm and went and sat on the step of the caravan, nursing it like a baby. Fear came down like a cage. I wished I was at home. My own doctor, Dr Brazenose, would know what to do. These foreign doctors, maybe they weren't so up to date. Or maybe it was some sort of Spanish condition. The doctor didn't seem so surprised about it, after all.

I looked over at the dark windows of Hooch's caravan. I could hear the faint murmur of her radio. When it wasn't Noël Coward, she listened to the World Service – fat, plummy voices growling on and on about foreign uprisings, dysfunctional economies and obscure election results in former Soviet states. I heard Jamie and Felicity scuffling about and Jamie skipped over and jumped on my back. 'Careful of my sore arm, darling,' I said.

'Let's have a look. Have you still got a hole in it?'

'No, it's OK,' I said. I didn't want him to see it like this.

'What time are we going to the water park?' he said.

'When Mum gets up. I'll go and see if she's awake.'

In the bedroom I shook Georgina. 'Georgina, look at it now,' I said 'Look.' I let the arm dangle down. I could still move it, although it did take a bit more effort, but it was now a good six inches longer than it should be.

She sat up and reached for her spectacles. When she put them on she gasped. 'Oh my God, Roger, what did you do?'

'I didn't do anything.'

'What did you do?' she repeated. We both stared at the arm for a long time. Then she said, 'Come here,' and she hugged me. 'Don't worry. We'll take you to the town. There's a hospital there. A big one. They'll know what to do.'

'What if…?' I said.

'Don't be stupid,' she said. 'That's not going to happen, have you ever heard of that happening to anyone?'

I got into the shower and gave myself a really good wash ahead of the hospital visit. I was using the affected arm to wash under my other arm when the situation got much, much worse. There was a kind of twang at my shoulder and the arm fell away, the upper part hitting the shower floor, the hand falling to rest against my thigh. 'Shit,' I cried. 'Fuck. Oh no.' I looked at the shoulder, expecting to see blood. But there was nothing. I stood with the shower gushing and steam gathering around me. I bent and gripped the arm by its hand. Then I rested it on the floor and with my good hand examined the place from where it had fallen. It was completely smooth, as if the arm had never been there. I bent down and felt the severed end of the detached arm too and it was smooth as well.

I turned off the shower. How was I going to explain this to Georgina and the kids? Waves of guilt and despair swept through me.

I wrapped the arm up in a towel and set off across the site to the main gates. I walked and walked, holding the arm close to my chest, tears burning my cheeks. I walked for about an hour but eventually the heat got too much and I collapsed on to a bench. I unwrapped the arm and looked at it. It didn't look any paler than the rest of my body. I touched it. It didn't feel cold, like a dead thing; it felt the same as before. I interlocked the fingers of my good hand with the fingers of my severed arm and sat there. Cars swished by on their way to the beach. I closed my eyes against the scorching sun.

Some time later there was an angry crump of gravel followed by Georgina's voice, sounding tight and clenched. 'Roger! We've been looking for you everywhere.'

I climbed into the car sheepishly. 'It's my arm,' I said. Georgina looked at the swaddled bundle then the stump at my shoulder. 'Oh, Roger, grow up. Are you ill?'

'Well, no.'

'Well, if you're not ill you're just going to have to get on with it, aren't you? Sometimes your self-indulgence is so pathetic. Don't ruin everyone's holiday over this.'

Felicity and Jamie were quiet all the way back. But I heard Jamie say quietly to Felicity, 'Dad's arms fell off,' and I heard Felicity giggle.

Hooch was standing outside our caravan when we got back.

'You've got a blockage,' she said, accusingly.

'Oh,' said Georgina.

'It's affecting the others on the row so I will have to fix it, like. Do you mind if I turn you off for half an hour?'

'Well, I was just about to cook,' Georgina said.

Hooch stared at her, unsmiling. 'I'm doing my job,' she said.

Hooch fixed the blockage then lay down in her hammock to read, with her CD player leaking out Coward's usual sentimental drivel.

Till you know that you know
Your stars are bright for you,
Right for you.

We didn't go down to the bar that night. Jamie and Felicity went to the playground on their own. They were upset to see the arm so I agreed to keep it wrapped up while they were around. But I kept it near by so I could see where it was. We sat outside and drank wine and looked at the stars. You could see Venus. Mercury too. When it was time to go to bed, I unwrapped the arm, pulled back the covers and laid it on the sheet on my side of the bed. Georgina looked at it in horror. 'What are you doing?'

'I'm going to bed,' I said.

'With that?' she said.

'But it's me. It's my arm.' I didn't want to be parted from the limb. I had a vague notion that during the night it might rejoin my body in the same way it had strangely become detached. I got in next to it and cuddled it close. A cold, clammy hot-water bottle.

'If you are sleeping with that arm then I am sleeping on the sofa.'

'Fine,' I said, and rolled over.

The next evening Georgina told me that she was going to stay with

Hooch for a few nights. 'This... you know... this arm thing... it's a bit... eeeuch. You know how I am with snails and things like that.'

'Hooch?'

'Just till the end of the holiday.'

'I can't imagine you staying with Hooch.'

'You can't imagine *me*? You *don't* imagine me, I'm just there.'

We looked at each other for a few moments in silence.

'Snails?' I said.

My face burned with shame and anger as I watched her drag her suitcase through the gravel to Hooch's caravan. Hooch was at the table doing her ledger and she didn't even look up as Georgina lifted the case up the step and into Hooch's home.

Georgina stayed with Hooch for the last three days of the holiday. We were about to set off for the airport when Georgina discovered I had packed the arm into my carry-on luggage.

'Roger, I can't believe you still have that. You can't take it home with us.'

'Well, I'm not leaving it here. What would I do? Chuck it in a skip?'

'You know what they said at the hospital. They couldn't reattach it. The nerves were all dead, like it had never been attached. You're so sentimental, Roger. It's an arm, that's all. The human spirit is not present in that piece of flesh. There's nothing of you, the man I love, in that arm.'

But I was adamant. 'The arm comes with me,' I said. 'I don't care what anyone says.'

At the airport it showed up on the X-ray and they took me into a special room. The police became involved. It took a long time, but eventually they were made to understand that there was no crime involved. But they wouldn't let me take it on the plane. They spent some time deciding on its classification. It wasn't a dead body, so what was it? They eventually decided it was meat.

'My arm is not raw meat,' I said.

After some discussion they let me take the arm away with a promise to return the next day with the right paperwork, and Georgina stalked off to the boarding gate without looking back, pulling behind her Felicity and Jamie, who twisted their necks to stare at me, eyes wet, faces red, lips trembling.

Hooch was standing outside her caravan with a suitcase. She was waiting for a taxi to the airport. She told me, in blurting, breathless sentences, all about Georgina and her. I pushed her inside the caravan, and from that point everything went badly.

But now it was all going to be all right. I stopped on the hill and looked down at Hooch's caravan. Empty. People come, and people go, then disappear. That's about it really, that's all you can say. I took a swig of water, felt giddy as if with the first touches of flu. Has the Perrier gone straight to my head or is life sick and cruel instead?

Hooch's caravan still smelt of Georgina. I made tea, and went outside and sat in the hammock. I picked up Hooch's mobile and listened to the messages. The light in number 46 was flickering, the shower tray in number 49 was leaking, there was a smell of gas in number 94. I would attend to these problems the next day. I picked up Hooch's book. A page was folded over a third of the way in. Two-thirds of a story she would never hear.

I looked over the site to the mountains. I could see an eagle high in the sky, slowly circling at its great height. I wondered whether it could see me.

A room with a view and you and no one to give advice.
That sounds a paradise few could fail to choose.

I thought of Georgina and Felicity and Jamie. One day I would go to the beach again and build another sand palace. It would help me remember that once there was more than just us. Still, I am better off here, in the sun. Nothing ever seems so bad when the sun is shining. I looked over to the box where my arm lay. Later I would take it out, sit with it in my lap again, as I did most nights. Otherwise I would forget. *It* would forget.

I want to remember every minute, always, always to the end of my days.

People had moved in to the next-door caravan, our old caravan. They kept talking to me, trying to get me to go out with them, down to the bar, to be sociable. To share. They once asked me what I was holding, what was in the bundle, what was so precious. Was it a baby? they joked. They were worried about me. I ignored them. I like to be alone. I want the freedom and I want the guile. I clicked on Hooch's CD. I won't share, I won't. Some things are private. So don't worry. I won't share you. I won't. I won't.

We'll bill and we'll coo and sorrow will never come,
Or will it ever come
Always torn, always thinking what if,
of possibilities, of the way things could have been
if only
I'll see you somewhere
I'll see you sometime
Darling...

Oscillate Wildly

Alison MacLeod

I loved the high-energy silliness of the title. It's like some surrealist slogan demanding we live life fully. I also loved the homage of a pun on Oscar Wilde. The song itself is a rare instrumental, all coolness and melancholy – very haunting – until it suddenly lifts off into something joyous, something big. I wanted to write a story that took that kind of running leap – a sort of tribute to someone I knew who was particularly good at running leaps.

Many years after his great-uncle laid the solid round of it in his hand, he would think of the carving. In the stillness of near-death, as the nurse pressed the sponge to his lips and dribbled water over his tongue, he'd see in his mind's eye the creamy white stone gleaming on his desk beneath the skylight. His fingertips would remember the broken edge where the vandal's hammer struck all those years ago. He'd spare a thought for the poor, notorious penis that had been severed with the blow and rested now, inert and foreshortened, on its cushion of testicles. Were he able to move his mouth, he would have smiled a final time at the comic vulnerability of those stone genitals, naked atop a pile of utility bills – his Great-Uncle Gaston's erstwhile paperweight and, now, for a brief while longer, his.

In those moments, when time forgot to breathe, he sensed every detail of his, literally, fleeting life with a radiant clarity. He did so in spite of the injections of diamorphine – of sweet, merciful heroin – that his brain now required to forget the tumour pain and to bypass the sensation that something, an animal, was tearing into his gut.

On the stairs to his room, the voices of his life lapped at the edges of him. He heard his ex-wife Shelley's muffled dramatics through the floorboards and thin rug. He heard the nurse's spoon stirring the brown sugar crystals at the bottom of her mug. He heard the bass line of his neighbours' music reverberating through their shared wall. He heard the tight, compressed breathing of Eoin, his brother, as he turned the pages of the *Independent* beside his bed. He heard his lover, Abi, turn in her broken sleep on the floor near his deathbed. He heard the slow shuffle of his elder daughter's grief in the room, and the bracelets of his younger daughter jingling with an energy, an angry restlessness, she couldn't contain. And, twice an hour, he heard the trains hurtle past the nearby crossing, loud as avenging angels at the dead-end of his street. He was fifty-two.

He had expected a heart attack. His doctor had explained that tumours need blood; that, in time, there wouldn't be blood enough for him and them both. He had imagined himself reading at his desk as the ghostly boot-blow was dealt to his chest, and Abi or one of the girls finding him, upright, in his black jeans and green pullover, resigned, gone, but OK. He hadn't expected to wake, without actually waking, to cold, soaked sheets below him; he hadn't expected the sensation of a catheter being threaded through his penis. He wouldn't have believed that he, he who'd always been so able to turn a phrase, would some day communicate his final, urgent thoughts in a code of stuttering eyebrows and eyelids.

Nor would he ever have imagined, thank God, the agony of his body as it was rotated every five hours, day and night, at Shelley's insistence

– she had arrived after twenty years with clinking bottles of wine and a horror of bedsores. (He would have laughed if the joke hadn't been, so inescapably, on him.)

More than anything, he would never have dreamed that his body was capable of such stillness.

So this was that bleak fate he'd believed would never be his: a cancer coma.

The brightness of the room seeped through his eyelids. How many days had passed like this? Flies buzzed and thudded against the skylight's pane. *Abi. Was she still in the room?*

Then he felt her hands on his feet, rubbing the soles. 'I promise,' she'd replied months before. 'I'll be with you. If it's humanly possible, I'll be with you.' And he'd felt his love for her would burst the banks of his chest.

Downstairs, Katie – or was it Sonia? – thumped across the floor to answer the phone. Beside his bed, a newspaper rattled. His brother had entered the room. Abi said, 'I'll just go for a Nescafé, Liam. I won't be long. Eoin's here with you now.' Then, as if taking her cue, Eoin's hand, cold with nerves, found his beneath the sheet, and Liam felt again the vibrations of his life.

He'd last held his brother's hand in 1957 as they queued to see *Calamity Jane* at the Imperial Cinema. Calamity had arrived in Belfast in '54, but she didn't make it to Newry until three years later. Liam was six years old; Eoin ten, and already grave; grave for their father's sake, who didn't want his sons picking up the habits to which, he feared, they were, by birth, predisposed. Drink. Wildness. Music. Fast talk. Shallow charm. Hadn't his own brothers been prone to the worst excesses? Wasn't the border only a stone's throw from Newry? Weren't his own people, the native Irish, prone to trouble?

In the queue for the Saturday morning show, Eoin ignores his younger brother's pleas for an ice-cream soda and lemon sherbet balls. He squeezes the half-crown in his thin, hot hand. It is the first time he has been trusted with money that is not his own, and he is not about to be whined out of it by his little brother. Throughout the show, he clenches the change, his palm sweating.

Liam, however, has forgotten about Eoin's locked fist. He has forgotten about the lemon sherbet balls. He wants to be Wild Bill Hickok throwing Calamity Jane on to the horse-drawn cart and yee-hawing her out of Deadwood. He wants to be a squawling Sioux brave, running in her wake. At the very end, when Calamity Jane swaps her buckskin and boots for a wedding dress, he wants to be the gun beneath her dress, strapped to her nice bit of leg. Calamity Jane is Liam's first love, and all the way home, he swings on Eoin's arm, begging him to turn back for the afternoon show. 'Just once more, Eoin. Please, Eoin. Come on. Let's just see that fil-im again. It was something, wasn't it? Didn't you think it was something? They won't even be home till suppertime. There's money enough. Let's just, why don't we, we've still time, and I'll give you my next week's allowance for the collection plate *plus* my Atlas bodybuilder's book. Come on, Eoin. Eoin? Please, Eoin. Come on, please now, be a legend, let's just...'

He swings madly on Eoin's arm.

Older now and bigger. At the strange cemetery a wind is blowing. The trees are bending and scraping like a rich man's servants; the pansies are bowing and dipping besides, and he's running into the wind, his legs like pistons, his cheeks flattened and red with the wind slapping.

His mam and his Great-Uncle Gaston have slowed on the uphill walk. '*Attends! Attends!*' his mother calls, a ribbon of a voice in the wind. It is the first time she has spoken to Liam in her native French. He doesn't like it.

He runs past flowerpots with rotting stems; past sad-faced stone ladies with their gowns sliding off their titties; past funny street signs at the junctions of the paths, as if this is actually a town of the dead; past graves that aren't graves but fancy stone houses with only one room because, he supposes, the needs of the dead are few. (*Why are cemeteries surrounded by fences? Because everyone's dying to get in. Ba-dum!* Tommy Murphy told him that one.)

He decides it is better to die in Ireland than in Paris because in Ireland the outdoors looks like the outdoors and gravestones are mossy and chipped, and the letters wear down with the wind and the rain so everyone gets forgotten in time and life flies on.

But he won't tell his mother's uncle as much because Great-Uncle Gaston is sure to die soon himself – he's the last of a generation, his mam explained, and that's why she's come and brought Liam for company, because he is such good company – when his finger isn't in his nose, that is – and he will make her old uncle laugh. It doesn't need to be said: neither Eoin nor their da would ever be able to make an old French uncle laugh. 'Oncle Gaston is big in his 'eart,' she says. 'E made me laugh when I was a little girl. This is where you get it.' It seems odd to Liam. An old uncle who likes to laugh who has worked all these years as a cemetery keeper.

When they are at home in Newry, Liam never thinks of his mam as French. In Newry, she's just 'foreign', and for Liam she's just his mam with her sing-song voice and her full lips that push out more than everyone else's when she speaks. He knows Jimmy Gannon from school fancies her when he serves her at the butcher's on Saturdays, and Liam could flatten him for it.

She arrived by accident in 1946 when the bus she was travelling on with her elderly boss, a respected French chocolatier, broke down in Newry. They were on their way from Dublin to Belfast where she was meant to take notes on chocolate distribution at J. Lyon's and Co. When his da spotted her, smoking elegantly under the bus shelter on Canal Street, he drew breath at the sight of her legs crossed at the ankles and the red silk scarf tied prettily at her neck. He was twenty-three and already bored by Irish girls and their eagerness to marry. When he heard her speak – to ask about lodgings for the night – he was beside himself with emotion for the first and last time in his life.

Liam knows the story. His father let it slip last year on St Stephen's Day after his annual glass of port. But the truth of the matter occurs to Liam only now as he runs towards the cemetery's far side: that he, Liam O'Donnell, came into the world because of a bus's broken water pump. It makes him laugh so hard he has to gasp for air as he runs, and spit runs down his chin. Wait till he tells Eoin that he's also on this earth because of a broken water pump. Eoin won't like it. Not one bit.

He's relishing that thought when he comes up short and panting at the sight of the angel.

It's not a pretty angel this time with soulful eyes and a slippery dress. No. It's a big fucker with broad square wings rising from its back. And the face is ungodly, as Father Hurley might say. ('Ungodly' is Father Hurley's favourite word at morning mass.) In fact, the angel looks too disdainful to bother with the likes of either Father Hurley or Liam. It looks in a mood, like Mr O'Flaherty the history master when he turns away from the boys, disgusted by their ignorance.

But the wings mesmerise Liam. They're powerful things that rise above his head, with long feathers carved into the stone, feathers that are longer even than those on an Indian brave's headdress.

He steps closer and, bending, takes a look at the naked angel's undercarriage, as a farmer might a bull's, because the angel isn't upright like a man. It has flanks, not a torso, and – he has to look twice – a broken stump of a penis without balls. Another faulty water pump.

He turns at the sound of voices. His mother and her uncle have caught him up at last, and she is wiping tears away from her eyes, tears brought on by both the whipping wind and a fit of giggles. It is the one time in Liam's life that he will see his mother helpless with laughter. Because, as she and Uncle Gaston turned the corner, she spotted her son, and, more to the point, her son's hand, cupping the famously vandalised genitals of Oscar Wilde's angel.

Liam looks at his white-haired great-uncle in his blue serge uniform. His uncle regards him sternly through watery eyes. Liam backs away from the stumpy remains but hardly knows where to put his offending hand. Then Uncle Gaston coughs with laughter and crooks an arthritic finger. '*Viens*,' he rumbles. '*Je veux te montrer quelque chose.*'

They return to the keeper's house, a house which Liam is relieved to discover has three good-sized rooms, not the single room the dead seem to favour in Paris. It is good to know that Great-Uncle Gaston *is* indeed alive, even though his skin is almost see-through.

At first, it is hard to see after all the sunshine outside. Liam has to blink himself back into the world. When he does, he finds his great-uncle pointing to a dusty metal desktop beneath the single window. And there they are, on top of a pile of invoices. Oscar Wilde's angel's bits.

His uncle lifts the fragment of stone from the desk and lowers it into Liam's hand, wheezing with laughter.

'Heavy,' Liam says, his voice cracking unexpectedly.

'*Mais oui!*' the old man booms. '*Très lourd!*'

Years later Liam will read about it: the public outrage, the tarpaulin, the plastering-over, the cumbersome fig leaf, the unveiling, then the infamous blow of the hammer. But unknown to the official histories, the following morning the dutiful keeper collected the fallen fragment, wrapped it in a piece of chamois leather, and returned to the keeper's house where he deposited it, sheepishly, upon his desk.

There it would remain. At the end of his tenure, he would bequeath the bollocks to the next keeper, who would in turn bequeath them to the next and so on, up and down the decades, until the day the *commune* took over from the *arrondissement* and deemed there would be no more permanent keepers. Uncle Gaston was the last of a line, and in more ways than one. He and his wife had never had children.

The Newry postman could have had no idea of the contraband he delivered to the O'Donnells' door three years after the visit to Oscar Wilde's tomb. The beloved bollocks arrived one summer's morning in a bundle of newspaper and a box marked 'M. Liam O'Donnell'.

Liam's father and brother frowned at the sight, but his mother reached up, put her arms around her son, who was a head taller than she was, and whispered in his ear that he should be proud. This was art. History. Tradition. The sculptor wanted to show *life*, didn't he?

Just months later, on a November's day that never grew light, Liam would return home late after school, late from dawdling in the record shop with Patrick Dunn, and find his mother dead in her bed.

'A stroke,' Dr Kearney pronounced. 'I'm very sorry. She was a good woman, and too young.' Liam's father had nodded morosely. 'I used to tell her she needed to quit the gaspers. I'm afraid she smoked for France and Ireland both.' He looked up to see his second son glaring at him.

Years away from Newry, in his attic room, on his deathbed – a bed that obliges the visiting nurses to bend lower than their union permits – Liam hears once more his uncle's rumbling, laughing voice somewhere in the space between the bed and the eaves. And as Abi lays her hand, cool and light, on his forehead, he hears his mother call again, *'Attends! Attends!'*

Because he's climbing into the van with the others. He should have run but it's too late now, and he's trembling like a fly on flypaper because the one in the black balaclava has already shown them the handgun beneath his donkey jacket. Liam has no idea where they're going. There are no windows in the van. All he can see is Neil in the seat across from his worrying a stick of gum in its silver foil like it's a flaming rosary, and he has to shout over the roar of the engine, 'Neil, will you sit quiet, for Christ's sake!' But the one in the green ski mask stands up and punches him in the eye for speaking, and he's sure it's Jimmy Gannon who used to fancy his mam.

When they tumble out, there are only trees, tyre tracks and a few empty food tins by a fire pit. Their captors line them up against the van, heads down, hands where they can see them, legs spread – Seamus O'Shea, Tommy Murphy, Patrick Dunn, Neil Flynn and himself – all the Newry boys who are aiming for university – and Liam wants anything but this. This waiting. This limbo of dread.

All because Pat Dunn mouthed off in the pub last week. He dubbed the Provos – Jimmy Gannon's gang – the goddamned Mafia of Newry and now, now hours pass with the lot of them spreadeagled against the van and the warning still ringing in their ears: 'The first one of yous that turns round is the first one to get it.'

Liam's hands are splayed against the dirty side, and he doesn't dare turn his face even an inch to catch the eye of Tommy, who's beside him. He doesn't dare do anything but train his ears on the darkness, listening for any sign. He hasn't heard so much as a twig crack since before nightfall. Maybe his father was right about the Irish and trouble – because that's what they're calling it on the telly every night – the Troubles – and he's never been in such trouble in all his seventeen years.

By dawn, Seamus O'Shea is so sick and crazy with sleeplessness that he forgets *not* to look over his shoulder when the wood pigeons wake and flap in the trees. And, 'Thank Christ,' he says. 'They've fucked off. It was a goddamned wind-up.' But no one's laughing. Neil is throwing up into some bushes. Tommy is crying because he's shat himself. Seamus and Pat start to row about Pat shooting off his mouth in that pub. Liam lies down on the ground and stares, with the eye that isn't swollen shut, at a sky he thought he'd never see again. There's a sliver of moon so sharp you could cut your wrists on it.

A warning. Get out of town.

So he's on the ferry chucking up over the side and dodging Father Hurley, who's going to visit his sister in Kilburn; he's old now but Liam can't forget how he used to try to get him to talk dirty in the confessional, so he lets Father Hurley smell the stink of vomit on his coat and he doesn't see him again.

Then it's 'No blacks, no dogs, no Irish' in every lodging-house window, and he's busking at Piccadilly, singing because that's what the English think the Irish should do at street corners, and he's got no address for Eoin, who's God knows where in London, so things go from bad to worse till he starts pushing dope, which is how he meets Shelley. It's not love at first sight there in the subway below Piccadilly but he doesn't want romance – he just wants shelter, shelter – and Shelley is his harbour, all safe and mothering, and earning a wage too in an office somewhere. They're OK – she's not Calamity Jane and he's not Wild Bill– but it's OK, he makes her laugh, and they marry because Shelley can't get into the civil service if they don't. The new flat isn't much and he can't afford to finish his A-levels, but pushing is still better than busking, and soon enough he gets a real job, putting up sheds in the big gardens of rich Londoners, so, for a while at least, at last, he and Shelley rest easy.

Only the carpet is sour. Why does the carpet smell sour? Did he knock over his beer? But he can't stop to think because they are on the floor, Shelley all soft and warm beneath him, and they're making a baby – 'Get drunk for a girl,' they used to say in Newry – but for all his humping, he can't come and Shelley says she's getting sore with him going at it. It's been nearly half an hour, and can't they turn the telly off? It's nearly over, he says, trying hard not to laugh at Frank and Betty Spencer, who are in a hotel room for their second honeymoon. When Frank lowers Betty on to the bed, the bed collapses and Betty's shapely bottom bobs up, which is when Liam gives way at last, the tendons in his legs trembling like slingshots. Shelley lifts her legs into the air and stays like that, staring at the ceiling, all dreamy like, while Liam watches the end of the show. Then nine months later, Katie is born, and Liam falls in love all over again as he and Shelley fall out of love, if love – married love – it ever was.

By the time they decide that Katie needs a brother or a sister, Liam has been sleeping on the sofa for nearly two years. At least he gets the work for his A-levels done – better late than never – and after that, his degree. It's amazing how two people can share a home by stepping gingerly around one another. It's also uncanny how other women seem to know when you're not sleeping with your wife and put temptation in your way. Liam can only be grateful. And there's the garden centre van too, his home away from, with his *Hamlet* exam quotations Sellotaped to the dashboard. But when Shelley tells him the calendar says go, all systems alert, he smiles cooperatively, and slips into his old room and in and out of her again, so that by the time he returns to the sofa – his sperm more fervent than he – Sonia, his beautiful girl, is conceived.

The trains at the crossing are getting louder and louder. Twice an hour they tear past, as if, at any moment, they'll explode into the room and bear him away. The four walls shudder, and he wonders blearily whether death is as lonely a thing as those days long ago, after the split, when he ached for his baby girls – could it be worse? – and he worries for a moment about how the undertaker will get his body down from the attic – the staircase is narrow, steep and bending – it's a black comedy in the making – and he'd be the first to laugh if he weren't in a goddamned coma – *ha-ha* – and there weren't already tears slipping down his cheek. *Ba-dum!* 'Liam,' Abi lulls, 'sssh now. Ssh, sweetheart. I'm here. You're not alone.' He doesn't know whether to blink once for yes, as in *Yes, I hear you, I understand* – or for, *Yes, I am alone, I'm alone in here and frightened.*

Abi.

It's the college picnic and already he loves her but she's married and it isn't right, it isn't right, he knows full well, but it's midsummer and the grass in the clearing is long and beckoning. It waves him on as he pulls off his shoes and socks, and runs madly forward into the handspring, his arms, back and legs moving into line… Then he lifts his left leg, extends his knee, plants his hands as far as he dares from his final step, and kicks his right leg up, his body a perfect vertical, his abs tight as the blood rushes to his head. He pushes his arms back, arches his ribs, then springs forward to land, miraculously, on the balls of his feet.

It is thirty years since he captained the gymnastics squad in Newry, and he is lucky he didn't snap his spine. But she turned to watch. Abi turned to watch, her glossy dark hair flying in the breeze and her wide, wide smile getting the better of her face.

She was born on the November day, the very day, they buried his mother. He was fifteen, lost and winded at the graveside in the hour Abi came keening into the world – and somehow that makes her dear to him, a gift. She's not fooled by his charm or his black Irish eyelashes like other women but still, still she laughs easily, and her words run deep within him, like a hidden stream. And she should, she really should, but she doesn't recoil from the bite of him when he goes mad on the booze and the shame of what he hasn't become. She doesn't turn and run from the homeless, rabid thing that curls, miserable, within his gut and is turning, little by little, into the tumour they will cut from him years too late.

'Listen,' she says, her head next to his now. Pillow-talk. He dreams of her breast, lovely in his mouth. 'Can you hear it? The music. Next door's.' It's an instrumental, faint through the wall. He can't quite get it, though he was once an encyclopedia of song. It's a loop of sound: cool, restless, spooky – music for a cold war soundtrack – then, against the odds, out of nowhere, a rising crescendo of something that sounds like joy…

And Abi's breath warm on his cheek.

Only there are footsteps, heavy on the stairs – she's lifting her head off the pillow and Liam can't hear the music any more because Eoin is talking from the foot of the bed. His brother, his long-estranged brother, his sombre sibling who hardly knows him, is saying, 'Abi, leave him. The girls should be at their father's side.' But Katie and Sonia are fine where they are, in the corner of his room, sifting old photos, content, near him but not so near that they're frightened by the sight of his wasted body beneath the sheets.

Abi goes quiet. He can feel the sudden strain of her hand on his. She is afraid of Eoin, of his deadly earnestness. She is afraid to argue, to disturb the calm of the room, and Eoin is speaking to her as if she is a servant of the house. *How dare you?* Liam wants to shout, but his lungs can't find air, his lips won't move. Then her hand is leaving his, her voice is fading, he can hear her step on the stairs, he's losing her – *Jesus, no – no, Abi—*

And he's on his feet, running – somehow – he has no idea how he's managed it – down the stairs – *Abi, don't leave me* – he's breathless behind her – why doesn't she turn? – *Abi!* – every muscle in his legs is driving him forward as—

Great-Uncle Gaston's cemetery flies past: the women in the slippery dresses, the houses of the dead, and his mother too, a red scarf tied at her neck. The stone bollocks are heavy in his hand but he feels as if he could run for ever – *Abi!* – or does until he finds himself face to face with Oscar Wilde's angel. He draws breath. His uncle is at the tomb already. The old man nods. Liam knows what he has to do. He unwraps their paperweight from the piece of chamois leather. He moves to the angel's side. He bends down and slides the bollocks and their stump of a penis back into place.

The angel's flanks shudder to life. Its feathers ripple. Liam backs away and sees the impassive eyes blink, the mouth tense. He watches, dazed, as the monumental wings quiver, then beat the air, loud as a windmill's sails. He turns his face to an unsettled sky and stares as the angel heaves itself into flight.

And in those moments, in that dizzying commotion of shadows, air and light, Liam feels again the wild oscillations of his life: the swinging, the running, the trembling, the chucking-up, the busking, the pushing and the humping; his sperm swimming, his babies babbling, Hamlet soliloquising, his body handspringing, his eyelids blinking, the joy rising and those wings spreading, defiant and tremendous, as the train at the crossing tears past.

Sweet and Tender Hooligan

Charlie Williams

I was probably just a little bit too young when I watched the Smiths performing 'This Charming Man' on Top of the Pops. *Took me years to get over the gladioli but I made it, eventually, some time in the mid-nineties. I was in a record shop in Leadenhall Market and 'What Difference Does It Make?' came on. It struck me like a call to arms and that moment has left its print on my memory. The eighties were full of tribes and 'Sweet And Tender Hooligan' reminds me of the one I was in back then. Which explains my problem with the gladioli, perhaps.*

'Do us a bag o' chips, Trace.'

'Is that all?'

'Erm…' Bean drummed his fingers on the counter, leaving dirty prints on the greasy surface. 'Nah, chuck a saveloy in there an' all.'

'I didn't mean that, I meant *Is that all you're gonna say to me?*'

Bean shrugged.

'You stood me up,' said Tracy, looking down at the chips that she was shovelling. 'I waited for over an hour.'

'When?'

'Monday. After work on Monday.'

Bean drummed his fingers some more. 'Eh?'

'You was meant to meet me. I waited nearly an hour.'

'You said over an hour.'

'You was meant to meet me.' She paused to wipe a tear from her eye, leaving a smudge in her eyeshadow. An exquisite lock of dark hair fell in front of her eye. She brushed most of it aside, the rest sticking to her forehead. 'Wrapped or open?'

'Open. I don't remember sayin' I'd meet yer, Trace. (Can you put some more vinegar on, mate? Ta.) Monday, you say?'

'Yeah. You came in about seven and asked what time I clocked off, then winked and said "See you later". You did.'

'I never winked, Trace. I don't… I mean, I never meant it like that. I weren't askin' you *out*, like.'

She put the food on the counter and turned away.

'No,' said Bean. 'No, I don't mean that. I mean, I never even knew you liked us. I thought—'

'I don't,' she said, turning to face him again. 'I don't like any lad who don't mean what he says. That'll be a pound fifty.'

'A pound fifty… Er, Trace, I mean, if you wanna go out with us, I'll… I mean I never even thought you'd—'

'You've had yer chance, now give us a pound fifty or I'll get Frank out.'

Bean looked behind her at the open doorway, from which came TV sounds. A large gut was visible over the side of an armchair, rising up and down. Suddenly the gut flinched and Frank sat up, rubbing his hands and shouting: 'Wahey! That's us into Europe. Ha ha! *Yoo-rop! Yoo-rop! Yoo…*'

Bean put his last two pounds on the counter and walked out, hoping that Tracy would call him back with his change. She didn't, although she did say:

'You're just a boy, really, ain't you?'

Bean ate his chips in the park, spinning slowly on the merry-go-round, tossing the occasional lump of batter to the pigeons. He cheered up when he saw Joe approaching, one hand in his pocket, the other holding a fag. There was another fag behind his ear. His head was turned sideways towards the road. He looked the other way, revealing yet another fag behind that ear.

'Bean.'

'All right, Joe.'

'Got a fag?'

'Nah, soz.'

Joe sat beside Bean and took a chip. It was the large one that Bean had been saving, but he didn't mind Joe having it.

'I'm collectin' em.'

'What? Fags?'

'Yeah. Case I gets sent down again. So me mam can bring em in for us, see. I don't want her shellin' out for my fags all the time. I loves me mam, me. And I ain't afraid of sayin' it. You know why I got expelled from school?'

'Well, I dunno all of it, but didn't you—'

'Cos the cunt called Mam a… a… ah, summat horrible. *Horrible.* And do you know what I said back to him, as I bounced his head off the wall? "Anyone," I says to him. "Anyone who upsets, hurts and/or talks shit about my mam, I will fuckin' *kill* that man. Fuckin' *kill* him." Heh. Anyway, you want a fag?'

'Well, I wouldn't wanna—'

'Yeah, yeah. Just have one.'

'Oh, ta, mate.'

Joe and Bean smoked and finished off the chips and watched an Austin Maxi go slowly past on the road. The driver was either a young boy or a very small person with a tiny head. Bean smiled at this thought. He was in a good mood. Joe had never given him a fag before. Things were looking up after all.

'You skint?'

'Yeah.'

'Me 'n all.'

A seagull, hopelessly far from the sea, flew overhead and dropped a wet white shit on the tarmac in front of them. Bean watched the bird fly away, hoping that it would find the river and follow it all the way downstream until it came out in the ocean (although he didn't know for sure that the river came out in the ocean). Joe, meanwhile, just watched the shit as it hardened in the gentle autumn breeze. After a while he said:

'I heard you got blowed out.'

'Who off?'

'Ah, so you did, then?'

'Who told yer?'

'Frank at the chippy.'

'Fuck sake, that fat fuckin' bastard. I never even got blew out, Joe, I just… Ah, don't matter.'

'You gotta have a bit of wedge behind you, Bean. You wants birds to go out with yer, you gotta shell out. You can't take em for a bag o' chips at the park. Specially not yer older ones like Trace from the chippy. You gotta impress em, like, show em how the other half lives. Like… like motors, and that. You gotta have a motor. You can't expect em to walk everywhere. How you gonna shag em if you ain't got a motor? And togs. No offence, mate, but how long you had that old bomber? Fuck sake, Bean, you just don't *wear* bomber jackets no more. Tell you what you gotta do, you gotta get yerself a nice leather box jacket. Burgundy. And them pumps you got, you need slip-ons, pal. Nice grey slip-ons, with a burgundy stripe down the front and some white socks to set em off. And some baggies. You needs a pair o' baggies.'

'Baggies?'

'Yeah. Five pleats. Six, even. Burgundy.'

'Oh.'

'Or grey. Mind you, baggies, slip-ons… all that costs. That's why you needs wedge, pal. And yer skint, Bean, ain't yer?'

'Well…' He thought of the 50p change that Tracy had not given him, and wondered whether that had been deliberate, so he would have a reason to go back. Probably not.

'You are, though. Yer skint.'

'Yeah.'

The seagull flew back overhead, landed behind them, and started pecking at the screwed-up chip paper that Bean had tossed. The bird was driven half crazy by the smell of food, but he would find little or no sustenance within.

'I got a bit o' work. Two-man job.'

'Oh yeah?' said Bean. 'What doin'?'

'How's you with windows?'

They found it down near the river, in a street lined with large trees. Bean didn't know the name of the street, and didn't recall ever being there before. He was excited and kept clicking his tongue. Joe ignored him, concentrated on watching the house with his hawk-eye. He stood motionless, face upturned, mouth hanging open and breathing hard through it. After a while he hopped into the tiny front garden, opened a low iron gate, and disappeared down a dark side alley. Bean followed and found him at the back of the house, back pressed against the wall. He motioned towards the window next to him.

Bean moved in.

'Is it movin'?'

'No, think it's locked.'

'It ain't locked.'

'How d'you know?'

'Cos you can't lock these types of windows. All you got is a latch, and… Fuck sake, Bean, I thought you was all right at windows? Just fuckin' stand aside and giz a go, I'll show yer.'

'I am all right at…' Bean trailed off. Joe wasn't listening anyway, busy as he was with the window.

'*Nnnng. Mmmmmpf.* There yer go. Piece of fuckin' piss when you knows how. Now, you can climb through, can you? Want us to give you a leg-up, or summat?'

'Course I fuckin' can. You go first, though, eh.'

'You don't wanna go first, is it? Oh, I see. Well, perhaps you don't wanna go in at all? That it? Perhaps you was talkin' shit when you says you was up to it, eh?'

'I *am* up to—'

'Go on, fuck off. Have a nice, borin', skint life with no birds, no motors and no nice togs. And don't ever cross my path again, you bottlin' cunt.'

'I ain't bottlin', Joe, I just mean…'

'Well, shut yer face and get in there, then. And keep yer fuckin' voice down, fuck sake. Them in there, they're deaf, but the neighbours ain't.'

'How d'you know they're deaf?'

'Cos they're old, you twat. Why'd you think we're here? Old people is piss easy.'

'Yeah, but how d'you know old folks lives here?'

'Cos… cos I cased the fuckin' place, you twat. Honestly, you dunno fuck all about this line o' work, does you? I wished I'd of knowed that before I asked you. Fuck…'

Bean looked at his shoes, which he couldn't actually see, such was the darkness. 'Not all old people is deaf, though,' he said. 'My grandpa ain't deaf.'

'Oh aye? How old is he?'

'Well, he's dead, right now. But he was old before he died, and he—'

'Fuckin' shut up and get in there, you twat.'

Bean went in, followed by Joe. They started feeling around. There was a funny smell but, this being the home of old people, neither burglar was surprised by that. Bean located the mantelpiece and found what he thought was a carriage clock. He squeezed it into the pocket of his bomber jacket and went on with the feeling process.

'Here, Joe.'

'What.'

'Look.'

'What?'

'This. Fuckin' look at this.'

'How can I look at that? It's pitch dark and I can't even see where you is.'

'I'm here.'

'Where?'

'By the telly.'

'Where's the fuckin' telly?'

'Hold up.'

'Hold up for what?'

'Here we go… *ta-da*.'

'Turn the *fuckin'* light out, you twat!'

'But you—'

'Turn it off!'

'All right, it's off.'

'Now it's gonna take fuckin' ages.'

'What will?'

'Night vision. Me night vision was just gettin' going then when you turned on the light.'

'I dunno why we can't just use torches.'

'We don't need torches. God gave us night vision for robbin' houses, not torches.'

'But—'

'Just sit tight and shut yer face. It's *your* fault, this is. What d'you wanna show us anyway?'

'A pair o' false teeth.'

'A pair o'…?'

A few minutes later (after Joe had stopped berating Bean in sharp whispers) they were creeping up the stairs, being careful to step only on the outside of each step. This was one of the ninja tips that Joe had told Bean beforehand, when he had briefed him in the park. Another was that you should not turn on any lights. There had been many others, Joe being well schooled in ninja techniques, and it was probably too much to expect Bean to remember them all, him being a relative novice. At the top of the stairs, Joe reached back and placed a hand on Bean's pigeon chest and said:

'Shhh.'

'What?'

'You hear it?'

'Hear what? I can hear you whisperin'. Not very well, though. You just say "You hear it?"?'

'Shhh.'

'I was just—'

'That noise.'

'Oh. Oh aye, I do hear it. What it is?'

'Dunno.'

They listened for a while, standing on the stairs in the darkness, Joe feeling like a genuine ninja, Bean feeling like a genuine burglar. After about a minute Joe whispered:

'Stopped now.'

'Yeah.'

'Must of been snorin'.'

'Yeah, snorin' or summat.'

'Come on.'

'Where we goin'?'

'That door there. First on yer left. That's where he hides all his money.'

'Hides? How d'you—'

A muffled click and the door on the left was framed orange in the darkness. Both young men fell silent. The door swung open, spilling bright light on to the landing. In the doorway stood an old man in yellowed vest and Y-fronts. He looked confused, and there was some drool on his chin. The fingers of both hands curled and uncurled as if they were throbbing. Behind him in the room, on the bed, an old woman lay spreadeagled in her dark red nightdress, a book open on her chest. You could already see bruises on her neck. Her dead eyes were open.

'She... She was old,' said the old man, looking at Bean. 'And she would of died anyway, if...'

He was still looking at Bean but his face was changing, from confused to irate. He wiped the drool off his chin and seized control of his hands, clenching them into block-like fists, saying: 'Oi, who the blimmin' hell are you, you little hooligan?' He didn't seem to notice Joe, who had somehow slipped past Bean and down the stairs. The last Bean heard of him was the front door slamming. The old man stepped forward and took a swipe at Bean with an open hand that seemed as big as a frying pan. Bean stumbled back and lost his footing, tumbling down the stairs and landing by the front door (cracking his head on it). He tried to get up, but something had failed in his back, and hands and knees was as high as he could get. Hearing the old man coming down the stairs, he scurried into the living room like an abused dog.

'Blimmin' hooligans, breakin' into decent folks' houses!' the man was shouting, coming through the door and turning on the light. His arms were covered in tattoos. Bean noticed that one of them read I LOVE BITCH (although that last word was unclear and seemed, when Bean later thought about it, to be crudely adapted from the name FIONA). On the other arm was a long, twisting serpent. Bean traced it all the way down to the hand, which was flashing a military knife.

'You know what I do to hooligans, eh?' said the man, rubbing his crotch. 'I fuck em. Then I kill em.' With that, he came forward.

Bean, his back screaming with every movement, reached for something, anything. His fingers wrapped around an electrical lead.

'And in local news, an elderly couple have been found brutally murdered in…'

Bean put his fingers in his ears. The pain was too much. He couldn't localise it to any particular place, but it hurt. He gritted his teeth and pulled the duvet tight over his scalp, and rubbed his bare ankles together.

After an hour or so his ankles stopped moving. The radio droned on in the background, but no distinct words were coming through. Bean was in his own secret world of darkness and pain. It was no sanctuary, but it was better than the alternative. After three hours he fell asleep.

At some point he lifted the covers slightly to release some of the fart gas that had built up, and caught a few words from the radio. It was some sort of afternoon advice show, and the man offering answers had a sympathetic voice that inclined Bean to trust it. He thought for a while, then sneaked out of bed and on to the landing. He listened at the top of the stairs, then crept down. Mam's shopping trolley was not in the hall, so she must be out. He sat on the bottom stair with the telephone on his lap. Hoping that he remembered the number right, he dialled.

'Hello?'

'Hello. I've done summat bad.'

'Who is this?'

'It's Bean. Er, I mean… Bea… er, Beaver.'

'Beaver?'

'Yeah.'

'Your name is Beaver?'

'Yeah. But you ain't the feller off the radio. I wanna speak to—'

'Mr Cole.'

'Eh?'

'Old Jim Cole, "the wise old soul". Yes, if you could just hold the line, you'll be through to him shortly.'

Some music came on. Bean squeezed his eyes shut. The song was an instrumental version of 'Green Green Grass' by Tom Jones. Despite his anxiety, Bean found himself tapping his foot. He stopped when Jim Cole came on the line.

'And we have a Mr Beaver on the line. How are you this sunny day, Mr Beaver?'

'Fine, fine… Look, I got a bit of a—'

'Problem, yes, but let's not skip the pleasantries, eh? Do you know, I always find that—'

'I done summat bad, Jim.'

'Well, haven't we all? What is this thing you've done, er, Mr…?'

'It don't matter what I done. What matters is that it ain't as bad as it looks. I mean, I did do *summat* bad, but the main bad thing I done, I didn't actually do. Not on purpose anyhow. I mean, I never meant to—'

'Hold yer horses there, laddie. I don't know about the listeners, but I'm getting confused. Have you or have you not, in your opinion, committed an act that you now regret?'

'Yeah, but it weren't just me. There was two of us, see, and we was both doin' it. He made the first move, actually. I just went along with it, and… Well, it all went too far, like.'

There was a prolonged silence, followed by Jim Cole saying: 'I see. And now you're filled with shame, is it?'

'Yeah, I am a bit, as it happens.'

'Well, the first thing you need to know, Mr… erm, is that you should *not* feel ashamed. I wouldn't go so far as to say that what you did with that other young man was natural, but, well, we are all different, I suppose. And you're not the first to go through what you're going through, let me tell you.'

'I ain't?'

'No, no. There's many others like you. As you might know, society frowns upon young men like you… and for good reason, I might add, seeing as there wouldn't be any society at all if we were all of your persuasion. But there's a lot of it goes on in the background, you might say. In the dark corners.'

'Yeah, well, I ain't ever gonna—'

'Do you know what my advice to you is, laddie? I think you should go and talk to the other young chap. There's no good in suffering alone, and where there's two heads, there's a way. That's what my old mam used to say, and she was always right. What do you think of that, Mr… erm…'

Bean knocked on the door. No one came for nearly a minute, though he could hear noises inside. He knocked again. He had never been here before. He didn't want to be here now, if he was honest, but he knew that Jim Cole was right.

The door opened. A gaunt-looking woman with dark-rimmed eyes looked at him.

'Joe in?' said Bean.

'He's not well.'

'Ain't he?'

'No.'

The woman went to close the door but Bean said: 'Can I see him, though? I just wanna—'

'He won't see no one. He's... he's took it hard.' She seemed to have something in her eye, and rubbed it. 'We've all took it hard.'

'Took what hard?'

She was crying openly now, but made no attempt to hide it. Tears fell down her cheeks though she made no sound, and stood perfectly still. 'There's been a death in the family.'

'Oh. Oh, I'm sorry to... Look, I won't keep him more than five minutes. I just need to—'

'He was very close to em.'

'Close to who?'

'My... his grandparents.' She got a handkerchief out and blew her nose, then squinted at Bean. 'Don't you read the papers?'

'But...' said Bean finally. The door was shut now, however, and no one was there to hear him. He stepped away from the front of the house and looked at the upper window. A face looked back at him, then faded to darkness.

Afterwards, running home, Bean wasn't sure about anything.

'If you don't come out, I'll phone a doctor.'

Bean didn't move. He didn't breathe. The bed was warm and he felt safe under the duvet. There were some bad smells but even they were comforting to him. It was a sanctuary now. It had to be. There was nowhere else to go. Everywhere outside his tiny duvet kingdom was treacherous and full of danger. People wanted him. People hated him and wanted him in prison, or dead. And all because of that electric fire. That old man and his army knife, and his stupid three-bar fire that had swung like a demolition ball into his decrepit head.

Bean closed his eyes and saw the blood. He opened them again and, quietly, hummed a nameless nursery rhyme.

A shrill voice at the door. 'I wanna get in there and clean. You been in there for God knows how many days. Open this door. If you don't open this door I'll get Mr Jacks across the road to come up here with his toolbox.'

'No!' It felt bad, shouting. His throat was full of phlegm and he sounded like a sick, giant frog with an unusually high voice.

'Andrew? Did you say summat?'

'Don't get Mr Jacks.'

'Why not? I've got to get in there, and you won't—'

'Mam, I'm all right. I mean, I'm sick. I... I got a really bad headache, and I just need...' He didn't know what he needed. 'I don't need no doctor, though. It ain't like that. I'll be better soon. Honest.'

'Well,' said his mother, 'all right. But I want you to eat summat.'

Twenty minutes later, Bean opened the door and looked both ways. He picked up a plate from the carpet and brought it inside.

He ate the ham sandwich, looking out of the window. From there you could see the road behind the house, and the little alley off it that led you past the allotments and towards town. Walking along the alley, smoking a fag, was Tracy from the chippy. Bean stepped back from the window and peered around the frame, watching her. There was a strange look on her face, as if she had just realised that someone had tricked her, long ago, into accepting her lot in life. To Bean it seemed that she was slowly being crushed by the weight of the world, and yet was unaware of it. To him she was beautiful.

When she was gone from view he went back to the sandwich, which was tasting nicer the more he ate. After the food he felt a bit better. He looked out of the window again. New possibilities were opening up before him. Avenues into the rest of his life seemed open now, whereas before, only minutes earlier, they had been barricaded shut. But he had to be brave. If he did not have courage, there was no point.

'I'll give you twenty pounds for it.'

'Twenty quid?'

'All right, twenty-five.'

Bean stared, mouth agape.

'Thirty, then. And I'm goin' no higher, mind you. That's me final.'

'Thirty quid?'

The man behind the counter appeared to clench his whole body and let out a prolonged, quiet whine. When that passed, and he was able to breathe again, he said: 'It's a good clock. I've not seen too many carriage clocks like this one. But it's, erm, it's got some corrosion. You see that there? Corrosion. Thirty quid, take or leave. I'm doin' you a favour.'

Later, in another shop, Bean asked: 'Do you do these in burgundy, though?'

Later still, walking up the hill, he gazed longingly at the second-hand cars in the forecourt of Ernie Bast & Sons. One in particular caught his eye: a lovely Austin Princess, five years old. It was burgundy with a thin grey stripe all around, and seemed perfect for him. Bean was a long way from being in a position to buy a car, let alone a prestigious model like this, but it gave him hope. It reminded him that there are things in the world worth working towards, and that you should never give up on them.

He tried the door handle, glancing over his shoulder at the showroom, then carried on up the hill, holding his bunch of flowers.

Just over the crest of the hill, across the road, stood the chippy. Inside it was brightly lit but the windows were steamed up, so you couldn't see whether the beefy arms frantically shovelling chips behind the counter were those of Frank or Tracy. Bean crossed the road and, using the dark window of the house next door as a mirror, straightened the lapels of his (fake) leather box jacket and adjusted his hair, which felt sticky. The barber had put something in it without asking, and although it smelt nice, it hadn't reacted well with the fine drizzle. An irritable, middle-aged face loomed out of the darkness behind the mirror-window, and Bean stepped back.

Both Frank and Tracy were working behind the counter. One orderly queue of eight customers wound around the edge of the floor. Bean took one step from the doorway and joined it. All eyes were on the menu on the wall behind the counter. Fingers were totting up prices and stomachs were growling at the thought of a piece of halibut or a fishcake, so no one noticed Bean standing at the back, dressed head to toe in burgundy and holding a bunch of deep red, market-bought carnations. As the queue moved forward people came in behind him, and may or may not have found something curious about his apparel, or the way he was chewing the filthy fingernails on his killer's hands. But Bean didn't notice them. All he saw was Tracy. *Please please please*, he kept saying in his head, although he never got around to adding *let me get served by Tracy*. Before that could happen, and after perhaps forty-five *pleases*, Joe walked in.

Bean didn't notice, intent as he was on studying Tracy's face. Her expression changed from blank to panicked, and Bean blushed, crestfallen, thinking that this was her reaction to seeing him waiting. The queue was going down fast, most customers wanting just chips. Bean felt his shoulders sagging more and more the closer he got. He even hoped now, just a little bit, that he would get served by Frank. But then his turn came.

She shouldered Frank aside and leaned over the counter. 'Go out the back,' she whispered. 'Don't turn around, just go out the back.'

'Eh? Why?'

Frank was watching her now, ignoring his customer, who was going on about the football. She grabbed Bean by the lapel and yanked sideways, wanting to drive home the message but only tearing off a handful of cheap PVC. Bean turned and looked outside. Nobody there. A bus went past with no passengers on board.Tracy lifted the partition and hissed: 'Bean!' She grabbed him again (by the elbow this time) and wrenched him through the back room and into a dark corridor. It smelled of damp and rot. Sacks of potatoes lined one wall, many loose and squashed on the concrete floor. Tracy faced Bean and said: 'You gotta leave town. He wants to kill you.'

'Who does?'

'Joe.'

'What?'

'Joe wants to kill you. You killed... He says you upset his mam.'

'I never upset his mam.'

'It don't matter, he thinks you did. He told me all about it, Bean.'

'He what? When? Why'd he tell you?'

'Last night. On me way home from… Look, it don't matter. I don't believe it anyway. I can see you'd never do summat like that. You're not the same as all them others, Bean. I can see it. Don't let no one tell you different.'

Bean stared back at Tracy, shaking his head so slowly and slightly that Tracy didn't notice. His mouth was hanging open, and she lunged at it with her own, clashing teeth and splitting his lower lip slightly. But Bean didn't notice that. He felt himself standing on the edge of a vast precipice and he threw himself off, diving with perfection into a warm, calm sea of soft lips, fleshy arms, tight aprons and the smell of chip fat. He forgot who he was and where he was, and knew only the moment that he and Tracy had created together. Then she stepped away from him and opened the back door.

'Run,' she said, looking at the floor. 'Run away. Leave town. He'll kill you.'

Before he could argue he found himself outside in the drizzle, the door shut behind him. He was in the yard behind the chippy, which was strewn with old potato sacks and unemptied dustbins. Around the edge was a brick wall about seven feet high, and in one corner a wooden gate. The gate opened and Joe stepped in, then stopped.

The drizzle had stopped and the sun had come back out for what time it had left, and it perched low behind Joe's head, obscuring his face. It was the same dark face Bean had seen in that upstairs window. Joe popped a flick knife and held it out sideways, as if pointing at one of the upturned dustbins and demanding to know who had upturned it.

Bean went for the wall, jumping off the one remaining upright dustbin and getting just enough spring off it before it went over. He briefly straddled the wall on his way over, only to meet the jagged glass embedded all along it. He yelped in pain and tried to fall sideways away from the yard, but a large hook of glass snagged his inner thigh and held him firm for a couple of seconds before snapping off. He landed shoulder first in an alley and ran. His thigh was numb and something didn't feel right between his legs, but adrenalin and Tracy's final words kept him moving. At the end of the alley he met the main road and kept running. A few people were on the path but they all moved aside for him. He ran hard for a long time, and when he stopped he keeled over on to the grass, paralysed by screaming lungs and a stitch in his side. When his body allowed him, many minutes later, he pulled himself up and sat for a while. He saw the shredded material between his legs, the drenched trousers and the white socks turned red, and started sobbing loudly, leaning back on a large piece of masonry.

Joe entered the twilit cemetery and stood still, sniffing the air. He heard no sounds other than the traffic on the road behind. He moved on, keeping low, blade out. Within a couple of minutes he saw a cruciform headstone with a figure slumped against it. He crept close, then walked tall. Five yards away he stopped. He looked at the face drained of colour, and the dark red spreading through the white marble gravel, and frowned. With a boot he prodded Bean's shoulder. Bean fell sideways and remained still. Behind him, on the headstone, were the words: IN THE MIDST OF LIFE WE ARE IN DEATH.

Joe put his knife away and walked home.

You've Got Everything Now

Catherine O'Flynn

The Smiths were the perfectly timed soundtrack to my teenage years. Their first single was released as I turned thirteen. At fourteen, I saw them on the Meat Is Murder *tour. By the time I was eighteen they were gone. Throughout it all I endured the knocks and jeers of pastel-shaded Duran Duran and Wham! fans shrouded in my old man's coat and ridiculous hair. What I loved most about The Smiths was the way they made me feel nostalgic and wistful for something I'd never had. 'You've Got Everything Now' is a typical example of that. I've tried to write a story that captures the song's sense of regret and desire, and I'm very sure I don't come close.*

Quinn sits at the front of the class. I suppose he feels some protection from the teacher, though of course the back of his head and shoulders are covered in ink and gob. There's something prim about Quinn. His uniform fits him, his movements are neat. He is small and dapper in a way that the rest of us aren't. I look at Millsy, distorted by hormones, some hideous halfway stage of the experiment, pustules on his face, limbs too big to control, wiry hair trying to escape his head. Quinn is not half-boy, half-man. He is a mini-man – tiny, but perfectly formed. On the rare occasions he speaks, his voice is deep and clear. On the rare occasions he speaks. Mr Edwards is late for class, the volume rises. Banks throws an apple core at the back of Quinn's head. It hits him in the neck. Wet, white debris sticks to his skin. We laugh. He turns around and looks at us. Always that same look.

Now at night, in bed when the house creaks and Alison's breath catches in her sleep, I still see that look. It waits behind the eyelids. I get out of bed and go and look in at the children. Amy lies face down, spreadeagled as if dropped from the sky, her hair pasted across the side of her hot and sticky face, her breathing deep and ragged. She engages in gruelling battles during her sleeping hours, deep, intense struggles that never quite break into nightmares. Her night-time self is somehow more corporeal, more burdened than the sunlit wisp she seems during the day. Eddie sleeps neatly on his back, his face turned a little to one side, his expression untroubled. Each morning when I take him to school I scan the faces of the other boys. I look for groupings and patterns in the playground. I look for bigger boys and idiot friends. I look closely at his face for signs of worry, indicators of anxiety. I stroke his head and try and breathe.

We smoke all through dinner break. Behind the sports pavilion we consume coke and fags. Our insides fill with gas and clouds. Banks runs to Greggs and brings back five cream cakes. Millsy wants to know who's going to miss out on a second cake. Banks answers by stuffing the surplus two in his mouth at the same time. He laughs so hard at Millsy's outraged expression that cream bursts from his mouth and nose. I lie on my back and let the winter sun press against my eyelids. If I try hard enough I can forget that Millsy and Banks are there. If I try hard enough I can leave this place behind. I imagine I'm lying in the middle of a vast prairie. The grass is high and moves around me in the breeze. My horse is tethered to a tree. A stream runs somewhere nearby, and there by the stream under the shade of a tall tree, someone is waiting for me. I sit up suddenly and find myself blinded by the light. I stare ahead waiting for my vision to clear. A group of girls emerges from the shadows, one of them turns and smiles just at me.

In the evenings I tell Alison about my day at work. She understands the challenges I face, the targets I have to meet with a team made up of other people's discards. I'm supposed to turn them around when everyone else has failed. Alison understands because she has wide managerial experience. She doesn't treat my commentary as whining, she takes it seriously. She thinks about it and makes recommendations. I listen to what she says. I've never been the kind of man to feel annoyed by his wife's advice, I'm grateful for it. After talking something over with Alison, there's always a clear path out of the woods.

Before school I see him first. Quinn emerges from behind the science block and steps out into the playground. I feel a tightness in my stomach but carry on talking to Millsy and Banks. They are asking me what I did with Sally Meadows. I'm choosing not to say. I'm pouring petrol on the fire. I stamp my feet and blow on my hands but the damp air is deep inside me. Banks is staggering around like a drunkard trying to keep the ball bouncing on his head as he wheedles and cajoles. He asks me what happened over and over again. When I don't answer he says he knows what happened anyway, then he tells me what happened, and says, that's what happened, isn't it? Then he asks again why don't I just tell them what happened.

Millsy interrupts:

'Quick, give me the ball. It's Queen.'

He takes the ball from Banks, places it on the wet ground and then kicks it hard across the playground. The full force hits Quinn in the side of the face, whipping his head sideways.

''Shot,' says Banks.

Quinn takes a moment to register what's happened and, as he does, the side of his face blooms deep red. He turns and looks directly at us. Millsy holds up his hand and smiles:

'Soz mate'. Quinn walks off. We laugh. The redness creeping up his face is there when I close my eyes, like a sunspot.

We drink wine at night to unwind, but it doesn't seem to work so well for me. I watch Alison sip and see the way it smoothes her out and slows her down, but inside myself I sense a quickening, a heightened awareness. I find myself thinking about the inside of my head, I become more and more conscious of the clutter in there. The same thoughts and images orbit endlessly like the abandoned husks of satellites and dropped spanners floating through space. I wish there was some way to empty my head, to let go of certain images for ever. Alison and I sprawl on the sofa and on each other and watch DVDs. We love *The Sopranos*. The words fly around us. I can't follow all the dialogue but I like lying there and staring into the glow.

Quinn attends classes less often now. He appears for afternoon registration and then he vanishes. I look at his empty seat in double geography. I find it hard to concentrate during these long afternoons. Sally Meadows looks across and smiles at me from beneath her fringe. Millsy kicks me beneath the desk. Mrs Dixon talks about glaciated u-shaped valleys, truncated spurs and corries or cwms or cirques. The second hand on the big clock seems to move back and forth. We are locked forever in the firm embrace of 2.41 p.m. The noises around me fragment and then re-combine in a pulsing soundtrack. Dixon's voice, ticking clock, sighs and yawns, Banks clicking his pen on then off, endlessly repeated. I rock back on my chair and arch my neck backwards until I am looking through the windows at the back of the classroom. I see the world upside down. The grey clouds below, the empty playground above and beyond it the tangled branches of the woods reaching down like roots in to the sky.

We have two, but it should have been three. We lost someone between Eddie and Amy. At the hospital the screen was just black. The nurse moved the scanner from place to place, pulling us through the dark universe inside Alison, sending out signals that weren't returned. She tried for a long time, then apologised and told us that the baby had bowed out, had declined our invitation. Its coming and going were silent, marked only with secret symbols.

A faint blue line on a white stick meant I am here. A black screen meant now I'm gone.

The only movement on the screen were our own reflections, like phantom signs of life. The nurse wiped the magic jelly from Alison's stomach with a blue paper towel and that was the end of the film. We grieved, and in time we moved on. Amy was born and stamped herself on us and on the world. But I can't forget what I saw on the screen. I can't forget the emptiness that I recognised there. On summer days my arms are covered in goose bumps. I feel the chill of the void inside as I cast around desperately for a pulse, for any sign of life.

Sally Meadows tells me secrets. She buys me gifts. She tells me she loves me. I say I love her too. She's the prettiest girl in the class. I buy her a Valentine's card bigger than an Alsatian dog. She says that she feels short of breath when I walk into a room. She sees me frown and I turn it into a smile. A wide, gleaming, luckiest boy in the world type smile.

I spend lunchtimes at Sally's house. I know all the posters on her bedroom walls now. I catch the dead eyes of pop stars as I lie on top of her. They are unmoved by the spectacle. Afterwards I pull my clothes back on and leave by the back door to avoid nosy neighbours, I climb over the garden fence and walk up the dusty road by the garages. I break into a run as I near school, realising that I'm late for afternoon registration again. As I run along the corridor I crash into someone rounding the corner. Quinn looks straight at me. I should tell him to get lost. I should punch him, but instead I stand and look at him and then I run on. I leap up the stairs two at a time, but my feet move slower until they stop. I close my eyes. A moment passes. That look again. I turn around and start to walk back down, and gradually my feet speed up. I keep on running till I see him in the distance. I slow to a walk and try to catch my breath.

He walks casually across the playground and down the playing fields. At the bottom I see him pull back the fencing and disappear into the woods beyond. I run down and climb through the fence, I stand still until I hear his footsteps over to the right. I pick my way carefully through the undergrowth, the wind moves through the trees and covers the sound of my pursuit. I follow him along pathways I've never seen before and then he stops. He is standing in a clearing and I watch from the tangled branches. His perfect frame is perfectly still. He starts to hum and I hear the voice so rarely heard – deep and clear. That voice calls me and I shake in response. My head feels clear and light and my body moves forward, but as I take a step there is a rustling in the bushes to my right. A man emerges. He wears a suit but no tie. His hair is grey at the temples. Quinn smiles at him – the only time I see him smile. They walk off to the far edge of the clearing and disappear into the leaves. I stand alone.

Sometimes the only way to get to sleep at night is to climb in with one of the kids. I know it should be the other way round. The enormous heat they generate passes through my skin and softens all my edges. They never wake up, they just shuffle over in their sleep and murmur. I could weep at their generousity. I close my eyes, I listen to their fast, shallow breaths and when I open my eyes I'm always standing at the edge of the clearing. I'm still a boy and so is Quinn. Bernard. His first name was Bernard. I'm watching from behind a tree, there is a rustling in the bushes nearby, but before the man emerges Quinn turns and looks directly at me. That same look. Level, steady and with some unspoken challenge. I walk out of the shadow and follow him.

I Want the One I Can't Have

Matt Beaumont

The song I wanted was 'You're The One For Me, Fatty', but it's a Morrissey number and I wasn't allowed. 'I Want The One I Can't Have' it had to be, then, obviously. Morrissey really appreciated envy – 'We Hate It When Our Friends Become Successful', another solo title and probably his best. I suspect he realised that envy is the uranium 235 that fuels the nuclear reactor of human relations. Or something.

It's an enduring regret that I never got round to seeing The Smiths. Honestly, I kept meaning to, but suddenly and terminally they went and broke up. Unlike Duran Duran. Will they ever have the good grace to fuck off?

'Who was that on the phone?'

'This guy with a short story commission.'

'Interesting?'

'Yeah… yeah, I think so. It's for a collection called *Ordinary World: Stories Inspired by the Songs of Duran Duran*… What's so funny? It's a good idea.'

'Duran *Duran*, though?'

'Cultural icons standing at the epicentre of a fascinating and unjustly maligned decade.'

'Excuse me?'

'Like them or loathe them, they were an important band.'

'They made glossy, disposable pop songs and had silly hair. That's "important", is it? What's next? *Snooker Loopy: Stories Inspired by Chas & Dave*?'

'Now you're being ridiculous.'

'Am I?'

'You just don't like Duran Duran.'

'They were all right. I bounced around to 'Girls On Film', had a snog to 'Save A Prayer', but, you know, you move on, don't you? Anyway, you're the one that hates Duran Duran. Why would a music snob like you have anything to do with it? Won't you feel tainted, soiled, cheap?'

'I told you, it's not about *liking* them. It's about acknowledging their place in the cultural panop— Do you have any idea how stupid you look when you raise your eyebrow?'

'I just can't believe you're taking this seriously. I'd think carefully before you agree to do it.'

'I will. I've got plenty of other stuff to be getting on with at the moment. I'll most likely say no.'

Word document (unsaved):

Wild Boys
Story notes:
Post-apocalyptic landscape
Spencer, 15
Reluctant leader of group of undernourished feral youths
A Frankenstein's monster of a car created from scrapyard automotive corpses
Pimp overlord – looks like Keith Allen in Kiss wardrobe
Piles of burning tyres, smoke charring blood-orange sky
Pile of bollocks

'What are you doing?'

'Nothing much. Surfing a few porn sites.'

'No you're not. What's that window you just closed?'

'Nothing.'

'You're writing that story, aren't you?'

'What story?'

'Don't give me that. The Duran Duran one. You said yes, didn't you?'

'It's a *good* idea. I'm between books anyway. And I'll be in some good company. A lot of pretty decent writers are contributing.'

'Like?'

'Not sure. The guy didn't actually say. But, you know, I got the vibe it'll be Granta names. It's not going to be trash.'

'Yeah, yeah. You shouldn't have said yes. You will regret it... Duran *Duran.*'

Word document (trashed):

Hungry Like the Wolf

Spencer emerged from the subway as the last of a vanilla-fudge-sundae Sunday melted submissively into a glowering dusk. The rawhide tails of his trenchcoat trailed a perturbing musk of liquor, testosterone and barely leashed power. His measured stride across the open concourse as he sought Her was one weary cliché after another and why the fuck am I even typing because if I commit another word of this drivel to my hard drive I will

'How's it going?'

'How's what going?'

'Your Duran Duran tribute.'

'It's not a tribute. It's merely a story that takes one of their song titles as a starting point.'

'Whatever. How's it going?'

'It's... going... Jesus, it's difficult. Have you ever listened to them?'

'Of course I have.'

'No, I mean actually *listened*.'

'I know the chorus to 'Rio'. It's about a girl, I think... Or a river.'

'I downloaded their greatest hits. 'Hungry Like The Wolf'... Wow...'

'You like it?'

'*No*. I never really paid attention to it before. I played it five times straight through and... I think it's about a rapist. It's like this weird celebration of stalking a woman across a city and then... possibly... *raping* her.'

'So is that your title?'

'No, way too sick. I think I'll try 'Union Of The Snake'.'

'What's that about?'

'It's completely indecipherable. It's exactly the sort of blank canvas I can work on because it doesn't fill my head with any images whatsoever.'

'Two snakes having sex? Or forming a trade union?'

'You've ruined it now. It'll have to be 'The Reflex', then.'

'What's that all about?'

'An only child? Called Reflex...? Haven't a clue. Strange. I read *Finnegans Wake* at uni and it made more sense.'

'Maybe the lads were more profound than any of us gave them credit for.'

Word document (trashed):

The Reflex

Spencer sat on the window ledge and waited. Waiting had been his life. Waiting for he knew not what, but waiting all the same. For an idea? Some tiny glint of inspiration to rise up from the depressive quagmire of a commission accepted in haste and repented at agonising, endless bloody leisure? And as he waited he thanked the Lord Jesus Christ for the soothing *bong* that announced an incoming email and a brief respite from this hell

'*Fuck*!'

'What's the matter?'

'Email from Beaumont.'

'He's usually pretty harmless. What's he done to upset you?'

'He's writing a story for *Paint a Vulgar Picture*.'

'Don't tell me. Stories inspired by The Smiths. Now *there's* an iconic group standing at the cultural epicentre.'

'Cunts.'

'I thought you liked The Smiths.'

'Not The Smiths. Beaumont, the rest of them. *Cunts*. He knocks off throwaway, so-called 'comedies'. Why's he been asked? Don't just shrug. *Why*?'

'Maybe they think he'll lighten the mood. The Smiths are liable to inspire a lot of gloomy introspection.'

'Bollocks. You're just falling for that lazy, knee-jerk Morrissey the Miserablist rubbish. The man was the wittiest writer pop has ever seen.'

'A bit like Simon le Bon... Ah, touched a nerve there. Coffee...? I'll take that as a no.'

Word document (trashed):

Skin Trade

Spencer pushed the flimsy bark canoe over the shale, then watched it slump in the water, weighed down as it was with the dozens of beaver pelts acquired over eight weeks of patient trapping. He wondered how much they would fetch from the French dealers that waited downstream. And he wondered why he was being jemmied into a tale of colonial fur traders when the author's head was swilling with three minutes of glam-funk tripe about a prostitute because, after all, who wouldn't rather be in a sub-Jackie Collins story about a hooker than freezing his knackers off on the upper reaches of the St Lawrence?

'How's it going, then...? That badly...? Why don't you call Beaumont and ask him to do a swap? He won't mind, will he? If he's as flippant and shallow as you say he is, he's probably got a secret crush on le Bon. Or at least on his missus. You can never tell with him... I take it from that look you already asked... I hate to say it... No, I won't say it... OK, I'll say it. I told you you'd regret it... *Jesus*! You could have had my eye out with that.'

<u>Word document (trashed)</u>:

Planet Earth
Spencer sat in the toothpaste-tube confines of his orbiting re-entry capsule and wrote the opening lines of his last will and
No, fuck it.
He wrote his shopping list.
Marmite
Jaffa Cakes
Organic mince
Lenor
Tea bags
Stock cubes
Oh, the phone. Remember check fridge before resuming list

'*Yes*?'
'Hi ... I haven't caught you at a bad time, have I? You sound a little... fraught.'
'No, I'm good. What is it?'
'I just wanted to know how the story was coming on. I don't want to be a pain, but the deadline was a couple of weeks ago. My production people are getting a little agitated. I emailed you, but perhaps you didn't get it.'
'It's... It's... It's going all right. Coming along... nicely.'
'Good, fantastic. So when can I expect something?'
'Soon. Yes, quite soon.'
'In the next few days?'

'Yeah, a few days.'

'Sorry, but I'm going to have to press you to be specific. You know, *deadlines*.'

'Look, to be absolutely honest, I'm struggling.'

'Oh. Would it help to talk it through?'

'I know the title thing is just supposed to be a jumping-off point, but I can't get the songs out of my head.'

'Right.'

'And they're not helpful.'

'Uh-huh.'

'In fact, they're shite. The worst kind of shite. Shite that dresses itself up in tight leather pants and a gold lamé jacket so you don't know it's shite until you tread in it and it's too late.'

'I wish you'd said how you felt about them when we first spoke about the project.'

'You didn't tell me about the Smiths collection when we first spoke, did you? I could do a story for that.'

'I've got my full quota of contributors for that one, I'm afraid. If anything, it's slightly oversubscribed.'

'Of course it is. It's The bloody *Smiths*. Tell me, how did you decide?'

'How do you mean?'

'Who got The Smiths and who got Duran Duran.'

'I don't know... It was pretty much a lottery.'

'A *lottery*?'

'I didn't have an agenda, if that's what you mean.'

'Of course you didn't. You just stuck a pin in a list of names, yeah?'

'Well, not quite, but it's not far off the mark. Look, are you going to be able to finish the story?'

'I said I'd do it so I'll do it.'

'Good, thank you. And what about *Church of the Poison Mind*? Shall I slate you in for that?'

'Oh, yes, absolutely *brilliant*! The eagerly awaited Culture Club anthology.'

'You're being ironic, aren't you…? Hello…? Hello…?'

Word document (trashed):

A View to a Kill
Frenzied, hysterical, utterly detached from any vestige of reason,
Spencer plunged the knife into

Post-it left on fridge:
Gone to murder one of the Taylor brothers. Either will do.
Both would be a bonus. Don't wait up.

Nowhere Fast

Jeremy Sheldon

I chose to write a story inspired by 'Nowhere Fast' because I couldn't get the following line out of my head: 'And if the day came when I felt a natural emotion, I'd get such a shock I'd probably jump In the ocean...' Now it seems I can't get Leo, the narrator, out of my head and he's developed into the central character of a longer piece.

'Leo, for heaven's sake...'

I looked up from the washbasin to see Sorrel standing at the door. For a moment, I wondered what I'd done wrong, then realised that I'd forgotten to switch off the tap while I was brushing my teeth, the latest development in her plans to save the planet single-handedly.

'*How many times do I have to remind you?*' she snapped, reaching in front of me and twisting it closed before I could move.

I grunted an apology through the toothpaste foam, long accustomed to what the girls and I sometimes called 'Mummy's Rules' (usually when Mummy wasn't listening), but Sorrel had already marched downstairs, eager to start preparing for the arrival of 'Marcus and Opal', some new friends she'd invited to the house for dinner that evening. A few minutes later, I joined her to find that she already had a list of chores waiting for me to attend to while she went out to the shops. Scrubbing the toilet. Sweeping the front path. Mopping the kitchen floor. Later, I was sipping a mug of tea and surveying my handiwork when she returned with the food.

'So,' I asked, 'who are they?'

'Marcus is another colum*nist* at the paper,' Sorrel replied.

I could have guessed as much. Recently, our whole lives had started to revolve around 'the paper'. But when had she started pronouncing the 'N' in columnist? I wasn't sure.

'He writes about design,' she added, somewhat vaguely it seemed to me. 'Opal is a yoga teacher.'

'And you met them when?'

'I haven't,' Sorrel replied. 'Marcus emailed me out the blue the other day to tell me how much he's been enjoying my column. I thought it might be nice to invite them over. Perhaps you can wear that shirt I bought you last Christmas.'

Sorrel spent the rest of the day fretting about 'the state of the knives and forks', hoovering every horizontal surface in the house, placing tea-lights in the freshly glistening bathroom and roasting a butternut squash. Whether the fact that her column that weekend extolled 'the wholesome beauty of gourds' was a coincidence or part of her grand design wasn't clear. Either way, I spent the rest of the day washing and polishing new (new!) wineglasses that she'd bought in Crouch End, ironing a tablecloth and driving the girls to St Albans to stay with their grandparents. I returned to find the hallway transformed with strings of tiny 'box' lights (where she'd stashed the girls' clutter, I never found out, but it reappeared piece by piece throughout the following week) and new 'throws' tossed over each of the sofas in the scrubbed sitting room.

'What do you think?' Sorrel asked. 'I thought the place could do with some sprucing up.'

'Very nice,' I replied, taking it all in and thinking that it looked as if we were about to redecorate. Who were this 'Marcus and Opal'? Whoever they were, they were clearly too important for Sorrel's standard 'take us as they find us' approach to those that called round.

Half an hour later I was ready and eager to welcome but then had to wait another forty minutes until the doorbell finally rang.

'I'll get it,' I called out, and pulled open the front door to find what appeared to be a pair of sixth-formers waiting on the doorstep.

'Hi there. You must be Marcus and Opal?'

The boy pulled a hand out of a pocket and thrust it forward.

'Marcus. You're Lionel, right? Good to meet you, pal.'

I hadn't had time to correct him before Sorrel shunted past to welcome them both, kissing them both on each cheek, I noticed, even though she'd met neither of them before.

'Marcus, wonderful to meet you finally. And you must be Opal? So glad you've braved your way to the wilds of Finsbury Park.'

'We brought bubbles,' Opal mewed in response, proffering two wrapped bottles.

'Champagne, how thoughtful,' I said, taking them from her.

'*Prosecco*, actually,' Marcus corrected. 'There's this really good offie on Columbia Road. Family business, literally been there for decades. We never go anywhere else. Thought champagne was a little *obvious*.'

'Well, we're even more thankful for it in that case,' I mumbled, drowned out by Sorrel's encouragement that we should move to somewhere 'more comfortable'.

I led Marcus into the sitting room and offered him a seat on one of the newly shrouded sofas while Sorrel and Opal went to the kitchen to fetch some glasses.

'Sorry we're a bit late,' he started, a gold signet ring flashing through his spiky hair. 'I was writing copy for a mate's website. Totally lost track of the time.'

'I understood that you were a journalist,' I said.

'Oh, I do all sorts of things,' he replied, as if the idea of doing one thing was impossible. 'Viral marketing, art, DJing…'

'I see. That all sounds very interesting.'

'And what about you? What do you do?'

'I'm a teacher.'

'Oh yeah? What subject?'

'Well, my subject's History. But my responsibilities pretty much keep me out of the classroom.'

'Responsibilities?'

I replied that I was a headmaster.

'Headmaster, eh? Don't look old enough.'

I wondered whether I needed to qualify that, at thirty-nine, I was the youngest headmaster in the borough (a source of some pride when the appointment was first made) or whether to respond by telling him that he didn't look old enough to write for the colour supplement of the weekend edition of a national newspaper. It was then, however, that Opal and Sorrel reappeared with a tray of glasses, a bowl of Japanese rice crackers and an opened bottle of 'bubbles'.

'Opal's just been telling me about a new initiative she's come up with,' Sorrel chimed as she set the tray down.

'Really?' I asked.

'She's got this brilliant idea of teaching yoga at schools. I was saying that she should discuss it with you. Maybe there's scope for a pilot scheme at St Stephen's?'

'It sounds like a lovely idea, in theory, very progressive,' I replied. 'In practice, it's challenge enough to get pupils to focus on the basics. It might be hard getting them to respond to something quite so... unconventional.'

'There's nothing more basic than yoga,' Opal chirped. 'Children today are so out of touch with their bodies, it's no wonder that none of them can sit still long enough to learn anything.'

'You should give it some thought,' added Marcus. 'No one can afford not to think outside the box these days. Might give you another string to your bow.'

I held back from various responses, relieved to be able to concentrate on pouring drinks while Sorrel continued to enquire about Opal's yoga classes and suggest she might come along to one. *What form did Opal teach?* Apparently she'd just recently returned from a retreat in Thailand where she'd 'got into Bikram'. *Was Bikram really more dynamic?* Sorrel asked. *Didn't a hybrid of the Ashtanga and Iyengar forms provide a better balance?* Opal mused that 'no form was better than its teacher' and this pretty much set the pattern for the evening that followed. I was used to some of Sorrel's more exotic ideas, her macrobiotic fasts, her Ayurvedic consultations, her implementation of a bokashi bin in the corner of the kitchen, her insistence we all use fennel toothpaste, her abhorrence of plastic carrier bags (and bleach and meat and monocrops and television and supermarkets and a whole detailed portfolio of other evils). I was more than used to being on the fringe of conversations whose terms I could only just decode (I'd spent my whole working life ignoring frenzied childish chatter about a vast array of alien objects, anything from Pokemon to P Diddy), but I was surprised to find three adults having a conversation in my kitchen in which I was barely included, let alone able to understand. Marcus seemed to lead at all times, his topics ranging from 'New Transgressionist' literature and the 'Brick Lane Jazz-Artcore' scene to 'Africanism' and 'Modern-Classic' design (the syllables of this last item crunched together without space for breath). And of course there was talk of his and Opal's most recent trip to India ('sourcing various *things*,' he admitted mysteriously) and talk of his various installation projects ('I'm making work for a couple of spaces at the moment…') and a tremendous amount of time spent outlining the plans he had for his and Opal's loft apartment on Vyner Street.

'Are you going for a Modern-Classic look?' I asked as politely as I could.

'Nah, something more Revisionist-Ethnic.'

This opened half an hour of discussion about Opal's fondness for South African fabrics that somehow segued into a report on Marcus and Opal's planned trip to New Zealand.

'What about the carbon emissions created by such a long flight?' I asked, choosing not to bother adding that their recent flights to Mumbai and back had also produced the same, and waited for Sorrel to add her own concerns. Our most recent summer holiday had been taken on the Scilly Isles rather than Paxos (my first choice of destination) and it had taken all my skills of negotiation to ensure that we hadn't had to bicycle our way to the West Country. Yet no such concern left Sorrel's lips, only a murmur of approval at Marcus's announcement that he and Opal would offset the carbon footprint of the journey with a payment towards the Forest Stewardship Council.

'Very clever,' I replied.

'Well,' Marcus sighed, 'none of us can keep taking and *taking* from the planet without giving something back.'

This comment seemed to mark a lull in the conversation and I wondered whether Marcus had finally run out of steam. Not a chance. Sorrel suggested we sit 'soft' (like pronouncing the N in 'columnist', this was a recent addition to her vocabulary) and busied herself preparing a pot of green tea (and a cup of vervain for Opal) while I led the way back to the sitting room, where Marcus launched into a new phase of the evening. This seemed to take the form of an interview. *Had I tried the new Jaliscan restaurant in Hoxton Square? Had I logged on to reaganomicon.com (a website dedicated to the 1980s 'but in an ironic way')? Had I heard of Tinariwin?*

'Where's that?' I asked.

'Not where, Lionel, but *who*,' hooted Opal.

Marcus was in the process of telling me that they were a 'sub-Saharan blues band' when Sorrel reappeared with the drinks and Fair Trade chocolates and I breathed a sigh of relief that Marcus could resume directing his commentary at her rather than me. And still it continued, Marcus and Sorrel exchanging information on a range of people they'd seen at 'launches' and 'private views'. *In Marcus's opinion, Mikey Fischer was a shameless 'rock slagger'. Did Sorrel know that Pip Tomkins was cheating on her magazine-editor husband with Jakey Smallbright? Had Marcus seen how poor Vic Morton's last show had been?* ('Poor?' he'd replied. 'It was fuckin' destitute.') *And what*

about Kane Pullet-Smith, seen desperately schmoozing with Chloe
Forbes at the Alarm Bar the previous week in an attempt to get his
own column?

How did Sorrel know all these people? When had she met them? I thought back over the last year or so since Sorrel had started writing her articles. She went out perhaps once a fortnight to 'a work thing' but always dismissed the events as pretentious and tiresome. According to Marcus's testimony, it all sounded like a backstage orgy at a rock concert. 'Parky' (whoever he was) had been '*busted doing it in the toilets with some cocktail waitress by his missus.*' Other characters had variously been caught 'boffing', 'doinking' and 'thrumming'. And there was the consistent if unspoken implication that everyone was taking drugs all the time, Marcus included (he'd build on a sequence of smug inferences before pulling up short and claiming he'd better 'plead the fifth' with a sideways glance in my direction).

Opal sat there listening to it all, batting her eyelids at Marcus. As for me, I tried not to look at my watch too often and contributed little to the conversation beyond the addition of a few neutral grunts for the hour that elapsed before they ordered their cab and finally left.

'That was fun,' Sorrel exclaimed once we'd waved them off and walked back inside.

'You must be joking?'

'What do you mean?'

Perhaps I should have sensed the warning signals, the speed of her response, the sharpening of her tone. But I'd drunk more than my normal amount and was in no mood for circumspection.

'I mean,' I said, piling the dirty teacups on to the tray and carrying them through to the kitchen, 'that he must have been the most pretentious person I've ever met.'

'I thought he was charming and interesting,' Sorrel replied. 'You might take note of that. You weren't...'

She broke off.

'I wasn't *what* exactly?' I asked, slamming the tray down on the kitchen counter and turning to face her.

'There's no need to be aggressive.'

'I'm not being aggressive. Tell me what you were about to say.'

Sorrel started clearing the kitchen table.

'I was about to say,' she began, eyes focused on the dirty plates and cutlery, 'that you weren't exactly the most enlightening company tonight. I think you could have made more of an effort. I always make an effort to back you up in your work...'

'More of an effort! I'm still trying to work out why I've spent half my weekend cleaning the house so that you can impress those fools. I thought you had better judgement than...'

'Leo,' she interrupted, 'you've drunk too much and you're embarrassing yourself. Perhaps you should just go upstairs to bed.'

'He was an idiot and you know it.'

'Marcus is one of the most respected writers at the paper...'

'Of course, the *paper*, I wondered when that was going to come up. Do you know how ridiculous you sound? It's not as if you're writing the leader column for *The Times*. All you're doing is writing a few hundred words about bloody diets once a week. It's hardly...'

I stopped, realising that I didn't want to finish my intended sentence. Sorrel had stared back at me for a few seconds.

'You know,' she replied quietly, 'I think you're jealous.'

'Jealous? Of *him*?'

'No.' She sighed, pushing a strand of red hair back from her face. 'Of *me*. I've finally been given the chance to do something I believe in. Now you're not the centre of attention round here, all you can do is undermine me.'

She walked out of the room at that point. Moments later, the sound of our bedroom door slamming echoed down the stairs. I stood there in the kitchen without moving for a few moments, cheeks and fingertips burning, heart thumping away. Had I been unfair? I didn't think so. I'd been putting up with 'Mummy's Rules' for long enough and every time I broke one of them, I was reprimanded as if I were a little boy. How come she'd let some trust-funded chancer behave like a spoiled brat and decided that I was the one at fault?

Weren't Marcus and Opal the kind of middle-class hypocrites that Sorrel loathed?

Perhaps not. Perhaps I was being unfair. What had Sorrel and I been like when we were in our mid-twenties? I thought back to our PGCE days, both of us giddy with high ideals and convinced we were going to transform the lives of young people. We were going to foster social change in the classroom, the 'sharp end', as Sorrel was fond of saying back then. And now? Even I had to admit that spending my days managing budgets and staff felt as far away from those lofty ambitions as one could get. Perhaps everyone deserved the chance to change as life's realities closed in.

I turned off all the lights downstairs and trudged slowly up to the bathroom, where I brushed my teeth (the tap dutifully switched off during the brushing itself) before opening our bedroom door as quietly as I could and creeping inside. Sorrel was already in bed with the lights off, her back facing me.

'I'm sorry,' I whispered in the darkness. 'I guess I got carried away just now. Can you forgive me?'

'Sure.'

I took my clothes off and slid into bed next to her, pulling the covers tight around us.

'I really am sorry.'

'It's OK, Leo. I just want to forget about it.'

I tired to gauge her tone. Her anger seemed to have subsided but I couldn't be sure. We lay there for a few moments, the sound of her breathing faint in my ears, before I reached an exploratory arm out towards her and tried to gather her closer to me. Would she shrug me off? No, her body shifted a little and soon her back was pressed against my chest, her buttocks pressed against my groin. Before I knew it, I had an erection growing in the space in between. Had Sorrel noticed? I tried to focus on some kind of quotidian image, anything (marking, morning assembly, staff meetings) to will it away, only for an image of Sorrel churning beneath me to flash up in its place.

Slowly, my fingertips pulsing with heat, I reached round to cup her breast in my hand. It had been months. Perhaps all we'd needed was a row to clear the air.

'Sorrel…'

'Go to sleep, Leo. I've got yoga in the morning and you have to collect the girls.'

There Is a Light that Never Goes Out

Helen Walsh

The year was 1991. I was bunking school, killing time in one of the greasy spoons up near Piccadilly Station. A mob of young scals with baby fringes and glue-sniffing complexions pour in. Behind them, but clearly with them, is this waif in a Smiths T-shirt. He's thirteenish and he's unbearably pretty and he stands out against the other urchins in their shell suits and LA Fox trainers. I'm besotted, I can't stop staring at him but only when he speaks do I realise it's a girl. I think about her non-stop and I return to the café the same time each week in the hope that she might be there. About six months later I see her down on the canal with some of the urchins. She's wearing the same T-shirt, the same ragged cardigan. I'm with my boyfriend at the time and he tells me that that's where the rent boys hang. I'm fourteen years old and at this stage in my life I'm bang into acid house and ecstasy and up until now The Smiths' clever conceits and gorgeous melodies are lost on me. Over that winter I buy all their albums and I fall headlong in love with them. I never see the girl on the canal again but 'There Is A Light That Never Goes Out' will always remind me of her.

Manchester, late November, 1989

Mac is waiting in our usual spot down by the canal. He looks different, tired perhaps, his face heavier set and wizened against the gangrene haze of the underpass. I check my watch. Only half of its crap illuminous face flashes up. I'm early. I drop back in the shadows of the footbridge and wait.

I've known him for nearly two and a half years, Mac. I've had sex with him over a hundred times and still I couldn't tell you how old he is. Could easily be anything between forty and sixty. His face, his whole look, is timeless. He'll be exactly the same when he's seventy, no doubt: slim, full thatch of hair, same cathode-blue eyes, a hue so sharp you could nick yourself on them.

He's wearing a navy Duffer of St George's parka, the toggles fastened right up to the throat; distressed denims and expensive training shoes. Forest Hills, I think. On anyone else it might look vulgar, ridiculous. But Mac? He just looks hip. Dangerous. And yet, in spite of the urban attire and the dead cool posturing – one foot cocked up against the wall and tugging on his joint like a fucking Hillbilly – he can't help but radiate elegance. Effortlessly so. Mac hums of taste and style and the moneyed finesse of suburbia, and he cuts a queer figure among the soaks and scavengers dragged blinking and stumbling by the rising moon.

This hundred-yard stretch of canal is a greasy netherworld of pimps and pushers and pariahs where the hamster wheel of sex and drugs is forever spinning. Even in the filthy scourge of January when the festive fever sweats itself dry and the dozen or so boys that work the Drive-In are slogging it out for a measly hand job with some whinnying foul-breathed suit, this little strip – or The Rack as its known to those who shop here – is always bustling. Always on heat.

The Rack is the maze of backstreets that sits roughly between the Village and the Northern Quarter and is predominantly the haunt of Chicken. The predators who feast on us are getting younger and younger – my last john was barely eighteen – but then so is the Chicken. Rash, the new kid on the block, is nine and he's by no means a novelty. I'm telling you, you ain't worth fuck all this side of rentland if your voice has broken. The Rack is also where the cranked-up trannies tout their trade with their fat weeping lips and botched titties and, if you squint hard enough through the darkness to the other side of the canal, you'll see Eugene, the bag-head amputee, stumping along on his crutches. The Rack is where the freaks show out. The Rack is where Mac came, all those years back, to find a freak like me.

I'm surprised he's showed, in all honesty. Since JT's body was pulled from the canal last week, trade has been dead slow. Tentatively, it's starting to pick up again, not that rentland feels any safer for it, mind. The sick fuck that battered JT, stuffed his anus with grit and sand and dumped him in the canal is still out there, roaming, stalking, possibly even slowing down right now on the other side of the carriageway, signalling with a double click of the beams for the young kid with the red Nike cap to get in. And I was half hoping Mac wouldn't show, tell the truth. I'm a little tired myself, a little frayed round the edges. Heavy limbed. Skittering head. Coming down with some big mad lurgy. Man, you should've seen the grey furball I coughed up in the basin this morning. It was *alive,* I tell you! Prodded the hirsute bastard with the end of my toothbrush and it jumped up and socked me between the eyes. And it's not like I really need the money. Since Richie blew himself up in his caravan crank kitchen out on the moors, I've been clear. I've been clear for five weeks now. Another five and I'll be clear for good. I'm here out of force of habit. Comfort, company, you know, all the usual suspects. Tonight, though, I'm sick. Can only function. I need Mac to stick to the script.

I come down on to the towpath. There's a slight gladdening of the heart as I draw level with him. The fact that he's here, waiting for me, is testimony to much more than his wretchedness. Mac *needs* me, and boy does that feel lovely. Like a big fuck-off shot of temazzies. A couple of Chicken are sniffing around him, draughting hard and deep on the stench of his money that hovers around him like a halo. They're wary, though, even the cocky Hulme half-caste sashaying his hungry black arse up and down the path. He's itching for a fix, eager to blow the old don and convert his sterling into hard white rock, but Mac's regality, his dead fucking calm – even with the filth crawling all over here last week – hacks through his drug daze and he flounders comically. He freezes, his face a staccato burst of terror and panic. And you can almost see the light bulbs popping behind his crazy black bug eyes:

Is it *him*? Is that the *one* that done JT?

The whites of his eyes are bulging now, the bang bang bang of his heart fracturing the night calm. He backs off, nervous, fades into a sly shadow. And I don't know if I'm imagining this, because everything's been dream-blurred since I spewed the crank, but behind Mac's stubble moustache I think I see the corner of his mouth twitch up into a smirk. He knows what the lad is thinking and he's half buzzing off it, he is.

Before I introduce you to Mac I'm going to freeze-frame us for a moment and tell you about JT, the lad in the canal. But don't be doing any crazy arithmetic and drawing some half-cocked conclusion from this, yeah? It wasn't Mac. Hasn't got it in him. How do I know? Nearly a thousand nights on the street, that's how. So just banish the idea. I want to tell you about JT because the boy deserves some kind of eulogy. The press never ran his story, no mention, nothing. Not even the gay press. Those Stone bitches that run *Village News*, they shunted his story to Obituaries. *Obituaries,* can you fucking believe? JT was kidnapped and tortured and disposed of in the most hideous way and his memory, his whole fucking life, has been silenced. Denied. He was rentboy trash and he was better off dead.

JT
Jay Trab 1974–1989

Used to work the Drive-In at the NCP. So called because the punters drive in, eye up the meat, place their order with the flash of a beam then seek out a slot in the car park and wait for the goods to be dispensed to their door. The system works well enough. The boys feel safe and so do the johns. I remember the first time I saw him, JT, this skinny Smiths kid, taking his place against the wall with all the whey-faced seasoned regulars. He made me stop and look and stare and smile. He had that dizzying combination of big lips and eyes with that Bambi-caught-in-the-headlamps kind of look, the ones that always seem to be shining on the edge of tears. His freckles were cartoon symmetrical, and so perfectly spaced apart they looked as though they'd been drawn on with the blunt nipple of an eyeliner. The vulnerability, the soft, clipped accent and the coy dimple smile with which he wooed his punters was a front, of course. Beneath the angelic veneer was a gutsy street urchin. His bony little fist could sit you on your arse in one solid uppercut and he carried a Stanley in the lip of his Beetlecrushers that he was not afraid to use. I loved the way his features deceived, the way they made cold, heartless bastards limp with desire. Surgeons, barristers, politicians – they all went to bits over JT, and not even the hard men that fetched up from Mosside and Salford were invulnerable to his rapt, sensual sadness. You could see their eyes warring and it made me laugh – could never quite make out whether they wanted to fuck him or father him. JT was turning nineteen, twenty tricks a night. He'd been pissed on, smeared in shit, fisted to an inch of his life, burnt, battered and knifed and he still managed to affect the same fresh-faced humility of the new kid on the block. He was a fucking legend and he worked harder than anyone I knew. Didn't do crank or rocks or any of the other shite that got peddled his way. Always played safe, no matter how much they were offering. He was savvy, man. He was going back to college. He'd packed away a little nest egg and was looking to call time on it all. He was getting himself a bedsit in Rusholme, on the curry mile, he said, and he was going to dine out every fucking night. Still can't believe he's gone. The night he was taken, he was working the Drive-In with Rash, the nine-year-old stowaway he'd taken under his wing. It was just the two of them and it was past one. Late for the Drive-In – even by Saturday night standards where business usually grinds to a halt around midnight. Rash says this car pulls up and signals to JT. Doesn't recall anything distinctive about it. Says it was big and expensive, the kind of car that all the big city bruisers own, the kind that pulls in here all the time. Another punter materialises, flashes for Rash to get in, and when he re-emerges there's no sign of JT – or his john. So Rash waits for him. Waits and waits. Goes back to the Molly house, perches on his sill and waits some more. A blast of cold cleans the night air, shocks it to daybreak. Rash is still looking out from his little watchtower and JT still ain't come home.

He's found two days later, washed up among the flotsam down by the locks, his dead, gutted body mummified in chip-shop wrappers, spent rubbers and junky paraphernalia. Not even a mention – one measly fucking sentence.

Jay Trab. 1974–1989.
Sleep easy, little angel.

I forge down the steps and on to the towpath, wending my way through the evening snarl of wraiths and monsters. Mac stands out, slouched and mellow, mugging oblivion to it all. Every now and again, though, he'll shift position, scan and scatter the furtive shadows nipping at his ankles. But as I draw close I register the little coal of anxiety in his eyes, the tight rectum of his mouth loosen and then tighten around his cigarette. He smiles. A double-edged smile. And that slight gladdening of the heart, it pinches down to nothing. As we walk along the path, I feel him pull back a fraction and rake his blue-burn all over me. My stomach sinks and hardens to a stone as I catch him in a sidelong glance, taking in the flesh-filled contours of my body. We climb the steps and peel left towards the back of the station where his car is parked. As he's wrestling with the key in the lock he appraises me across the roof of the car, a hot little flare of disgust scorching the icy air between us.

You look different, he says. Meaning, you've put on weight. His voice is bare and stripped of emotion but his eyes give colour to what he's thinking.

I leave the revelation dangling for a moment, and then I say, so is that a good or a bad thing?

He says nothing, just shrugs and nods for me to get in the car.

It's been coming for a while. Ever since I kicked the crank. A slow and steady softening of the flesh. Creeping out in all the wrong places. My denims so tight you can see the swollen outline of my genitals. October 10, my seventeenth birthday, I filled a B-cup for the first time in my life. I looked in the mirror, looked deep and hard at myself, and I vowed to: Go for a run. Use the dumb-bells. STOP EATING SHIT. I went for a run. I hammered the dumb-bells so hard that I couldn't so much as lever a fork to my mouth. I starved. Binged. Rammed my fingers down my throat till blood vessels spattered my cheeks and my heart punched up through my mouth. My denims granted me some reprieve and loosened their grip around my waist. My hip jowls shrank down to nothing and so did my tits. But there was nothing I could do to correct the broadening pelvis, the dimples that flecked my thighs. All this starving and running and lifting was pretty fucking pointless. It was going to take a fuck of a lot more than a six-pack and a tight arse to stave off the inevitable pull of biology. You see, physically, there ain't that much difference between the pubescent male and female, but once your hormones gather momentum, once your body starts ripening and revolting against what nature intended, you have to make a choice. Some of the trans kids on the Rack are shooting test. They got the deep voices and the facial hair and all the fat from their tits slowly migrating south to their stomachs. And I've thought about it, sure. Still jerk off about going all the way. The scrag of my neck stands on end when I imagine how it would feel – the round, smooth density of my surgically constructed balls pulling on my surgically constructed penis. But, by and large, I'm at ease with my anatomy. Half buzz off my girl's body, the way it rubs up against my boy's brain, challenging, defying, denouncing. I'm like a smorgasbord of different gender cues. A chromosomal riddle. I can invent and reinvent myself. And I *love* my clit. Love it when a straight john figures me out and becomes hopelessly aroused, reaches down and slips a finger inside and feels out for the lurch of his cock straining against my cunt wall. I love my downy man rectum. My weather-lashed hands and my thick yoke of shoulder muscle. I love the soft strip of skin between my tits. I love this skewed take on gender, I do. Mac, though, he doesn't like ambiguity, not where X and Y is concerned. He never ever uses my cunt. Won't go near me when I'm on. The stench of bad blood – iron and salt and yeast seeping up from my boxers – appals him. When we have sex, I lie face down, always face down.

When I met him I was fourteen, a late developer. And then I got into the crank and, even though my periods came and my tits started to bud, I was still skinny as hell, my arse and legs taut like a pullet's. I fooled him at first just like I fooled all the others. We'd go to the end of the canal. I'd suck him off. Occasionally, he'd fuck me in the arse. And then, one night, he asked if I'd go back to his house. I had no choice but to come clean. I put his hand between my legs, let him feel my scrotum-less crotch. He reeled back and, for a moment, I thought he might hit me. I asked him if he still wanted me. He nodded, his eyes giving out a little charge of self-loathing. That night was the best sex we ever had.

So Mac has hitherto been complicit in this duplicity, but only up to the point where my body is able to deceive him. The soft cushion of fat that now veils my hips and has plumped up my arse disgusts him. I'm almost a woman now, and it's only a matter of time before he calls time on our trysts and trades me in for Chicken. He slips on the blindfold, softly removes a stray swatch of fringe that has become trapped between my eyes and the felt. We sit silently for several minutes while Mac struggles to start the engine of his old green Jag.

You should get that fan belt looked at, I say.

I feel him smile for a moment and the tightness in my tummy relents a little. He snaps on the radio. Kills the possibility of further conversation. I do my thing of tracing the route for a while, giving up as I always do just past the Wilmslow turn-off. Dunno what he does here – whether he doubles back on himself or doesn't come off at all, just slows right down on the hard shoulder – but the red herring screws me every time. In the distance I hear an ambulance siren singing. And then the deadweight of suburbia creeping up on us like some malevolent fog.

We're twisting and weaving through the empty lanes now and I know this last stretch of journey off pat. Two more lefts and a sharp right and we'll be pulling into his drive.

The only meaningful conversation I've ever had with Mac – the only time we've ever pared back the husk of our stilted business banter – was that first drive back to his house. It was Christmas Eve and the city was bouncing. He asked how it was that a nice kid like me had ended up here, working the Rack.

Talk me through it, he said. Shouldn't you be wrapped up in bed or something waiting for Mum and Dad to go to sleep so you can go sneak a look at your presents?

I used to get asked this all the time when I first started working the Rack, and how I chose to answer would be entirely contingent on how much crank I'd blown. If I was loaded, I'd ream off the most hideous shit and occasionally the punter would be struck with pity or shame and he'd slap me my fee and scarper. But, more often than not, he'd slap me, tell me to shut the fuck up and get on with it. With Mac it was different. I wanted to tell him the truth. I looked up to him, I guess. I liked what his eyes told me – they were cool and resigned and yet they were by no means cold, they were still open to possibility. And to me, there was something pleasing in that contradiction, something I saw replicated in my own eyes. Moreover, I was honest with Mac because he didn't reject me. He knew what I was and still he desired me. I told him:

Thirteen was a difficult year for me. While most of the other kids on the estate were coming of age – getting whacked out of their minds on gas and glue – my own rite of passage was played out in the steamy neurosis of the bathroom mirror as I came of gender, made the slow, painful transition from Nicole to Cole. Mum drank heavily.

It's not normal, she'd scream, her red freckled arms plunged elbow deep in greasy black dishwater.

I left home, the eve of my fourteenth birthday. I could see the mottled delineation of Mum in the bathroom as I thumbed a lift from the carriageway down below and, as I pulled off in the swish, souped-up car of some Asian homeboy, I finger-waved her goodbye. Just outside Manchester he swerved hard right into some industrial wasteland and asked me to suck him off. I looked him flush between the eyes and told him, no – not for nothing. He tossed a fiver in my lap, told me he'd double it if I saw him proper. It was the first time I'd felt a penis, the first time I'd felt the coarse down of a man's thigh, and I was sick with desire and envy. I fought hard to suppress a gag reflex as he blew right into my lungs. I felt clumsy and foolish, but when I got out of the car he handed me the rest of my fee and asked me if I was looking for regular work.

Doing what? I asked.

Doing what you just did for me.

I started work that same evening.

The crunch of gravel below and my heart stops waxing and waning, slows back down to normal. Love that sound. Little frisson of nostalgia that harks right back to my childhood. Mum used to clean for this rich couple in this big fuck-off mansion in Derwynt with wrought-iron gates and a never-ending drive. In the school holidays she'd take me with her and I'd horse around with their teenage son while she scrubbed the shit from their toilets and ironed their linen. He'd dress me up in his boxers and Y-fronts, he'd let me take a leak with him – him on the toilet, me straddling the bidet, piss shooting off in a dozen directions.

Mac helps me out of the car. I can hear the wind moaning and sobbing across the fields, and then it's on my face, fussing my perfect canting fringe awry, ripping the skin from the back of my neck and licking out my sweat patches. We step inside. The blindfold comes off. All the windows are shuttered in the house and, to this day, I have absolutely no idea where Mac's house is. I get the impression, though, by the nearby lowing of cattle, the way the darkness hangs so heavy against my blindfold, that we're deep in the country. Styal or Jodral, maybe. I go upstairs, shower – even though I showered before I left the hostel – and then I go into Mac's bedroom. He's lit some candles and there's a bottle of expensive-looking red wine uncorked on the bedside cabinet with two glasses. I decant the wine into the glasses, glug greedily and replenish. I lie naked and face down on the bed with my head turned out towards the shuttered window. Mac comes in, sips on his wine and sits down on the bed beside me. He undresses and togs up and the smell of KY and rubber knifes through the air, reassuring and warm like the smell of Johnson's when you're a kid.

There's no kinky shit with Mac. He likes it vanilla. Sometimes he has me dress up in small, schoolboy undies, the ones that have Superman or Spiderman flying across the crotch. Once, just once, he invited a third party. Some pretty young blonde waif with smack teeth and a posh voice. He dressed us both in white vests and blue gymslips and got us to rub up against one another like kids making out at the far end of the playing field on a balmy summer evening.

He takes longer than usual, and as he rolls off me I can smell the bitter tang of disappointment on his skin. As I'm dressing I catch sight of my curves and dimples in the wardrobe mirror, then catch sight of him watching me closely. He gives me a look that penetrates me so fully its like he's feeling my womb, my milk ducts. It's so final that I can't resist feeling it, letting it burn right through me, and so final that I can't stand feeling it. It's over, he's telling me. You're no longer required. I'm shaking with hurt and sadness as I put on my clothes.

As he drops me off later that evening and presses the familiar crinkle of notes into my hand, I tell him see you next week, then, and he just smiles with half his mouth.

Goodbye, then, I say.

He won't look at me.

I stand there in the sodium-pocked darkness, watch him right to the end of the road as he peels left and out of sight in a puff of smoke. The empty frozen street looks as stunned as I do. I stand there for a long while until the cold seizes my lungs, forcing me back to the Molly house. Forging back up the canal, I make out the diminutive figure of Rash, tearing towards me. He's waving his arms dementedly and he's shouting the same thing over and over, but it's only when he gets right up close that I can make out the words behind the spume of his breath:

They found another one. Another body in the canal. There's pigs all over the patch telling us to lay low for a few days. They're telling us to stay clear of punters with Jags.

Behind him, snow is starting to fall.

Rush and a Push and the Land Is Ours

Peter Wild

These days The Smiths are regarded as the most influential band that ever there was, but once upon a time they were a really divisive band. For everyone I knew who loved them, there were maybe ten people who would go on and on about how miserable they were. The number of arguments I sat in on, with people on one side pointing out songs like 'Suffer Little Children' and lyrics like 'In a river the colour of lead/ Immerse the baby's head' as proof of the utter choking bleakness, while others cited songs like 'Vicar In A Tutu' and 'Heaven Knows I'm Miserable Now' as evidence of just how funny The Smiths could be. There were other factions, too - like the fans who dug the adolescent yearning of 'Back To The Old House', 'Unloveable' and, of course, 'There Is A Light That Never Goes Out', or the quiff brigade, those girls and boys desperate to be Morrissey, who latched on to every cryptic utterance, reading Oscar Wilde and watching A Taste of Honey in order to... get... just... that bit closer to the man himself - but, for me, The Smiths were always at their most interesting when they became political and, occasionally, dangerous. From the aforementioned 'Suffer Little Children' through 'Panic' and

'Shoplifters Of The World Unite', The Smiths were never afraid to engage with the world as they saw it – and they occasionally seemed to take a malicious spite in talking about stuff that people didn't, you know, talk about. That was the attitude I wanted to incorporate in my story. Taking a song like 'Rush And A Push And The Land Is Ours' and using it as the basis for a misguided political campaign seemed handsomely devilish.

Sorry to bother you. I was wondering if I could take up a few small moments of your time.

I'm campaigning on behalf of—

Do you mind if we—?

Lovely, lovely. Thank you.

Tea? Well, only if you've got a pot on. You have? Splendid. *Yes.* Tea would be lovely.

You have a beautiful home, if you don't mind my saying. I particularly like what you've done with the—

Ah.

Thank you.

No, no sugar for me. *I'm sweet enough, so they tell me.*

Sssssssssssssssssssssssssssssp. Wonderful.

What lovely china! It's a family heirloom, is it? You don't get much of that any more, do you? Family heirlooms. Great tradition, that.

Of course, our man is a great believer in tradition. Morality. *Decency.* Law and order. These are the cornerstones of our campaign.

Believe it or not, I used to live around here. On this very street, as a matter of fact, yes. It must be—

Thirteen years. Give or take. A long time, at any rate. I can hardly believe it myself.

Oh, it was very different when I lived here, very different. This street has changed.

Mind, the entire country has changed. We've come a long way, haven't we?

Thirteen years ago, you couldn't move for credit crunch *this* and knife crime *that*, could you? Do you remember all that knife crime? Feral kids (so called) kicking law-abiding citizens to death on their own front porch. Out-of-control gangs in hoodies and scarf masks, their tracksuit trousers tucked into their socks, loitering on street corners.

All those no-go areas…

You don't remember?

No, no, don't worry. A lot of people have forgotten. That's the thing, you see. Life is so much better these days. And you're young, aren't you? You're young and life is good. It's easy to forget that a relatively short time ago, life wasn't so great. We had a prime minister—

You must remember—?

What a mess he made.

What a mess his *party* made.

Historically, that's what his party *always* did, though. Like a bunch of schoolchildren let loose on a table filled with cream cakes. Cream cakes for everyone! But, of course, you can't give cream cakes to *everyone*. There's no budget for that. So you end up with a royal mess. You end up with a decade of royal mess.

Which is where we came in.

A landslide victory!

I remember that day as if it was yesterday. All the crowds singing *Gordon is a moron, Gordon is a moron, Gordon is a more-ron*… as he was led away from Number 10.

Happy days.

Lovely tea, by the way.

We rode in on a wave of unprecedented support. Sales of the *Daily Mail* and the *Sun* went through the roof. The people – the people who voted for us in their tens of thousands – were asking for draconian measures. Hard to believe now but it's true. *We want draconian measures*, they told us in so many words. Thankfully, we'd had ten-plus years in the wilderness and we had a few draconian measures up our sleeves.

The previous lot said it would take years to find a solution, years to fix what they were calling a broken country.

You know why it takes years to fix a broken country, don't you?

Four words:

Jobs for the boys.

We told the electorate we'd fix things in a year and that's what we planned to do. We were confident. More than that, even. We were *right*.

We had a scheme. *Three and you're in.* You haven't heard of it? I'm not surprised. That's the culture we live in. People have become goldfish. *No offence.* There were billboards the length and breadth of the country. You couldn't move for the adverts.

Three strikes and you're in!

There was a tagline as well:

Separating the wheat from the chav.

That was mine. It's *good*, isn't it?

You don't know what a chav is? That just goes to show you how successful we've been!

The premise was brilliant: we took the idea of gated communities, islands of solace where the obscenely wealthy basked safe in the knowledge that they were among *their own kind*, and we flipped it: gated communities for the more *undesirable elements* – or not gated communities so much as gated *cities*, gated cities and gated towns.

Doncaster we closed off. Hull. Milton Keynes. Wigan. Bacup. Stockport. Walthamstow. There were others. We took these places off the map. Erected huge walls. To all intents and purposes, they were the same as they'd ever been. We just walled them off. *Left them to it.*

We equipped law enforcement with state-of-the-art biometrics, handheld PDAs.

We drew up lists of acceptable and unacceptable behaviour. I say we drew up lists. We'd had the lists for the better part of a half-century.

Sorry?

What do I mean by unacceptable behaviour?

…

It's funny. Thirteen years ago you would've known *exactly* what I meant by unacceptable behaviour. It just goes to show you…

As far as we were concerned, unacceptable behaviour covered any and all acts of petty crime. By which I mean, small-scale drug dealing, vandalism, threatening behaviour, the carrying of a concealed weapon. However, we consulted with focus groups throughout the country and, as a result, the list grew and grew. It got so playing music on your phone too loud was considered unacceptable behaviour. Truancy – unacceptable behaviour. Undue aggression in your tone of voice. *Obesity*. Casual racism. Ignorance. Unacceptable behaviour.

If the powers that be witnessed what we deemed unacceptable behaviour, you were given a strike, your thumbprint recorded by the police, your information stored centrally on a beautiful supercomputer the size of a Fry's Turkish Delight.

If you received three strikes, you were relocated, instantaneously, without recourse to the legal system. We gave the police their powers back. You had three strikes, you were gone. Decent society wanted nothing to do with you.

It does sound harsh, you're right – but you have to remember, these are people who were laughing at the judicial system. Prison was a holiday. More than that, even. Prison was a badge of honour.

There was an 0800 number too. You could report unacceptable behaviour. You could text. Our voters really liked that. Created so many jobs. Call centres and the like. Not that we accepted what people had to say, of course. We had a furiously complicated software system that cross-referenced who you were against everything we knew about you. If you had a criminal record, if you didn't pay your council tax on time, if you earned below a certain amount, we didn't take you seriously. At the same time, however, frequently, a nexus was established – lots of people reporting the same problem. In those instances, we applied a sort of cumulative corroboration. Not so much you're guilty until you're proven innocent as you're guilty. Full stop.

Of course, there were riots – at first. Dublin, *Dundee* – I'm sure you remember the rest.

The PC brigade had a real feather in its cap. All those think tanks, the Fabian Society, Amnesty International. We told them straight: we thought it partly their fault the country had wound up in the state that it was in. Always bloody apologising for the people we'd *let down*.

Everyone has a choice, I think.

You can decide to be good. You can decide to be bad. You can decide to do your best or you can decide that life will never be fair and react accordingly.

We cleared these towns so that they were empty. We walled them off. Then we repopulated them with ne'er-do-wells.

What struck me at the time was, when we cleared the gated towns and cities, there were large numbers of people who refused to leave. Gated, ungated, it was all one to them. They wanted to stay where they knew what was what.

Now, looking back, it would've been easier to relocate the *desirable* elements, but you live and you learn.

…

It was never going to proceed without controversy, though, was it? Revolutionary ideas never do. We anticipated the guerrilla film crews and the shocking documentaries that promised to spill the beans on life behind the wall.

Life was brutal in the gated communities.

Why would that shock *anyone*?

Our rationale was—

These people have *urges*: the urge to steal, the urge to cheat, the urge to fight and stab and, yes, kill. Behind the wall, they were free to do just as they pleased. If they were going to kill (and steal and cheat and fight and stab), how much better it was that they killed and stole from and cheated and fought and stabbed *each other*.

When people saw we were serious, when people saw that the relocations were final, irrevocable – three strikes and you were *in*, end of – antisocial behaviour disappeared.

We didn't see a reduction. It disappeared.

Society changed, overnight.

There were rumbles, of course, rumbles at home and abroad. But there are *always* rumbles. And when other countries saw the amount we were saving on community policing—

Well, it wasn't long before gated communities sprang up pretty much everywhere.

I don't suppose I could trouble you for a top-up, could I? You really *do* make a wonderful cup of tea.

...

Are these your children? They're beautiful. Where was that taken? Lanzarote, eh? I've never been there. Yes, yes, I've heard it has a bad reputation. But it's nice, you say?

I have three children myself.

I say children; they're all grown up now. But they're always children, aren't they? However old they get.

Time fair marches on, doesn't it?

Oh. Thanks.

Sssssssssssssssssssssssssssssssspp. Mmh. Lovely.

Time fair marches on and now, of course, there are people – people like your good self – who have forgotten the gated communities even exist.

No, don't apologise, I think it's a good thing. I'm *glad* you don't remember what the world was like before. I'm *glad* you have no idea what a chav is.

Of course, there are people who never forget. They're the ones we're up against now. There are people who think all the walls have to come down.

A flagrant abuse of human rights...

...

I know what you're going to say. I can tell from the expression on your face. *We've had our three terms in office. Isn't it time we gave the other fellows a crack of the whip? A change is as good as a rest...*

I'm not saying it's been perfect. We've had *issues*, as a government. All the sleaze. With us, it's always sleaze. It's what comes of public school boys, largely, getting what they want. And, I agree, we're very definitely past our sell-by date, in some respects.

But it was precisely *that* – that sense of our time coming to an end, that *intuition* that whoever comes next might overturn a lot of the genuinely good work we've done – that has led to my being here today.

We've had an idea, you see.

As far as those gated communities are concerned, quite possibly their time has come and gone. They were a good idea while they lasted but now the world has moved on.

OK.

Fine.

But the last thing that we want is to release all of those undesirable elements – undesirable elements, I should add, who have had a good long time to get worked up. If they were undesirable elements *before*, imagine how undesirable they're likely to be now…

So. What we're asking voters is this: give us one more chance. Let us fix this problem once and for all. I won't go overboard on the details of the plan. All that you really need to know is that we have a *solution* and it's pretty damn *final*.

What we're asking is this:

Come next Thursday.

When you find yourself alone in the voting cubicle.

With your pen hovering over the piece of paper.

As you weigh up the choices available to you.

Vote for us.

Just this one last time, if need be.

We'll make sure that this land of ours stays great.

You have my word on that.

Jeane

James Hopkin

I latched on to The Smiths around the time of the Meat Is Murder *album and, like so many bored and bony adolescents, I became a fanatic: well-gelled quiff, old suit jacket from Affleck's Palace on Tib Street, and dancing on one leg in the Hacienda, or Morrissey's former haunts such as Deville's. In fact, it was there I first heard 'Jeane', not even realising it was The Smiths, because I didn't have the right version of 'This Charming Man' and the production sounded so flat (though that is part of its appeal). 'Jeane' reminds me of Deville's: the sticky carpets, the dance floor not much bigger than a boxing ring, and then all these Morrissey clones – even the girls. As an honorary Manc, having moved to Manchester aged nine, The Smiths meant so much because the lyrics forever preyed upon the theme of belonging/not belonging and, er, longing. My devotion was rewarded when, at the age of nineteen and at Manchester airport, I was astonished to see a tall, immaculate rockabilly bouffant coming out of customs with my parents, whom I'd gone to collect. It turns out they had travelled back on the same flight from Florida, where the estranged Mozz had been recording the video for 'Suedehead'. I grabbed a pile of paper from a travel desk and rushed*

for autographs. He was witty and courteous and I accompanied
him to a black cab outside. When the cab pulled away, I turned
and saw an old school friend waiting at the bus stop. 'Jesus Christ!'
he said. 'Was that Morrissey?'

We were bent around a century and howling at both ends.
Your first words to me, well, they put it slightly differently –
your first words? There were others that tumbled through your
teeth. You were smoking, of course, or rolling to smoke or putting one
out or puffing. And God knows from where you'd suddenly appeared.
Perhaps through a gap in the grouting? But these were the first words
of yours that I remember: 'I grew up during the Thatcher years,' you
said. 'I have known nothing but loneliness.'

As you spoke, you turned as eerie as the corner of a pub half an
hour after chucking-out time. You looked to be scowling or spitting, in
silence, your eyelashes scratching at the lenses of your specs.

I didn't know if you were joking or quoting. But, no, you looked
sincere.

'Coming back?' you asked, big blue eyes unblinking. You see, it
really was half an hour after chucking-out time. Back in the days of
smoky snugs and lock-ins and those gleaming green tiles in the toilet.
The alternative? I had a bedsit, a box room, a mattress stuffed with
seaweed. At least, that's how it smelled. I wouldn't say no. I couldn't say
no. Despite your surliness, or because of it, you reeked of adventure.
And it was raining, of course, and the passing taxis carried silhouettes
of heads to somewhere louder or safer or lost, the gutter-puddles fizzing
with just-lit cigarettes. And what had happened to our friends?

You pointed out a fire escape twisting down the back of the
Victorian pub. The traffic lights lit up your wonder as well as your spiky
orange hair, though you seemed to stand either side of your smile. So
we loomed and shrank in the dark, gazing up at this iron staircase,
wondering how best to get away.

Your flat turned out to be underground. Where else? You claimed
to be a species of mould.

'My days are determined by ankles,' you said, looking to the railings on the street above. Then you added something about all a body's nerves ending in the feet. Down here, you were the closest to those endings. So you vibrate, you said, day and night, to a city passing by. You were situated at source, you said, at the very point where the jitters begin. A whole city's jitters. 'And it can be nerve-racking,' you said. 'At source.'

I didn't doubt it.

'When it rains on the gravel,' you continued, pointing to the tiny paddock in front of your window, 'it sounds just like piss. And when people on their way back piss through the railings, it sounds just like rain. And sometimes like a round of applause on the radio next door.'

Next door? I couldn't believe there'd be anyone else down here. Let alone radio reception. It felt right only for you, vibrating at your own frequency. For a moment, though, I thought I could hear shuffling behind the plasterwork, coughing in the pipes.

Then you disappeared. And in such a small space! You must have unstrapped shadows, ridiculed dimensions, skipped in and out of physics to get away with that. Aha, the kitchenette! A cupboard door to make you come over all diminutive. A squeaky hinge for a whimper. But you were betrayed by a nasal noise that you couldn't hide in a drawer.

'My gran,' you said. 'There's no escaping genes. Especially northern ones. Her sneeze carried right across the Pennines.'

Minutes later, you served up this lumpy green stuff in rough bowls probably not long off the potter's wheel. And it was tasty, this lumpy green stuff. Pea and potato? 'Another species of mould,' you said, spooning it up with glee.

'Anyway,' you said, getting all intrigued beneath your copper locks, 'what kind of cutlery are you?'

You vanished soon after with our empty bowls as if they were on short-term loan from whoever was living in the cupboard. Then your slim snout emerged between two mugs. Whisky. Or was it rum? We swigged like sailors in the hold pretending we were ashore. I started taking drags on your roll-ups, little bits of bitterness sticking to my mouth and teeth; on my tongue, traces of your lipstick. Ochre, perhaps, or magenta? In any case an optimistic Gothic. 'Did you inherit knitting fingers, too?' I asked, as you rolled another. 'Yeah,' you replied. 'I'm making cushion covers for my lungs.'

That first time we were bunkered for days – or was it weeks? – as we rattled through the registers from academic to tap-room Manc, discoursing on Orwell, Joy Division, Tetley Gold. There were orgasms and arguments, kitchen implements and ejaculations, and sometimes at the same time. When we ventured out, you were always a step ahead, with a movement between a skip and a stride, a rushing shuffle, pointing out fire escapes, one-legged pigeons, a postage stamp on the pavement ('the whole street wants to get away'). I trailed in your leather and tobacco wake, sometimes coughing to keep up, but when I complained that all this smoking makes you smell of wet pencils, you snorted: 'Perfume is for the menopausal!' We bought only milk, bread, eggs and one or two 'spinster snacks', as you called them. You had a thing for brown paper bags; you believed that anything that came in a brown paper bag was honest and simple and sacred. In the street I could hear you whistling like a kettle lifted just that moment off the hob, and I assumed it was the wind through your teeth, if not through your bones, if not through you, Jeane, if not right through you.

Sorry, I'm getting ahead of myself. Or behind. But nostalgia is a form of tenderness, isn't it? It comes sewn with soft regrets. And it's strange: even when we were together, Jeane, I was always looking for you.

Sometimes you rose imperious, too tall for your umbrella, other times your shoulders collapsed and it was as if the whole of you was trying to hide behind your nose. On our down days, we were stricken: you, big eyed, smelling of spent fireworks, as husky as a whore and just as desperate, wearing only knickers as you rolled on newspapers trying to erase the state of things. You could not be placated. You'd take a pitchfork to my platitudes, spear me up. Easy meat. Yet when I held you, your body felt like a child's. For a moment, you said nothing. Your hair had lost its spike. Then I felt your bones pressing against me. We were lost in this city. In the rust and fog. Even the river was running away! In these moments we realised – didn't we? Emphatically. Unflinchingly – that our quick wits alone might not be enough to get us through.

All this looming and leaving! I didn't think about it. Just part of your corrosive charm, I thought, just part of our underground life. Intellect with bristle and bone. How else to resist? Then again, you could snap like a trap on my best ideas. You could rubbish my motives with a sneer. It didn't matter. There we were, at source, trembling in propinquity.

But then you'd emerge from some other patch of darkness, laughing behind your own back, giving it the old Manc swank and middle finger, dragging me out of my mood with a kick up the arse and a dossier of brilliant ideas. 'What is a human being but a mix-up of tendencies? Today my tendency is to clean. We are nothing but our stains!' you'd announce as you set about the flat. 'That's all most of us leave behind: scent, stench, SPOOR!' Yellow rubber gloves up to the elbows, you'd scrub and mop and vacuum-clean, singing your head off as you ripped at the bedsheets, occasionally pausing to sniff ('I remember that one!' or 'Jesus, you must have needed that!'), or you'd babble about the time when you rented your flat for a fortnight to a pair of Bulgarian lesbians for whom you gloriously despoiled the bedlinen the night before their arrival – yes, and with a man you'd taken a shine to in the street simply because he had hiccups. (Well, there's no accounting for…) And you'd clean in such a fury that I sometimes wondered if it was your own spoor you were seeking to eradicate. (Though, admittedly, we were both from backgrounds where a wet tea towel and a boiling kettle cured most ills.) Meanwhile, once outside, your nicotine molars went ruby in the sun.

When the flat was tidy and there were fresh flowers on the sill (if carnations can ever be fresh, that is), you'd resume your quirky grace. Everything you tried on in charity shops fell for your aura, could not resist your frame, angled and insistent, even though your clothes were often inside out. But that's how you liked it. No high-street designers for you. 'A label,' you once told me, 'is merely a dead butterfly ironed on to fool the sick, the sentimental or the fookin' pig-shit thick!' And before you could say 'well, I'll go to the foot of our stairs', you were taking them all on, from the 'slappers and runts' who pissed in your paddock to some halfwit English graduate writing in the paper, from bearded students wearing Che Guevara T-shirts ('It's not revolution,' you'd hiss, 'it's merchandise!') to the 'bourgeoisie dropping off their blazered bluddy ducklings' at the private school down the road. There you'd be, a book in both pockets (well, you had to keep balance), careful not to break the spines of these living things, your roll-up a conductor's baton jerking to each syllable of your rant. My dear lady disdain! Such sulphurous scorn! No one could hold a match to you. No one *should* hold a match to you.

Once, you railed at the university secretary. Yes, she'd always get your goat, and why? 'She's just so fookin' prim and proper,' you snarled, your eyeballs rolling with the lacklustre menace of medieval shot. 'Middle-class immaculate! Utterly asinine! You know what I'd like to do to her?' And here your tongue emerged as if to lick a particle of poison. 'I'd like to drag her into the stationery cupboard and cover her in shit!'

You got yourself so worked up that your lungs had a pillow fight and your cough went on for hours.

But, Jeane, it wasn't so much that we wanted to leave, was it? I mean, didn't we just want somewhere to come back to?

After all, we were content enough in our Victorian pub, 'The Briton's Protection'. We'd laugh as we pushed each other past the 'death chamber', the name we gave to the empty back room with an unlit fireplace, even in winter, where we once sat and shivered even more than the loose sash windows. We preferred the snug, waiting at the wooden serving hatch, relieved not to be with those hanging by their ties on the city side of the bar. And we gazed through the windows beyond at the grand buildings going up to resurrect our city of dark bricks and rain: to the left, a train station transformed into an exhibition centre; opposite, a concert hall of sophisticated angles and evening silhouettes; to the right, apartment blocks elegantly disguising their expensive lack of space, and in the midst of all this glass and grind and brickwork, our pub stood firm behind its name in neon. OK, the diggers and cranes made the whisky bottles rattle on their shelves, but we saw these rows of bottles as the pipes on a fairground organ filling the place with music. With our backs to the canal, we sank into our green velvet seats and marvelled at the bulging, gilt-edged ceiling while wondering – don't you dare deny it! – when it was all going to come down on our heads. Yet we felt safe in the snug. 'Not so safe,' you pointed out. 'It's "guns" backwards.' And there were shootings on the streets that summer.

So, tell me, Jeane, when was it that you began to disappear? Or did I simply start looking for you more? 'I don't do love,' you told me, the first time you kicked me out. You went spiky, your hair, your shoulders, all of you shaping like a flint-edged projectile about to be flung. 'And I don't do people. And you are a people.'

'Fine!' I said, packing up my pride. 'You can keep a whole city's jitters to yourself!'

And the next time. Or the time after that. How did it go again?

'I'm clearing out the urchin-end of my acquaintances!' you declared, giving me a shove.

'What a coincidence!' I replied. 'I'm clearing out the orphan-end of mine!'

But we phoned most evenings and talked all night, with you so animated that, rather than take a break, you pissed in a pint pot nicked from the Briton's or I carried on talking while your grandmother delivered her sneeze down your nostrils or you rolled yourself hoarse or went mad with theories, teapots, utensils. We were still resisting and not just each other. Occasionally I brought you things in brown paper bags: a cheese-and-pickle sandwich, a pair of rubber gloves, *The Last of Cheri*. And that was one of my favourite visions of you: the reading Jeane. Because when you finally raised your head from a book, your nose would be twitching with all the scents of the story.

Yet increasingly when I came to you I found the blinds down and silence the other side of your door. Or else there was loud music. Perhaps another week-long seduction? You didn't answer the phone. I pissed in your paddock. I went to the Briton's and sat alone in the death chamber. I wondered: do we keep changing our backgrounds until we find a foreground that fits?

But I knew that your own fate was enough for you to ponder; you didn't want to get tangled up in anybody else's. You had to extricate yourself. You had to parade your estrangement. You had to remain odd in any epoch.

Finally, I heard that you had slipped out of the country having won a research post at the Frei University in Berlin. The land of long and angular women! So many posh Fraus for you to despoil! I pictured you in a backstreet *kneipe* smoking at the helm. I saw you undaunted by an exhaustion of U-bahns and courtyard magpies, by dark steel undersides and rivers of rust, by buildings held up only by graffiti and the mustard off your bratwurst. And finally I saw your red hair flattened by an easterly wind bringing brick-dust and winter and an untellable despair, like the cold shaft of dirt blown along the tunnel just before the train pulls in.

Before long, you sent me an invitation on a postcard of Kirchner's *Rheinbrucke in Köln* – just your kind of spindly beauty.

We walked under art-nouveau balconies in and out of the rain. Not in the fashionably downbeat areas of Friedrichshain or Prenzlauerberg (beer bottle, army jacket, ring through lip), but in the backstreets of Charlottenburg, the district of unfrequented galleries and out-of-date salons, where the ageing bourgeoisie measure the lost decades with slow and tiny steps, and we'd marvel at the lighting in an old jeweller's shop and peer through the doors of the Hotel Savoy to see a lift cage, an intricacy of brass and gold, looking like a royal carriage. Or we'd nip across to Kantstrasse to wallow in the seediness of 'Big Pimp Hotdogs', 'Kant Kino', 'Sex King Cascade'.

'It's not just history,' you kept saying. 'It's mortality!'

And it didn't end there, this living installation. You took me to the dim *kneipe*s of Wedding where we absorbed the stares of tattooed men wearing bleached denim and mullets 'fit to scour a frying pan', as you put it. Or else we'd dart into a stand-up *konditorei*, no seats, just high tables and leaning pads, which seemed perfect for your life of discovery and dash, and with your fingertips tapping the steaming bowl of *milchkaffee*, you raised your head and started reciting the names of the over-iced pastries on display: *Quarkplunder, Fruchtwuppi, Mandelschleife, Schweinsoren* – 'Christ,' you said of the latter, 'they made a right pig's ear out of that!' We nearly eloped with our laughter, raising ourselves to reverie, thinking of these wide streets, each one a song sheet, you said to me before giving it your best Lotte Lenya giving it her best Jenny Diver, and how full of song you were along those streets that were dark like tunnels without roofs, only bare trees marking the score and a few last leaves, 'also notes', you said, pointing to them, and I wondered in that moment if your whole life was a search for a song, you know, the right one, whether squeezed from your own lungs or from someone else's.

What am I saying? I'm not sure. Just that you were in your element in that Einstein-stadt, always this syrupy grin on your chops, you and your mortality finding ever new projects and liaisons: *untergrund*, an eroticized resistance, a whole city at source! You relished your breakfasts: 'two eggs in a glass', which you took with black coffee and three cigarettes. And you immersed yourself in a century's worth of second-hand shops, coming out one day like a 1920s lesbian in a pinstripe suit with one of your leaky roll-ups stuck in a cigarette holder, the next, popping out a punk in a green leather jacket and tartan mini. Then the Troedelmarkt on Strasse des 17 Juni snared you with a book cabinet, a silver flip-top ashtray, a shaving-brush (!), a Leipzig edition of *Neue Gedichte*, snuffboxes, hatpins, turn-of-the-century nudes – '*Mein Gott*,' you exclaimed. 'They didn't half love a full bush!'

But what was it? Though you thrived in academic research – 'my spirit has found a spine!' – the other Jeane, the Jeane without footnotes, seemed less focused, as if you'd been swept up by the faster, more dangerous rhythms of the 'jitters' of Berlin. We went to a party in a wardrobe in Neuköln. There were five guys present. On the way home you whispered to me that you had already slept with them all. Yes, it was as if – in your dressing-up, your doomed assignations – you were racing through eras and appetites trying to catch up with yourself. Or escape yourself – your spoor! – for ever.

In the entrance hall to your ground-floor flat the mould was no longer a metaphor. A sign warned of rat poison. The hall was always cold and suffered an ecclesiastical stench. 'Welcome to my chapel of rest!' you said, my first day there. You were smoking more and more. You were violently opposed to what you derided as the '*Gesundheit fascismus!*' now creeping across Europe, depositing smokers on pavements or in tents no bigger than an outdoor bog. Another thing I noticed: despite the nose-clotting, fingernail-filth of the place, your sneeze had all but disappeared.

One night, we found a dingy *kneipe* under an S-bahn bridge. 'This city can be measured by its iron bridges,' you said. 'And its fire escapes,' I added. The look you gave me: an intimate astonishment? Or should that be: admonishment? You swept the moment aside with a continental 'QUATSCH!' and vanished behind the heavy curtain hanging at the door.

A group of Ishyvoo expats, posh Home Counties boys, were mincing round the place in velvet and tweed. 'Human bluddy dressage!' you exclaimed. They were instantly around you, toying with you, insisting on their artistic credentials. One of them piped up: 'I always wanted a misfit for a muse!' You played along as they tried to outwit each other with their dandy quips and quotations. But you trumped them each time until they got fed up – how dare this northern lass! And you, tiring of their rich-boy routines and your own smoking tournament, finally took me by the arm and, gathering your trinkets and shawls about you, you put out all the candles on the way to the door. Then you turned back and screamed at them: 'CUNTS!'

Outside, still shaking, you stopped me on the steps. Your fierce blue eyes under the *kneipe's* lamp. Your bony fingers clamped my wrist, not taking my pulse but trying to stop it. 'And for your information,' you snarled, only your bad teeth showing, 'I have replaced my... my... fascination with fire escapes. I am now interested in dead neon. This city's full of unlit signs. The alphabet of mortality!' And with that you vanished in the darkness flowing beneath the bridge.

On the last day of my trip, things remained frosty between us. So much to say or to avoid saying. Silences every bit as awkward as those in an auditorium between movements of a concerto. On the train to the airport to see me off, you burst through our diffidence. You were thrilled to discover, at one of the stations, an entire wall of green tiles reminding you of the ones at the Briton's. Yet when you spoke, the former mood was quickly reinstated. 'When your world gets bigger,' you said, avoiding my eyes despite my efforts, 'it only means there are more doorways to stand in.'

At the airport, we embraced. But it felt as though we were both only checking to see if the other was still standing.

A few months later, I heard you had gone farther east. Perhaps to establish yourself as the girl from far away among more elegant, more treacherous femmes fatales? (Though I knew you'd be just as happy kicking your boots along broken pavements with old ladies in mohair bonnets.) Maybe you found a place there for your skittering spirit and those big rolling eyes of yours that roll up everything they see. And, maybe, having recorded the dead letters of Berlin – 'a meeting of treacle and smoke!' – you'd gone in search of other eras, other alphabets, other mortal signs?

Talking of which, did I tell you? The 'P' has gone from the neon name of our pub. (But don't read anything into that.) In any case, only the guns are still smoking!

Jeane, we're never going to get to the end of this conversation, are we? (Please have empty pint pots to hand.)

In other words, we just have to carry on, don't we? I mean, just like everyone else. We're all living like stowaways now. And there's no time like the present, Jeane, unless perhaps the past!

Which means: you do the onions, I'll do the mash.

On second thoughts, I'll put the kettle on, you keep singing.

The Boy with the Thorn in His Side

John Williams

I have a son who is sixteen years old now. He listens to The Smiths rather more than I ever did. And hearing their records blast out of his computer speakers, I'm struck by how well they have lasted, how much better than any of their post-punk contemporaries. But I still can't simply enjoy them the way Owen can. I think that's because he can just hear the music while I am assaulted by memories. I feel lost in the hinterland of the songs. I feel like I know too well the world they come from.

It's hard, now, to remember the first six months of 1980 with anything approaching fondness. At best, I suppose, living though that time was a toughening process, a long cold bath for the soul. I'm talking about me here, not the country as a whole, though Mrs Thatch's restructuring of our economy was having a pretty similar effect around the place. Certainly it was where I lived at the time, the small grey Protestant city of Cardiff. But you doubtless know all about Mrs Thatch, so let's get on with telling you some more about me.

I was living in a flat in Riverside at the time, just the other side of the river from the city centre. It was a first-floor flat with three rooms. For the past few months I'd shared it with two friends: Andrew, who I knew from the world of punk rock, and Blair, who I knew from the world of school. I took the middle bedroom. Blair took the back bedroom and Andrew slept in the living room. There was also a bathroom and a kitchen, of which I remember little. The street we lived in had a couple of chip shops at one end, and a warren of junk shops at the other end, which pretty much sorted out our basic needs. Actually most of our basic needs were sorted out by the mini-market next to the chip shop, a fabulously depressing place full of the kind of products people talk about with 'ironic' affection these days. Personally I find it hard to think of the likes of Findus Crispy Pancakes with wistful nostalgia: this was the kind of shit we actually lived on. Especially if Andrew did the shopping. Andrew was so shy he refused to buy anything that involved talking to the shop assistant. Everything had to come straight from the shelf or freezer cabinet.

Andrew and myself were signing on, Blair was in his second year of university. Blair was pretty much a normal person who had friends and girlfriends and went to lectures and stuff. Me and Andrew weren't very normal people. We were odd boys whose lives were full of music, thanks to a lack of anything else going on, who listened to John Peel and knew nobody who wasn't in another Cardiff post-punk ensemble. Nevertheless the three of us formed a band along with another student called Jeff. We were the Puritan Guitars and we made a deliberately awful racket. We rehearsed in the back bedroom when the downstairs neighbours were out or, on occasion, when they were in, which led to a certain amount of bad feeling. After three months or so of this Blair had had enough, and moved out to share a flat with some other students. What were we to do? The handful of people we knew already had their own flats. The thought of getting a stranger in was terrifying. Finally Andrew came up with a solution. His cousin Pete would move in after Christmas.

Pete was one of those people you heard about before actually meeting them. Apparently at school he'd played the saxophone, listened to free jazz and had ambitions to play in some kind of Henry

Cow-like art-rock ensemble. Soon after leaving school, however, he'd decided against this plan, and renounced music altogether. He retired his saxophone and decided to get rid of his record collection. Not for Pete, though, the normal solution of trying to flog them to your friends or taking them down Mr Kelly's second-hand stall in the market. Oh no, Pete decided that the thing to do with his collection of jazz and prog was to head down to the local primary school and give the records away to deserving-looking little girls. This was apparently easier said than done – not many ten-year-old girls show much interest in the works of Evan Parker.

In other bulletins I'd learned that Pete used to read the classics of anarchist literature incessantly, but now he'd become a postman. I know it doesn't follow, but what can I tell you, we were young.

It was Pete's job as a postie, as we most certainly didn't refer to them back then, that would enable him to stop living with his mother and move to Cardiff. I was kind of looking forward to him moving in. At least he didn't sound boring. And nor was he, at least not in an ordinary way. In person Pete was one of those people who are actually quite big but because they're embarrassed about themselves in the world they hunch over and hide it. He had sandy hair, the wide eyes of a child and the giggling laugh of a madman. He didn't say a lot. He got up very early to go to work, and went to bed similarly early to sleep. In between whiles he sat in his room and read. I asked him at first about the anarchism, did he still read Malatesta and Kropotkin and all that? No, he told me, he only read the Bible now.

After a while Andrew and myself pretty much left him to it. Every once in a while, maybe on a Friday, I would suggest going to the pub. Andrew didn't drink, so that just left me and Pete walking round the corner to the Mitre. We'd buy a drink each and sit there saying very little indeed. Sometimes, if I had few extra quid derived from selling bits of my record collection to Mr Kelly, we might have a second drink. It would be consumed in silence, us sitting there like a pair of junior old men, and then we'd walk back to the flat. Pete would go to bed and I'd listen to John Peel with Andrew.

It is hard to imagine now the significance that John Peel had for all us post-punk types, all the confused and lonely eighteen-year-olds in our charity shop and army surplus clothes, haunting the second-hand record stores of declining industrial towns. It let us know that we were not alone, that there were others out there. Every time you heard a session from Girls At Our Best from Leeds or Orange Juice from Glasgow it was a light in a window over the street, a beacon on a hill, a sign of life in the grey.

We wrote to each other back then, all us boys in bands and fanzines, sending the word from Cardiff to Nottingham or Sunderland to Glasgow, news of our microscopic scenes. And when we weren't writing to each other, we'd write to our bulletin boards, the letters pages of *Sounds* and the *NME*. We'd send jokes and complaints, messages from the regions. Some people, like my friend Colin B. Morton from neighbouring Newport, became regular names on the page. I read every word of the music press back then, of course. I knew the names of all the regular correspondents. Most regular of all, for a time, was one Stephen P. Morrissey from Manchester, whose particular thing was to work the New York Dolls into his letters.

After six months this existence of signing on, subsisting on chips with curry sauce, writing letters and playing music that sounded like rubber bands and biscuit tins and skronky guitars topped off by some bloke complaining about this and that and everything, of living with Andrew and Pete, began to wear thin. In the middle of a gig one night I realised that this was just too miserable an existence to be borne, and when I discovered that there was a room about to go free at our guitarist's student house I jumped at it. I even got a job working in an anarchist printer's for twenty-three pounds a week. I silk-screened and Letrasetted and wrote radical newsletters, and made an effort to meet girls, and slowly, gradually, things changed in my life, and let's skip forward three or four years to, I don't know, 1984, I suppose, thereabouts at least.

I was in college by then, Media Studies at the Polytechnic of Central London, and working part time in a record shop, and I hadn't listened to Peelie, as we definitely never called him, for years. These days I favoured London pirate soul stations like Kiss FM and LWR. I didn't write letters to the *NME* any more, I didn't even buy it, not every week anyway, not religiously. I bought *The Face* instead, aspired to being cool, bought clothes from Katharine Hamnett, tried to look good.

Anyway, one grey afternoon in this year that was probably 1984, I was back in Cardiff, visiting my parents presumably, and I was walking past Spillers Records in town when a voice called out to me. I turned round, clocked the sandy hair and the wide eyes. Pete. He was wearing a greatcoat. He looked like the kind of person that, if I was in London, I'd have made a point of avoiding eye contact with. He looked like the kind of person I was very keen to differentiate myself from.

'John,' he said, 'I heard you on the radio.'

I looked confused, said he couldn't have. I hadn't done anything to get me on the radio. He looked disappointed, said it was someone who sounded a lot like me. And he'd been expecting, you know, me to do something. I said, well, no I hadn't exactly done anything, though I was in college now and things were going, you know, great. And anyway, what was he doing here?

'I've come to see The Smiths,' he said.

'Really,' I said, 'but you don't like that kind of thing.'

Oh, but he did, he said. He loved The Smiths, he told me, and giggled the way he did, and said he'd walked here from him mother's place in Abercarn, fifteen miles over the mountain.

Ah, I said, and maybe oh. I knew of The Smiths, I guess they had an album out by this time and a few singles. I'd seen pictures of Morrissey and his carnations, heard one or two of the songs. I remember thinking that maybe, just maybe, if me and my boys had stuck at it, we might have ended up sounding a bit like that, a bit ironic and camp and triumphant in defeat, a bit northern (Cardiff then was really a northern city, dying Victorian grey: the first time I went anywhere that felt the same was the first time I went to Manchester. It's nothing like the cities of the west of England: Bristol or Exeter or, God forbid, Swindon). We'd even talked about trying to make a record with Sandie

Shaw, we went to see her in cabaret and asked her, but nothing came of it. And now Stephen P. Morrissey had beaten us to the punch, and us no longer even in the ring. I felt jealous and disdainful: they were kings of a world I'd left behind.

We went for a coffee, there was plenty of time. Pete had walked so fast through the valleys and over the mountain that he'd arrived half a day early. Pete demurred a little, he had arrived with no money whatsoever, would be walking back through the night. So I demonstrated my London big-shot-ness, and said I'd pay for a cup of milky coffee.

In the café it was like old times, when we used to go to the pub together. We sat with nothing to say: Mr Shy and Mr Ridiculously Shy. Eventually Pete started talking about the Bible and the ways in which we failed to understand the New Testament. After a while of this I had an idea as to what to do next.

So we went round to Spike's place. Spike was a guitar player and another old school mate of Andrew and Pete. He was reasonably pleased to see me, and looked to have that familiar mixture of alarm and fascination on seeing Pete. We had cups of tea and Pete started arguing religion with Spike, who by this time had swapped the faith of his childhood for a fervent belief in the Trotskyism of the WRP. They seemed to be enjoying the barney, and I took the chance to say that I had to get going. Spike said he'd have Pete to stay that night, save him walking over the mountain in the dark. I headed on out feeling like I'd got away with something, had slickly passed on the responsibility that was Pete.

It was only later that I heard that Spike had been so freaked out by Pete's Dostoyevskyan appearance and religious conviction that he and his then missus had not answered the door when Pete came round later that night, and Pete had indeed walked back over the mountain. I doubt that he minded. There was something not merely innocent but positively saintly about Pete back then. Something unworldly, born out of loneliness and awkwardness and a strange fierce intelligence. I'm sure I wasn't alone in finding it frightening.

And that saintliness was for the most part happy in solitude, but was still happy to have found a place on earth to commune that was not a dying chapel in a dying valley but a dance hall packed with congregants come to see a man with carnations in his back pocket and a hearing aid in his ear, one who gathered to him all the lost boys of my time, and for a moment made them proud in their aloneness and their shyness and their intelligence.

But me, I'd crossed over and walked on the other side of the road. Thinking only this, that there but for the grace of God go I.

Some Girls are Bigger than Others

Jenn Ashworth

Music is not an inspiration, it is a distraction. It is a noise spreading out behind cars and smoking the air like a second exhaust. It insists its way through open windows – advertising someone else's party. It comes out of jukeboxes in pubs, smothering conversation, and it makes me hate the students who live next door.

When I was writing a novel about a very overweight woman, embroiled in editing and Internet research about Fat Admirers, Feeders and BBWs, my best friend used to email me MP3s. Theme music. Tunes to write to. I don't work like that – I need silence – but when I was stuck, and because he was my friend, I would listen to them. Two stand out: 'Fat Bottomed Girls' and 'Some Girls Are Bigger Than Others'. This is the story inspired by the second, and dedicated to the friend who forced it on me.

Christine serves tins of Del Monte fruit cocktail in tiny glass bowls after Sunday dinner. She pours Tip Top into the bowls, but slowly, so it doesn't curdle the sugary water the fruit is sitting in. She always gives Garry the cherry, fishing it out of the tin first with her fingers.

Even when Derek is here, Garry still gets the cherry. They don't talk about it. They've never had a conversation about Garry possibly being a bit too old to have his sausage and mash made into a face on his plate: peas for hair, sliced carrot for eyes. Always getting the cherry.

Garry thinks that when he is an old man, coming home for Sunday dinner with a tie and a brown suit, Christine will still give him tomato ketchup in the glass egg cup, the special yellow bowl that he collected tokens for, and dodder over to the table with the tin in her hand, swishing the cubed fruit about with her fingers and proffering the cherry on her palm.

Derek never says anything about it. He doesn't say anything now, but bends over his bowl, stirring the Tip Top around with his spoon until every last piece of fruit is covered. Garry eats slowly, saving the cherry for last, and wonders whether Derek has noticed, and if he has noticed, whether he is bothered.

Derek eats like a machine. His elbow jabs the air and his mouth goes like a cement mixer. He grunts because he can't chew and breathe at the same time. He rattles the spoon against the sides of the bowl. Gary doesn't look at him, but looks at Christine, tipping her bowl to scoop up watery Tip Top as if it is soup, and smiling at Derek as he sucks and chews. They eat like this, the three of them, for a long time. Outside, the broken gate batters the fence and the long grass in the garden ripples with the wind.

Eventually, Derek pushes his bowl away from him and stretches. He looks out of the kitchen window at the brambles waving in the front window. It is grey outside, rain tapping the window and falling in dotted diagonals. Garry stares at the patterns the drops make. He wonders about Morse code. Dots and dashes. Wonders whether there is writing on the window, a secret message, a joke from the world to him.

'I reckon I'll start on those brambles this afternoon,' Derek says, 'I brought my clippers with me.'

Christine murmurs and spreads her fingers over his shoulders, takes his bowl away.

'You going to come out and give me a hand?' he says to Garry.

'No,' Garry says, 'I've got something in my room I'm working on. Homework. I've got something for a project.'

'Schoolwork, eh?' Derek says, and laughs. Perhaps he is making fun because Christine introduced Garry to Derek as 'the brainbox'. Perhaps he is laughing because he doesn't think Garry is going up to do schoolwork at all, but to open his flies and look at magazines and play with himself.

Garry looks at Christine's back: she is standing at the sink, blocking the view from the window. He can hear her hands dipping in and out of the water. The pattern on her dress hurts his eyes.

'Leave him, Derek,' Christine says, turning to touch his shoulder again, 'he'll be all right upstairs.'

'Head in a book,' Derek says, and mutters something about fresh air.

'He'll open the window a crack, won't you, love?'

'I'll open it,' Garry says, but Christine is giggling because Derek has reached up and grabbed her. His fingers sink into the softness under her ribs and above her hips.

'Derek!' Christine says, and squirms into him. Her wide forearms shake as she laughs, and Derek puts his head forward. The movement reminds Garry of a tortoise's turd-coloured head coming out of its shell. He bites her arm gently and she laughs again.

Garry goes upstairs.

In his room, Garry lines the matchsticks up carefully on his desk. He spreads glue on to one side of each matchstick with another matchstick. He sticks the matchsticks together to make a wall. He uses Christine's travel hairdryer with a folding handle to dry the glue. He likes the order of this. He likes the way the thing builds gradually: a lampshade, a model guitar, a ship, a house – whatever it will be, it always starts the same, one match against another and the sharp fishy smell of the glue prickling the pink rims of his eyes.

He's making a box now. The book says it's for jewellery, but Garry is making it for himself. A herringbone box with a lid hinged with brown string: something to keep his Stanley knife, spare blades, squares of sandpaper, tubes of glue. It's a hobby box.

Brainbox, Garry thinks, *my son the brainbox*, and doesn't laugh.

Derek comes to stay three or four times a week. Garry isn't sure whether it is worse that he is supposed to call him 'uncle', or that he's not supposed to notice that his mother lets her 'brother' bump her in the night.

Once, Derek came to pick up Garry from school. Garry saw his white Ford parked across from the gates, Derek's bare arm hanging out of the window, his hairy hand slapping the roof of the car in time to music. Garry had turned and walked quickly in the other direction. Smack into those three girls, who had laughed, and poked his shoulders.

'Where you going, *Garry*?'

They always said his name like that. Sarcastic, as if there was something wrong with it. He'd shaken his head and wondered whether 'Garry' meant something obscene in a foreign language. One those girls had been learning because they were in Set One for everything, and one whose existence was a secret from him because he was in Set Three for everything. Brainbox. He turned quickly, and brushed the tall one with the back of his wrist as he moved.

'Ugh!' she said, delighted. The other two cackled – the darker-haired one a beat slower, and less loudly than the others.

'Ugh!' she said. 'Garry just touched my tit! My tit!'

More laughter. Garry felt his face, his neck, even the parts of his head that were under his hair, turning red. He saw Derek leaning out of the car. Saw he had no shirt on.

'Did you want to see her tits, Garry? Check if they're as big as your mum's?' the tall one said.

'No,' Garry said.

'Not feel them?'

Garry shook his head again.

'So you wanted to suck on them? Like you do with your mummy?'

The one with the dark hair laughed, and put her thumb in her mouth. She put her head on one side and giggled around her thumb. Garry saw her tongue touch her thumbnail as she spoke.

'Your mum's a right fat get, isn't she, Garry?'

They shouted something else but Garry was running, his backpack banging against his side. Derek was unfastening his seat belt and staring. The girls were walking more quickly, catching up with some fifth-years, telling them that Garry had just marched up to them and grabbed their tits, told them he wanted to check whether they were like his mum's.

Garry reached the car, got in, fastened his seat belt.

'What was all that about?' Derek said. No hurry to drive away. He turned in his seat, put a puzzled and concerned expression on his face.

'Just a game,' Garry said, and, 'let's go.'

'Shall I have a word? They're big lads. Maybe need someone bigger to tell them what's what?'

Lads? Garry looked out of the window and saw the three girls with the fifth-year boys. The boys were huge. Dark hair on their top lips and real smells after PE.

'It's nothing,' Garry said. 'They're mates of mine.'

Mates was a good word. Derek laughed suddenly.

'Horseplay,' he said, 'best days of your life,' and started the car. They drove home and Garry remembered hearing Derek's voice on the landing in the middle of the night, consonants softened by Carling, whispering to Christine and saying 'fun bags' in the dark.

He pressed the tips of his fingers against the window until they turned white, looked at them, then did it again.

There are noises on the landing. Bumping noises, and giggling. A door opens and closes. It's three in the afternoon, but Garry hears the bed creak and Christine's special drawer slide open, and he wants to throw himself through the window. He bends over his matchsticks and thinks about Silverkin hairspray.

It comes in a gold can. There's a picture of a woman with big swaying hair on the side of it. Garry leaves his matchsticks, goes to his own drawer. Takes out the can. It feels cool and light in his hands. It took him weeks of furtive trips to the chemist's to find the right brand. He shakes it, pops the cap and sprays it on to a pair of briefs. They're not boxers: they're blue Danger Mouse briefs he's never worn, but he closes his eyes and inhales Silverkin and thinks about those three girls.

His head tips and he thinks about that girl, the one with the darker, fuzzy hair. Garry lies on his bed and breathes in hard and looks at the skin on the back of her knee. It's just a slice of skin: a rectangle between the top of her sock and the hem of her skirt. It's ordinary. It's white and shot with blue veins that wander like slug trails. Garry wants to touch the back of that knee more than anything else in the world. It is white and blue and it smells like Silverkin Mega Firm.

Derek doesn't come again until Friday. Christine is sulky and tells him he needn't bother expecting his tea making because she hasn't got anything in. Derek stays on the path, kicking the dead ends of the brambles into the lawn. One of the prickly stalks catches on his jeans and he swears and kicks it away.

'For God's sake,' Christine says, 'it isn't a snake. It's a twig.'

Eventually, Christine lets him in and they stand in the kitchen. Garry watches him, and Derek doesn't look. He knows he makes the uncles feel guilty, even if he doesn't talk to them.

'Did you stop by the offy on your way?' Christine asks, hopefully.

Her face is as pale and transparent as a shell. Something brittle and translucent – a vase in a posh shop. There are signs: you break it, you pay for it.

Derek doesn't say anything and Garry goes upstairs. He sits at his desk and cuts string for the lid of the brainbox and doesn't listen. An hour, maybe two, and the front door bangs closed. It always happens like this. They go, after a while. Mostly, they leave their presents behind them. Derek promised a drive of the white Ford on the beach at Southport, but it had never materialised.

After a while, Garry puts the glue away and goes down into the kitchen. His mother is sitting at the table, pushing her finger through a pile of spilt sugar.

'Well, that's that done with,' she says, and sighs deeply. 'Derek won't be coming round any more.'

Garry doesn't say anything. Christine draws a circle in the sugar, licks her finger and begins to push the grains into a pile.

'Don't be upset, love. It's for the best.'

'I'm not upset,' Garry says. He opens the fridge, checks there's milk, puts the kettle on to make her some coffee. There are dirty plates in the sink; clumps of scrambled egg and smears of brown sauce still clinging to them. He turns the tap on and washes them while he's waiting for the kettle to click. He ignores Christine: sees her shoulders shaking and her head go down. He can hear her tears hit the table. He touches her arm and slides the mug over to her.

'Silly, me going on like this.' She sniffs, rubs at her eyes, inspects the mascara on her fingers. 'He was no good anyway.'

'No,' Garry says. She starts playing with the sugar again. Garry wants to get the cloth and wipe it away. He can hear the grains scratching over the table, can see the way it is clinging to her fingernails.

She sighs again. 'I don't feel like cooking tonight. I think we need a treat. What do you think? A fish supper? Do you fancy that? Or a pie? A battered sausage?'

Garry thinks of the fat, of the cholesterol that is even now swimming around inside his mother's veins. He thinks of it like little bombs, tiny yellow mines heading towards her heart and brain.

'I can cook,' Garry says, 'I'm getting good at it. I learned quiche at school. Have we any eggs left?'

'Oh no,' Christine says, 'I can't be bothered with all that. Let's have something nice.' Her handbag is hanging off the back of the chair and Garry stands while she looks for the money.

'Come straight back afterwards,' she says, when he is standing at the back door. 'There's a film starting at seven. We can watch it together, can't we?'

Garry nods, and goes out without putting his coat on.

There is a bus shelter outside the chip shop. It's painted green – the same dark, dirty green as the doors in the toilets at school. Those three girls are there. He knew they would be. He walks past quickly, rubbing his fingers together in his pockets. He's been at his matches again and the brainbox is nearly finished.The glue peels away from his skin, forms little balls. He pulls a hand out of his pocket and inspects them. Tiny grey balls, like pieces of snot. He rubs his hands together and goes inside the shop.

It stinks of grease and vinegar, and there is a queue. He takes his place at the back of it. There are glass cabinets along the counter – heated cases with lights inside, and a shiny metal trim. There's battered cod and sausages, pies in silver cases, fragments of batter piled up like cornflakes. He looks at his reflection in the metal part of the cabinet. He looks at the girls in the bus shelter.

The same three, and always together. Two of them blonde, and the other one, who isn't as good as the others. Her hair is a fuzzy kind of brown, and her bag isn't as good as her friends'. There's something grubby about her school shirts. When they swish past him in the corridor, he can smell them. The other two smell like Daz and Body Shop Dewberry and Wrigley's Juicy Fruit. The other one, the one that isn't as good – she smells like damp towels and cigarettes and Silverkin. He stares at them in the metal. One of the blonde ones has got a yo-yo. They're laughing.

When it's his turn, Garry buys a pudding with chips, a polystyrene pot of gravy and a can of Coke. He opens the can of Coke – it's warm and the lid tastes like vinegar and dust.

'Are you going to come over here?'

Garry isn't sure whether they mean it in a nice way, or not. He stops. The bag is warm against his leg. The dark one stares at him.

'Come on, then,' she says. She doesn't shout, but Garry can hear her anyway – clear against the fizz of the traffic passing. He goes.

'What's in the bag?'

Garry shrugs. 'Just tea.'

'Give us a chip, will you? We're starving.'

Garry thinks about telling them the chips are for his mum, but stops himself just in time and hands the bag over. The tall one tears open the paper and half the chips scatter over the pavement.

'You going out tonight?' the dark-haired one says. Garry looks at her feet and shakes his head. She's got jeans on, but the back of her knee is still there, rubbing against the denim. He feels his trousers get tight and watches the bag of chips go from hand to hand between them.

'Why don't you come out with us?'

Garry thinks about Christine. She's sitting at the kitchen table, making a puddle on the Formica. She's resting her forehead on the back of her fat hands.

'I can't,' he says. It wasn't a serious offer anyway. Best to say no. Safest. The matchsticks are waiting at home. There's enough Silverkin to get him to sleep.

'He can't,' the tall one says in her sarcastic voice, 'he's got to get home to his mummy, hasn't he?'

Their laughter sounds like lots of little pieces of metal falling.

'He's got to go and suck on her titties, haven't you, *Garry*?'

'Garry, Garry, are you listening?' The dark-haired one leans forward. Her hair is curling over her forehead. The neck of her T-shirt gapes and he can see the dark place between her chest and the material.

'Listen,' she says, and Garry looks at her, lost in the whirl of a green eye.

'What?' he asks. 'She's not well. She's expecting me. That's her tea you're eating, you know.'

The dark-haired one grabs the bag, throws it at Garry.

'Have it, then,' she says mildly.

The pudding explodes against his chest. The gravy soaks through his T-shirt instantly and he jumps back, and holds the fabric away from his skin. It's burning hot.

'Get on, then,' she says, and laughs again, 'home to your mother.'

The tall one kicks at the chips and lumps of pudding on the pavement. The pieces skid over the tarmac to the kerb.

'Pick it up, then. Can't have her starving to death, can we?'

Garry shakes the pudding off him as he runs home. I'll burn this shirt, he thinks, and tell her the chippy was closed.

He goes into Christine's bedroom. The curtains are drawn, but it is still light outside. The room is filled with sticky, grey sunshine, and Garry can see Christine lying on the bed, her fat white feet hanging over the side. Her toenails are painted pink. She's wearing a dress, a big flowery dress made out of nylon. It's shiny where it's pulled tight over her breasts and belly: the buttons down the front are crooked.

All of her dresses are the same: wash-and-wear nylon from the market, dried quickly, no ironing. He looks at her face. All fat people, he realises, look the same. They have soft, piggy faces like babies. The fat under her skin has softly wiped away his mother's features, and now she is sleeping her mouth is slack, her hair stuck damply to her forehead. If it wasn't for the dress, the signature dress, and the signature stink in her room of feet and cigarettes and Carling, he thinks he wouldn't recognise her.

Yes. Garry steps into the room quietly, dodging shoes and crumpled clothing and teacups on his journey to the sagging bed. If this woman, he looks at her again, this specimen, and wonders how many colours the nylon dresses come in, if this woman was lying just like this, but in a park, or in a hospital, or in an entirely different dress, he wouldn't think they belonged to each other at all.

Garry lifts up his Silverkin, strikes the match and points the jet at his mother. There's a satisfying woosh, and the smell of burning hair. He feels the heat in his hands, sees the feet jerk and scrabble against the sheets, hears high-pitched noises coming out of her mouth.

She goes up like a Christmas pudding.

Paint a Vulgar Picture

Scarlett Thomas

Well, here's a little number about fame and what it can do tp people – and even dogs. I've been haunted by this song ever since I first heard it in my dingy bedroom, but one line particularly resonates: 'You could have said no if you'd wanted to.' But sometimes, of course, you don't, or you just can't.

'No, the story's about the ugly duckling *turning into* a beautiful swan...'

I'm sitting on a red plastic chair in a stock cupboard signing copies of my novel. Outside, in the main area of the bookshop, some kid won't stop howling. I can't see the kid, or its mother. I can hear the howling, and also rain hitting the thin roof of the shop like bitten fingernails on a desk.

The mother says to the kid, 'It's a nice story.' The kid still howls.

My name has come out wrong on seven of the ten books so far and I don't know what to do about it. On the next one I draw a sad smiley (i.e. not smiling) and write the words 'Help me!' Will this make the book more valuable? Less valuable? I've done them all in fountain pen, anyway.

Is this important to me at all? It was before I did it.

There was a story going around about this famous writer who signed her books and then added 'Buy Pete's book instead'. Pete must have been dicking her at every literary festival they went to together. When I first heard that story I didn't really know what to make of it but later I realised that when I saw the picture in my head of the author signing her books, it was me doing it, not her, and I was covered in silver tinsel. I haven't been invited to any literary festivals. My boyfriend William has been to a couple in the last few years, and I've tagged along. We went to one where members of the public had to wear red badges and authors wore green badges and every time I tried to speak to anyone they'd look at my red badge, then look over my shoulder and then walk off. William's last book only sold two thousand copies, and his publishers look like they're going to drop him, so his agent has sent his new novel around to everyone else, but no one's said anything yet. So no literary festivals for us. It's OK, though, because we're going on holiday next week and we're going to have our own literary festival with our dog, Oedipus Rex.

'I don't understand this whole book-signing business anyway,' I say to William when I find him outside the shop. He's looking in the window of the shop next door, but I don't know what at. They do engraving, stiletto heels and key cutting, and the only thing they have in their window is a rack of Zippo lighters. 'It's like, *Wow, she actually touched it...* Is that it? Whatever happened to the Death of the Author? Does the book mean more because I touched it? No. Less? Possibly.'

'Don't be a wanker,' he says.

'What? How am I being a wanker now?'

It's still raining and we haven't got an umbrella, or waterproof clothes. Last year we took Rex to a family fun dog show in the local park and it rained. I kept saying in a loud voice, 'Oh, no! We forgot our waterproofs,' and William kept saying, also in a loud voice, 'Why are you pretending we have waterproofs?' People looked at us. I still have a picture of Rex from that day. He's standing in a puddle doing his big dog-smile, having just won the Best in Show trophy. On the way home I promised him he wouldn't have to go in a dog show ever again, since he'd won the trophy, but I don't know why I promised him that, or why I thought he wouldn't want to go in another one. The people from the dog show arranged for his name to be engraved on the trophy, and we always point it out to people when they come to our house.

We're shopping for a tent for our holiday. But since we discovered that the local bookshops have copies of my novel already (it's out in August, i.e. the cruellest bookselling month apart from January, according to William), this has turned into a mini book tour where, in every bookshop doorway, William coaches me in how to say, 'Hi, I'm a local author, would you like me to sign your stock?' I'm disturbed by the word 'stock'. Also, I'd like it to be night, and I'd like to be wearing pale make-up and black clothes, and ideally a crazed fan or long-forgotten drug dealer would turn up and cause a scene outside, and there'd be so many fans waiting for me inside that when they all crowded to the window to look, their breath would steam it up and no one would be able to see anything.

The next shop is supposed to be an independent but it stocks the same books as Waterstone's and has posters up advertising Richard and Judy's book signing tomorrow.

'I'm sick of this,' I say to William.

'Just get it done and we'll go and find the tent,' he says. 'Just remember that if you sign them they can't send them back. And maybe they'll ask you to come and do a reading.'

'I only want to do a reading if hundreds of people are going to show up.'

'I know.'

'That's never going to happen, though, is it?'

'No.'

This time I sit on a chair in front of a desk in the actual shop. However, they only have two copies of my book. They have five copies of another first novel I recognise, by one of my rivals; however, these lie in a small pile in front of the sales desk.

'They waiting to be shelved?' I say.

'No. They're waiting to be returned. To be honest,' says the guy, 'you're looking at a month of shelf-life these days before we start sending them back.'

'You can't send these back, though,' I say. 'Not once I've signed them.'

'No. Well, that's a myth, actually.'

'Oh.'

'Oh well,' says William. 'You might be sitting on the same chair Richard or Judy will be sitting on tomorrow.'

'To be honest,' says the guy again, 'we'll probably use the nice chairs for that.'

We explode out of the shop, and run around down a backstreet laughing. We used to work together before we gave it all up to be writers, and sometimes we'd sit in meetings and not be able to look at one another because of the giggling fits. There was one time when we were discussing the students' action plans, and one of them had written 'I want too be faymus', or something like that, and we both had to leave the room. Apparently everyone heard us laughing outside. But it's only when we stop running that I realise this time I am just making a noise like laughter and my stomach doesn't hurt, and my eyes aren't watering, and I'm still thinking about tinsel and fogged-up windows. William leans against a wooden door.

'Ow,' he says, touching his chest.

'Yeah, I know. What a cunt.'

I light a cigarette with a match and then put the match out with my fingers.

'What's wrong?' William asks.

'Nothing. What's this place?'

We're not great shoppers, but I must have walked Rex past here a hundred times without noticing it.

'A museum,' says William, looking at the sign. 'Is it new?'

I shrug. 'Who knows?'

'What's it got inside it?' William moves toward the glass front. 'The

Roman city blah blah blah... Hey, this is cool. You can go underground and look at the Roman city.'

'Yeah, right.'

'No, really.'

'It'll just be another CD-ROM.'

There's a newsagent next to this. It has a noticeboard.

'What are you doing now?' I ask William.

'Looking at the noticeboard,' he says.

'We'll *buy* a tent,' I say.

'Yeah, but there might be one for cheap, or even for free...'

I smoke, and I don't look at the museum or the noticeboard.

'Family fun dog show,' he says. 'We could take Rex. It's tomorrow.'

'He went last year,' I say. 'We promised him he wouldn't have to do it again.'

'Oh yeah.' William touches his chest. 'Ow. Don't you think he'd enjoy it, though?'

'No. He told me not to make him do it again.'

'OK. Oh, what about the trophy?'

'What trophy?' I put out my cigarette. 'Oh fuck.'

Do normal people polish trophies? We didn't. When we take it off the TV it's full of dust, and dead flies. It's tarnished on the outside and on the inside and looks a hundred years old. We have to take it back tomorrow. I put it in a bowl of Ecover washing-up liquid, vinegar, salt and bleach and hope for the best.

William's upstairs checking his email. Has anyone made an offer on his book? No, they have not. If they had, he'd have told me. I go upstairs anyway, and stand behind him, looking at all the spam in his inbox.

'What can we say?' I ask him.

'What about?'

'We're both writers. Why haven't we polished the trophy *all year*?'

'We didn't give a shit?'

'*Will...*'

'Our arms fell off?'

'Yeah, whatever. Come on. We have to plot it so it's believable.'

'It's a good job I look at noticeboards, otherwise we wouldn't even have known.' He coughs. 'We could tell the truth.'

'What is the truth, though?'

'We couldn't be bothered.'

'I just didn't know it would tarnish so much.'

'Laurie?'

'What?'

'Don't cry.'

'I'm not.'

He looks around at me.

'OK, I am. I want to sit in a cupboard and cry about the trophy. I don't know why.'

'Go on, then.'

'Work out what to say.'

'I thought you didn't care about what these people think?' he calls after me. 'I thought you were over this.'

By the time we get to the park, the dog show is almost over. William takes Rex to sniff around the edge of the river, and I go over to the marquee. I'm wearing torn jeans and I have no dog. The trophy is in a Waitrose carrier bag, not the Londis one William originally used. I feel like the kind of ghost they find on cable TV: *She can't leave this place... She feels she's stuck here... She means you great harm...* I do not mean harm, but I have no voice and only the ability to make everything feel so cold that children cry.

I take the trophy out of the bag.

'I've come to return this,' I say to a woman selling raffle tickets.

'Sorry?' she says.

'The Best in Show trophy from last year. It's a bit... My husband got a bit overzealous about cleaning it and I think it went a bit too far.'

'Oh. Well, thanks.'

I hand her the trophy. I think of the clean patch it's left on top of the

TV, and I want to cry again. We had that trophy for a whole year, and we never touched it once. She looks at it and there's nothing I can say to make any difference.

'I think I've got a silver cloth somewhere,' she says.

'We're both writers,' I say. 'We get a bit eccentric about cleaning.'

She says nothing.

Outside, William and Rex are both looking at the arena, which is full of small hurdles and other things I recognise from agility trials on Crufts.

'My chest hurts,' says William.

'It's stress,' I say. 'You're very stressed.'

'I know. I am, but.' He coughs. 'My breathing.'

'It's this book stuff,' I say. 'Hey, this looks fun.'

Rex is wagging his tail and straining towards the arena.

'Is it too late to enter this?' I ask a woman in a green jacket.

'No, it's not too late. It's fifty pence, though.'

'Cool.' I give her fifty pence. 'He won Best in Show last year.'

She gives me a little ticket.

'I honestly don't think I can do this right now,' says William.

'I'll do it,' I say. 'I could do with some exercise.'

'I think I might sit down.'

'Are you OK?'

'No. Yes. You're right; it's stress. I'll be fine.'

At Casualty they ask for William's occupation and I say 'writer'. He's not here. He's been fast-tracked down the corridor, along a yellow line.

'Writer?'

'Yes.'

'Date of birth?'

I give the rest of William's details, which I know as well as my own. I do this while smiling without showing my teeth, with my hands out of my pockets, leaning against the counter to hide the rips in my jeans. I could have said 'lecturer'. William still lectures part time at the university. Should I have said that?

William used to joke about the conversation he had every time someone asked him what he did and he said he was a writer. The person would say, *A writer, eh? Got anything published?* And he'd say, *Yes.* And they'd say, *What? Just one book?* And he'd say, *Well, a couple, you know.* And they'd say something like, *Wow, a real published writer,* as if he were the Loch Ness Monster. And he'd say something like, *I just got lucky.* And then, without fail, they'd say, *So, is it mysteries you write, then, or what?* Always mysteries. He predicted that when my turn came around people would assume I wrote romances.

I follow the yellow line to the Cardiac Room.

'How are you feeling?' I ask him.

'It hurts,' he says.

He's wired up to one of those machines that flash your heart rate every second.

'Hey,' I say. 'I could kiss you and see what effect it has.'

'Yeah,' he says. 'You could give me a heart attack. That would be hilarious.'

'You'll be OK,' I say.

If he isn't, I know what I'll do. Once Rex has lived out his natural life, visiting his master's grave (with me) three times a day, I will Google 'Suicide Bombing' and work out how to strap a bomb to my body, and then I will go to his publisher and detonate myself. I'm surprised more people don't do things like this.

I can't believe I just thought him dead.

'Are you OK?' William asks me.

'Yeah. We never got our tent,' I say.

'We'll get the best tent ever,' he says.

Fuck. We're in a film. This is the last scene. He's going to die. He's going to die... He'll have his tent, all right, but in heaven. And St Peter will say 'Occupation?' and he'll say *Writer,* and even St Peter will think that's a little OTT (the hubris, the hubris…) and he'll get sent to Purgatory, which will be like a slush pile in the sky, and told to drink himself to death like real writers, and…

'What exactly is pericarditis again?' William asks me on the way home.

'It's like all the symptoms of a heart attack, but without the actual heart attack,' I say. 'Like the fictional version. I don't know. The muscle around your heart is inflamed, or something, but it's not dangerous. Only you could have an inflamed heart that isn't dangerous. I still think it's stress.'

I'm driving around the ring road, with William. William is alive.

'We can still go on holiday,' he says.

'Yeah. Next week. And we'll stop worrying about our books, and I won't cry any more because I think old women hate me, and everything'll be fine.'

'Poor Rex,' he says.

'I'll take him for a long walk when we get in.'

We were in Casualty for eight hours. Rex chews stuff and raids the bin when he's on his own for more than three.

'He'll still be pissed off, probably.'

'Yeah.'

The last thing that happened at the dog show before someone called an ambulance was Rex trying to bite this woman who was trying to make him run through a plastic tunnel.

'Fucking hell,' William says. 'Look.'

The traffic's moving slowly. We can both see the flowers on either side of the road, all tied to similar grey railings. One lot by the school; the other lot by the pedestrian crossing. They look fresh. Obviously they haven't been rained on yet, or bleached out by the sun. There's a small toy duck wedged in between two bunches of flowers tied next to the pedestrian crossing. I imagine someone fixing it there. Did they use string? Sellotape? Nothing at all? Did it fall down, and did the person have to try again? It's made of dark yellow fluffy fabric. It probably has a brand name on it somewhere, and care instructions.

'Shit, do you think there were two accidents, or just one?' I say.

Here's William's cue to say something stupid about bodies flying through the air and hitting both railings like something on *America's Worst Accidents*.

Here's my cue to say something about how tacky the flowers are.

Neither of us says anything until we are on the other side of the ring road.

'I hope no one steals the little duck,' I say.

Cemetry Gates

Mil Millington

I love the notion of 'meeting at the cemetry gates' – which is a splendid image, but especially so, I feel, if the gates are figurative.

'Sorry,' he said, tilting his head up away from the ground that had been holding his full attention.

He'd shuffled round the corner into the path of a woman walking in the opposite direction. The near-collision wasn't any more his fault than hers, but he felt that the burden of the apology lay on him: even if the wall hadn't been there, he wasn't looking where he was going. Though irrelevant in practical terms, the subtle and multifaceted points system of British manners dictated that he should obviously be the one to put up the first Sorry in this particular encounter.

The woman – a handbag clutched to her stomach and, it required only half a glance to see, Things On Her Mind – blinked with initial irritation, then lowered her eyes and quickly replied, 'No – you're all right, love.' She arced around him, farther around than could be taken as meaningless, and scurried away.

He took a breath, and then began moving again – his eyes returning to his feet. He wondered whether he looked like someone who was learning to walk. The thought provoked a wry smile. As he watched each leg slide alternately forward his worry wasn't that walking was something that he was struggling to learn, but rather that it was something that he was determinedly trying not to forget.

A dozen or so steps and, triumphant, he arrived at his destination. He paused for a moment; pleased, but affecting casualness.

'You've had a shave,' Helen said, glancing up at David as he carefully lowered himself into the chair.

She heard the surprise in her own voice and examined it with curiosity – as one would pick out an odd sound among the familiar noises of one's car; an unidentified rattle or an unexpected tick appearing amid the well-known hums and rumbles. Her mouth seemed to be suggesting, without consulting her, that she'd been confronted by the disappearance of stubble that she'd become accustomed to over many years. Yet that wasn't the case. That wasn't the case at all.

David, settling into his seat with a small, relieved sigh, wiped his hand over his cheeks. 'Yeah,' he replied, his voice woody but weightless – like a long exhalation. 'I never intended to appear all rugged and outdoorsy. It was inertia.'

'You look a bit weird clean shaven.'

'Thanks.'

'Well, not "weird".'

'What, then?'

'OK – "weird".'

'Thanks, again.'

'You backed me into a corner.'

David smiled and explored his face with his fingertips once more. If he stroked down towards his chin, his skin felt smooth (and a little loose too, but that was another matter). Yet, even though it had been only a few hours since he'd stood unsteadily before a steamy mirror, when he ran his nails upwards he could hear the crackle of bristles.

'Shaving is really dull,' he said. 'It's so, so dull. At least you get to play with your face – we just have to mow ours.'

'Play with my face?'

'Make-up. Women. You get to apply all those...' He waved two fingers at himself, indicating, possibly, his lips. 'Things. I don't know – colours and so on.'

'And that's playing with our faces, is it?'

'Yes, of course it is. You're creating something. It's like making a work of art – shaving is like stripping wallpaper. Have you ever stripped wallpaper?'

'I'm not sure. Maybe – I can't remember.'

'Then you've never stripped wallpaper. If you had, you'd remember. It's the most tedious thing that's ever existed – it's so boring it actually *hurts*. I can feel it now: the sound of the scraper on the plaster; the smell of dampened woodchip; the dust in your eyes; the aching of your arm; the sheer, punishing, bloody boredom of it. Nobody should ever waste their time stripping wallpaper.'

'Or shaving?'

'Yeah. Except we have to.'

'Because you'd end up with a beard.'

'Exactly.'

'And look like a twat.'

'Exactly.'

The sky was cold and bad tempered and looked as if it had slept in its mascara. David glanced at it through the window and was saddened by how distant it seemed behind the double glazing.

'And the other thing,' he continued, 'is that it bloody well outlives you. Your hair carries on growing after you're dead. Talk about tenacious. I'm going to show it who's boss while I'm alive, at least, because I know it'll get me in the end: beards pursue you into the damn grave.'

'That's not true, actually.'

'Yes it is.'

'No – it's a myth. Your hair doesn't really continue to grow after you die. People thought that it did because your skin shrinks and goes livid; it might look like you've got a five o'clock shadow when you shuffled off at midday, but, really, it's not that your stubble has risen, it's that your face has fallen.'

David didn't reply.

'Also,' Helen went on, 'before the courts got so picky about death certificates, they were forever burying people alive – particularly if there was a plague doing the rounds. They didn't hang about back then. If you had a funny turn and didn't seem very talkative, you were straight in the ground. They'd dig you up later—'

'Why would they do that?'

'Oh, a bit of body snatching, maybe. Or just for something to do of an evening – there was no televised snooker at that time. Anyway, they'd dig people up and see the body had a little hair growth. And – not nearly as rarely as it's pleasant to think about – fingernail marks scratched into the inside of the coffin lid too. I've read that this might have been the origin of the idea of vampires.'

'God. That's horrible.'

'More horrible than being dead? Can being alive ever be more horrible than being dead?'

'Being *buried* alive? Yes. That's more horrible – don't you think?'

Helen picked absently at the adhesive strip on her forearm. 'Perhaps... But I suppose there's always the chance of being heard and rescued – if you scream loud enough and long enough. It's terrifying, but there's still *hope*. There's still a good reason for screaming. Premature burial can't tear away hope. It's taken modern advances in diagnostic medicine to do that.'

'I...'

'Anyway, my face hasn't been a work of art for years. When you have children, you abandon make-up. There isn't the time any more. At least, you think you have no time, until you realise what having no time really is.'

David started to reach his hand out to Helen's... but then faltered and turned the movement into rubbing something that wasn't there off his knee.

'I saw your children,' he said.

Helen nodded, without looking at him.

David smiled. 'They look like good kids. I popped my head in, and they were here, so I left again. Was that you mother with them?'

'Yes.' The reply was stripped. Terse. Unemotional. Emotional.

'I thought so. Your husband...'

'*Ex*-husband. No, I haven't seen him. There's not a single reason I should, or would want to. They were with my mother.'

'Well... Good kids. I thought, anyway.'

'Yes.' She gave a small laugh, which segued into a larger cough. David reached across and poured some water into her glass from the bedside jug, but she waved it away. 'Worth the price of their idiot father, they were,' she added. 'Tallulah Bankhead said, "If I had to live my life again, I'd make the same mistakes, only sooner."' Helen allowed herself another tight, bitter laugh. 'Though she lived to be sixty-six – so, to my mind, she had a reasonably fair amount of time to enjoy kicking herself.'

David turned to the sky again. It was still there. Petulantly, like a small child making his presence unavoidably felt by leaning against his mother's legs while she was trying to get on with her household chores, it flopped on top of the buildings that formed the unevenly serrated skyline of the city. The roofs would decay, and crumble, and be replaced, thought David. They were fixed, but transient; while the sky was ever changing but immortal. It would be there – in human terms – for ever. For ever was a long time. Longer than brick and slate. And much, much longer than him.

'It's a pity,' he said, half answering Helen, half answering himself.

'A pity? A *pity*? I don't understand you.' She squinted at him and shook her head. 'Where's your sense of justice?'

'That's not really relevant, is it?'

'Yes it is. What separates us from badgers and mackerel is moral awareness; and that's really just a fancy way of saying that we instinctively and innately want things to be fair. Nothing is more definitive of what we are than our angry outrage when we encounter unfairness. Well, there are murderers out there – and they'll still be out there this time next year. Rapists are sitting on sofas right now, planning their summer holidays. Burglars, wife beaters and petty thugs will collect their pensions. Plain old shitty, selfish little creeps are going to be around to see their children grow up. Doesn't that make you angry? Doesn't the sheer, fucking *unfairness* of it twist your insides?'

'You shouldn't get worked up.' This time David did take hold of Helen's hand. 'It'll wear you out.'

'I've already worn out.' She tossed him a glance. 'Ha! I'm funny.'

She laughed, but also squeezed his fingers so hard that it took a serious effort for him not to wince. He even considered reaching down to the dispenser at his waist and giving himself a quick intravenous burst. But Helen soon noticed that her hand had embarked upon a small mutiny. She inwardly tutted with annoyance: tch – *really*; her voice, her expressions, her movements... keeping all the bits of herself under control was like juggling chainsaws. Her grip relaxed and, with a few gentle pats on his wrist, withdrew: she'd happily hold hands, but she didn't want it to seem as though she *needed* to hold hands.

'Do you know what else is funny?' she said.

David leaned back into his chair. 'What?'

'I still can't die.'

David shifted uncomfortably. Helen smiled.

'In my head, that is,' she added. 'I think about being dead, and I get angry – *furious*. It sets me shaking with sheer rage at the sickening injustice of it. But, really, I'm not thinking about being dead: I'm thinking about *thinking* about being dead.'

'Is there a difference?'

'*Oh* yes. I'll give you an example.'

'I'm all ears.'

He wasn't especially eager to know the details, but he was pleased that Helen wanted to explain them to him. She always livened up when she'd got a new bit of death that she was mulling over. And he sort of understood that; dissecting it put her in the driving seat – in the same way that gallows humour does: not waving, but drowning while giving the finger. Helen's preferred way to whistle a happy tune was to whistle through the graveyard. So, he was glad she'd found another point about which to become eagerly fixated. Though he tried to prevent her getting *too* worked up, he didn't try to soothe it away completely, even when she got angry about things. She seemed to draw strength from it. Sometimes he thought that it was only dying that was keeping her alive.

'Well, for a start,' Helen said, 'I hear my tenses.'

'A man goes to the doctor: he says—'

'Doctor, I keep dreaming I'm a wigwam and a marquee. The doctor replies, "I know what your problem is."'

'You're two tents.'

They both laughed like schoolboys.

'That's such a crap joke,' Helen said through crackly giggles.

'I know.'

They laughed harder.

'OK, OK – seriously...' Helen determinedly calmed herself. 'Look, the very worst thing is that I think about my children. I think about how I'll miss them. Did you hear it? I won't miss them – I'll be dead. But it's 'I *will* miss them'. Not a loss I'm feeling now, but a loss I imagine myself feeling, when I won't actually be feeling anything at all. I won't *be* at all. It's as though I'll be there, looking at myself *not* being there, and feeling the pain of my absent self. It's a mess. How can I have such a muddled, convoluted, nonsensical picture in my head? The answer is because my head simply can't assimilate being dead. Even though I know it; even though the miserable, cruel, imminent certainty of it fills my thoughts every moment, my head's still unable to grasp the reality properly.'

'You can't accept it. That's completely understandable.'

'No, no. I can *accept* it: but I can't imagine it. It's like accepting that time is relative. You go, "Well, OK. Einstein's proved it is, apparently, so I'm sure it's right. He wouldn't have said it simply for a gag – he was German." But you can't imagine it as a reality you're sitting in. You can only see it in the abstract.'

'Right. I get what you mean now.'

'And I bet you're the same.' She turned her eyes away from him and peered up at her drip; the saggy plastic bag hung limply from its shiny stand like a sad balloon two days after the party was over. 'Every day, I wonder whether you won't come to see me. You won't come, because you'll have…' – she tried not to pause, but the pause was too heavy for her to move it out of the way without an effort – 'gone.'

Once again, David remained silent.

Helen continued. 'Even though I *know* that I'm likely to go first.'

'Nonsense.'

'Oh, please. I'll go first.'

'You won't.'

'I will.'

'You have a very unattractive competitive streak in you, you know.'

'But – as you've thrown yourself so predictably into my trap – that's my point. I'm sure that when you think about us you don't think that you might not be here tomorrow; you think that you'll come and *I* won't be here.'

'I do not,' replied David chidingly. He was unable to hold her eyes, however, because it was true. Each day, as he shuffled in to see her, he had to struggle against the image of arriving to find an empty bed.

'You're such a liar.' Helen grinned. 'But such a rubbish liar. I wish I'd known that there were men who were so utterly rubbish at lying before I married Dan. It's like those women who get divorced and suddenly realise that sex can be great, it was simply that their husbands were useless and they'd assumed it was normal.'

'I wouldn't have lied to you anyway. If…'

'Ifs and buts. We'll never know.'

'I know I could have made you happy.'

'You have made me happy.'

'You've made me happy too. And sadder. It's so…' He tried to find a better word, but there wasn't one. 'So *sad* that we found each other, but found each other here.'

'Pff – you think it was an accident? I'm a divorced woman with two young children. It's a nightmare getting that second date – you've no idea. To be honest, I'm only dying as a way to meet men.'

'Hussy.'

'I'd show you, but our tubes would get all knotted. It'd take two orderlies the rest of the day to untangle us from coitus.'

'Oh, I don't like to brag, but pretty much every woman who's had sex with me has wanted to ring for a nurse at some point.'

'Enough, enough. Don't dangle temptation, David.'

'You started it.'

'Yes – sorry. It's always like that. Put me on a morphine drip and I'm anybody's.'

She grinned, but it made David consider, not for the first time, how much of what he felt – what they both felt – was down to a combination of extreme circumstances and medical-strength narcotics. Would he have fallen for her, and (even more of an issue) would she have fallen for him, if the situation had been different? If they'd simply struck up a conversation after reaching for the same tangerine in Safeway, would it have led to this? Was it real? It had all happened so fast – and wasn't that a giveaway? Limited time, limited choice and unlimited methadone: was that it? Would it have happened if they were two people with their whole lives ahead of them?

He decided it was irrelevant. After all, their whole lives *were* ahead of them – it was just that they didn't stretch very *far* ahead of them. What you feel is what you feel; it's its own measure – you don't arrive at it after adding up the As, Bs and Cs like a questionnaire in a women's magazine. And what was the downside to accepting their feelings? One thing was certain: they weren't going to live to regret it.

Happy with his reasoning, he welcomed in the sadness once more.

'Stop it,' said Helen, snapping her fingers at him.

'Stop it?'

'You're drifting again. You can be turned on or pissed off, but I won't stand for any "sorrowful introspection" nonsense.'

'I can't—'

'You can. Do it for my sake – do it for *our* sake. We'll be a couple, visibly, if we both go spitting and scratching into that good night.' She took his hand in both of hers. 'Promise me something.'

'What?'

'Promise me that, with your last ounce of strength…'

'Yes?'

'You'll punch a consultant in the neck.'

David smiled and shook his head. 'You really are…'

Helen raised her eyebrows questioningly.

'Beyond hope,' said David. He pulled up his arm and kissed the back of her hand.

Helen reached out to him and touched his cheek. 'Awww – you say the sweetest things. There's nothing so irresistible as a man who makes you feel like you work on two levels.' She ran a fingertip across his lips. 'I bet my knees would go all wobbly, if I had any sensation below my waist.' She grinned again. 'A woman wakes up in hospital. She says, "Doctor! I can't feel my legs!"'

'The doctor says, "Yes. We had to cut off your arms."'

They both crumbled into another fit of giggles – worse than the last one. It went on and on; each time they thought it had run its course they set each other off again with a look, until, gradually, it ebbed into a silence that was almost like an afterglow. Finally, David spoke again.

'I ought to get back.'

'I know…' Helen clicked her teeth. 'If you go missing for too long they'll probably give your place to someone else. Shortage of resources. There's a great queue of people who simply can't die until there's a bed free.'

David struggled to his feet. He hated leaving. On top of the terribleness of not being with her, added even to the nauseous knowledge that she might be gone the next time he returned, was the fact that each journey was more difficult than the last. He dreaded the appearance of a moment when – for all the power of his desire to see her – his traitorous body would refuse to carry him through the antiseptic corridors to her bedside.

'I'll come back – as soon as I can,' he said; insistently, so his limbs would hear and be committed.

'I'll be here.'

'Of course you will.'

'But, if you can't—'

'I *will*.'

'But if you *can't*, it'll only be a detail. We aren't these failing organs and collapsing cells, David. I've learned, now, not to mistake intimacy for holding hands together as we walk in the summer rain, or wandering around IKEA picking out bedding – all arm in arm and our pockets stuffed with a thieving excess of tiny pencils. If I never touched you again, you'd still be with me. You'd be with me *here*.' She placed her hand on herself.

'Your crotch?' David asked, peering.

'Yeah.' She pulled a face at him. 'What? You'd prefer me to point to my heart? It's just a muscle. I've got better places to keep you than that. Do you *want* to be lodged in my aorta?' she asked derisively.

'No. Your crotch is good. I can live in your crotch – no problem.'

'You will. Live.'

'Until the next time, at least,' he said.

He stood for a moment, looking down at her, and shook his head. 'I feel lucky.'

'Me too.' She smiled.

He turned and began to walk away. Without looking back he said, 'See you soon.'

'Yes,' she replied, closing her eyes. 'I can see you now.'

Death of a Disco Dancer

Nick Stone

Morrissey didn't like discos much. In 'How Soon Is Now?', he goes to one, can't pull and goes home and cries and wants to die. In 'Panic', he wants to hang the DJ who responds to the apocalypse raging outside by playing inane, irrelevant pop. And here, he watches some wannabe John Travolta get killed in a nightclub and looks away.

Miami, 1981

'Gennelmen,' Major Hartman addressed Detective Sergeant Al Rodgers and Detective Larry Edwards with a broad grin. 'You're gonna be movie stars.'

Rodgers and Edwards looked at Hartman and then at each other, nonplussed.

'OK, that's an exaggeration.' Hartman chuckled. 'But there's this Hollywood producer I know wants to do a pilot for a cop show based in Miami. He's heard all about us and the fine work we do here. He needs two detectives to show him around, take him through their day, let him see life through their eyes. His characters are a salt 'n' pepper duo. I immediately thought of you two.'

Miami PD frequently got asked to help out on movies, TV shows and the like in one capacity or another and usually refused, unless a big-name star contacted them in person and the project was resolutely pro-cop.

'So what *exactly* are we supposed to do?' Rodgers asked. He didn't like the idea one bit. They had work to do and lots of it. Homicides in the city were already up two hundred per cent thanks to the cocaine cowboys' daily shoot-outs and the new Cuban intake, killing their way into the American dream. Rodgers hated cop shows and most cop movies – not his bag, being entertained by a cartoon version of what you did for a living every day.

'I want you two to play at bein' cops for the day. Put on a show. Imagine you're two characters in a movie, and the guy's your audience. Impress him, wow him, *inspire* him.'

'*Huh*?' Rodgers grunted.

'I got a little scenario in mind. Take him for a spin around the city for about an hour, point things out to him, let him see the luxury and the misery. Then, at about eleven a.m., you'll get a call from Dispatch sayin' there's a stiff on a boat in the Marina. You go over there to investigate with the guy, show him what you do – the whole process, boarding the boat, securing the scene, discovering the body, witness canvassing – no paperwork, though, that's boring.'

'Who's the stiff?' Edwards asked.

'Some rich guy turned up dead ten minutes ago. It don't matter.' Hartman lost a little of his jovial glow as he addressed Edwards, impatience stealing the sheen off his smile. Hartman was an old-school Miami PD who'd started his policing in the late '50s when the force was segregated and the crime rate was negligible. Back then night patrol for Miami Beach had consisted of exactly one patrol car.

'PD'll take over once you guys have done your *thang*,' Hartman said, testing Edwards the way he always did, throwing some condescending jive his way, letting him know his place. 'As you're drivin' around, tell the guy war stories, entertain him, give him stuff he can use – shake down some hookers and dealers, if you like.'

'We gotta spend *all day* with this guy?' Rodgers groaned. Hartman nodded. 'Want us to take him home with us too?' Rodgers joked.

'Cute.' Hartman smirked. 'When your shift's over, bring him back up here. Think you can handle that?'

Rodgers grunted his assent.

'Remember, this is about makin' a good impression. So don't get him killed. And Rodgers, ain't you got a better suit of clothes you can wear? You look like you woke up in what you're stood in.'

'I didn't know we'd be on show today – or else I woulda come here in my dress blues,' Rodgers retorted. 'White gloves and decorations. The whole nine yards.'

Rodgers was wearing black jeans, a black T-shirt, his houndstooth jacket and black-and-white suede Nike Cortez sneakers. He hadn't shaved. Edwards was smartly turned out as ever, navy blue suit and open-necked white shirt and polished black leather shoes.

'Edwards, can you wait outside, please?' Major Hartman said.

'Yes, *sah,*' Edwards whispered, his pointed sarcasm bypassing Hartman's radar completely.

Hartman waited several seconds after Edwards had left before speaking, which he did in a quieter tone, leaning slightly forward over his desk.

'Just so's you know, Al, I'm puttin' up some of my own money into this thing against a share of the profits. I consider it a good investment. The series comes off right, the country'll get a picture postcard of Miami beamed into its living room once a week. No better ad for this city than a popular TV show. It'll boost tourism and bring in the money. God knows this place could use some clean cash.'

America was in the middle of a crippling recession, but you wouldn't have known it in Miami. Business was booming in every direction – real estate, construction and retail – thanks to the millions the cocaine traffickers were pouring into the city.

'That's *if* it works out,' Rodgers said.

'Of course.' Hartman nodded. 'But this guy knows what he's doing. He's worked for David Jacobs. And David Jacobs is the guy who put *Dallas* on the map.'

' "Who shot JR Ewing?" ' Rodgers remembered with a rueful smile. 'Two of the quietest nights in the history of Miami law enforcement.' On 21 March the previous year, the streets, bars and clubs had nearly emptied for the hour that cliffhanger episode of *Dallas* had aired – a phenomenon repeated in nearly all major American cities. And they'd been deserted all over again on 21 November when the shooter's identity had been revealed. Rodgers hadn't watched either episode, but he'd had the lowdown from virtually everyone he knew, as well as a constant barrage of newspaper headlines, magazine covers and TV reports wherever he went.

'You can't argue with the power of television.' Hartman grinned. 'This series comes off it'll be great for the city and great for us.'

Good for *you*, you mean, Rodgers thought, but didn't let it show in his face, giving Hartman a mild nod of approval.

'Sure,' he said. 'What's this guy's name?'

'Roman Rich.' The film producer stood up and introduced himself with a hand extended in Edwards' direction. He'd been waiting for them downstairs in reception, black notebook in hand.

Rich was in his mid to late thirties and stood slightly over six feet tall, but his was a strictly blow-away-in-the-breeze build, as if his skeleton had been put together with matchsticks. He was the sort of guy who coordinated his colours. His sharply creased beige chinos matched his pastel yellow complexion; his maroon Lacoste polo shirt whose sleeves billowed around his long, thin arms went with his polished leather loafers and the frames of the large square-framed glasses he wore, both exactly the same shade of maroon. His small brown eyes were magnified by the thick lenses so that they appeared to hover over and in front of his head like a pair of greasy bees, seemingly disengaged from the rest his face, which was as thin and pointy as a rodent drawn by a bored architect with ruler and pencil. Rich's straight hair was the same shade as his eyes. It was cut short at the back and left semi-long at the front, so it fell over his forehead in bangs, which he'd parted in the middle. He wore a gold Rolex on his left wrist and a thick gold chain around his neck, which reminded Rodgers of the kind of very expensive collar rich, misanthropic old women bought for the ugly dogs they named after dead husbands.

'You must be Detective Sergeant Al Rodgers,' Rich said to Edwards, in a voice that couldn't have fitted his physique better – thin, reedy and slightly nasal.

Edwards gave Rodgers a slight look that Rodgers acknowledged with a meagre nod, giving his partner the go-ahead to bullshit. It was an easy enough mistake to make and one people made regularly – Edwards looked more authoritative than Rodgers – but Rodgers had already taken a dislike to Rich before meeting him, simply because they were having to waste their time sucking up to him on Hartman's say-so. This meant that nothing the jerk could say or do short of pissing off out of their lives that instant would ever be right.

'I must be,' Edwards replied with a smile.

'Pleased to meet you!' Rich smiled broadly for a few seconds longer than seemed natural or normal, as if his lips had got stuck to the top of his gums – which, Rodgers noticed, went very well with his shirt, glasses and loafers. His teeth were as white and straight as the best American dentistry could make them, but when he smiled Rich reminded Rodgers of stuffed and mounted roadkill.

Rich looked at Rodgers.

'And you must be Detective Larry Edwards?'

'Right again,' Rodgers deadpanned.

'So, er, how's this gonna work?' he asked Edwards.

'What we're gonna do is drive you around some. Show you a few sights and – if we're lucky – we might get to do some business,' Edwards said jovially.

'Business?'

'Yeah, you know, cop business. Arrest us some bad guys.'

'Sounds good.'

'Good is what it is – after you.' Edwards motioned Rich to the glass front door and they followed him out. Edwards made a jerk-off sign behind the producer's back and Rodgers nodded and smirked.

They took MacArthur Causeway to Miami Beach. It was a nice day out, the bright morning sun boosting the shimmering blue of the ocean against the ashen concrete of the bridge.

Edwards drove. Rich sat in the back, grinning like a kid who's been allowed to stay up late. Edwards told Rich war stories about hundred-mile-an-hour car chases across MacArthur and how the bridge was a popular spot for jumpers. Rich was writing everything down in his black notebook with a gold pen. When the details were to his liking he'd gasp an excited 'Wow-yeah!' – which came out as 'Wah-hair!' – or a curt 'Neat!' – or, if they got particularly juicy (anything with coke and multiple homicides), he'd make a long low sound somewhere between a choked gurgle and a pleased moan, as if he were getting the blowjob of his life and being throttled at the same time.

Rodgers said nothing whatsoever, left it all to Edwards, glad he didn't have to entertain this arsehole.

They had the radio on. Edwards would stop in mid-tale whenever the dispatcher came on.

'What's QSM mean?' referring to the way the dispatcher started every call out.

Quit Shooting Your Mouth, Rodgers thought to say, but kept his peace.

'It's a code requesting a response from an available unit. So, what she just said – "QSM a unit to respond to 714 Northwest Eighteenth Street in reference to male stabbed" – means any cars in the vicinity go to this place. Then the car in the area will answer QSL, then give their car number and say they're on their way.'

'Neat!' Rich said as he scribbled, his pen making the sounds of rat paws scuttling back and forth across a ceiling.

They went down to South Beach, which Edwards told Rich was called God's Waiting Room, on account of the majority of the population being over sixty or the kind of lowlifes who wouldn't make it past thirty.

'God's Waiting Room – wah-hair!'

Ocean Drive and Collins Avenue fascinated Rich, as Edwards pointed out spots where epic gun battles had taken place or mutilated bodies had been found in parked cars. His pen scratched furiously, like a dog with stubborn tics, and his fellated hanged man noises got louder and more intense, embarrassing the two cops.

Edwards stopped right in front of the building where Rodgers lived and gave Rich a long talk about how the once glorious and fashionable art deco hotels had all turned into near-slums from the new Cuban intake, or doubled up as brothels, shooting galleries and squats. Rodgers mouthed 'fuck you' to Edwards, who merely winked at him. Rodgers had never seen Edwards happier on the job.

They rolled down James Avenue, past the derelict and boarded-up Albion Hotel and into a strip of poverty, where failed cafés, cheap motels, used-tyre stores and scrap-metal lots dominated either side of the street. They turned off at 18th Street and went down Washington Avenue, passing bars and clubs, Edwards reeling out more stories about shoot-outs between rival posses of cocaine cowboys that had happened right in the middle of the dance floors, with the cops caught in between.

'What kind of guns do you guys carry?' Rich asked.

'Mine's a .45 Colt M1911 automatic,' Edwards said.

'That work out for you OK?'

'Sure,' Edwards said. 'I'd be happiest with a revolver, though – a .357 Magnum or even a .38 Special – 'cause they don't jam and they're next to always reliable – autos jam and stovepipe like crazy. But this is the Wild West out here and you need to get off fast rounds. We carry a couple of Ithaca pumps in the back, plus two M16s in case things get real heavy.'

'Have they?'

'This is Miami, man,' Edwards said. 'There's always a war on somewhere.'

Rich let out a long and very satisfied moan at that and they heard him squirm in his seat before he grated some more in his book.

'What about you, Detective Edwards?' Rich asked Rodgers. 'What do you carry?'

'9 Mil Sig Sauer P220,' Rodgers mumbled.

'A *what*?'

Rodgers repeated himself and spelled the name.

'They ain't that common here yet,' he added. 'They're Swiss-made. Double action, no safety, so once you pull it you're good to go. It's low recoil, very accurate and reliable. I regularly put ninety per cent of a clip dead on centre of a target.'

'Where d'you get it?'

'Company sent some over for us to try out,' Rodgers lied. He'd kept two of the pistols on a raid of a Finnish arms dealer's warehouse in 1978. The guns were brand new and still in their boxes. He kept the other one at home.

'Can I see it?'

'Askin' a cop if you can see his gun is like askin' a man to show you his dick,' Rodgers said.

'Come on, Edwards, be a sport.' Edwards grinned. 'I *do* hold rank here.'

'I'll show him mine if you show him yours, *Sarge*,' Rodgers said.

'Deal.'

Rodgers took out the Sig and ejected the clip. He passed it to Rich, who took the gun – which weighed slightly under a kilo – in the palm of his hand, admiring it.

'*Real* neat!' he said, and wrote down some more notes.

'So what's this show of yours about?' Rodgers asked when Rich handed him his piece back.

'It's not a show as such yet. It's a pilot.'

'Pilot?' Rodgers asked.

'Yeah, a pilot's like a feature-length episode that gets made ahead of a projected series. Sort of a trailer for the series. Introduces the characters, what they do, who they are, where they're at. It gets aired, and if it does OK, a series gets commissioned.'

'Like a TV movie, then?'

'Kind of, yeah, if you see it that way,' Rich said in a slightly condescending tone, which Rodgers picked up on.

'This pilot got a name?' Edwards asked, passing Rodgers his black Colt.

'Yeah – Cap'n Crunch!' Rodgers joked.

Edwards guffawed, more to let out a few hundred cubic metres of trapped laughter than because of Rodgers' witticism.

Rich didn't laugh at all.

'I was thinking of *Miami Homicide*,' he said, coldly.

'That's real positive,' Rodgers said, ejecting the clip and the spare round in the Colt's chamber before passing it back to Rich.

'Miami *is* Murder Capital USA, right now,' Rich remarked. 'But this series isn't *just* going to be about crime. I want to make it into a – a – a *poem* to Miami. I want to capture the city's beauty – not just the cupcakes in bikinis either, but its cultural diversity, its – its – its ethnicky beat.'

'"Ethnicky beat"?' Rodgers turned around and looked at him. 'The fuck is *that*?'

'He means gunfire.' Edwards laughed.

Rich didn't reply. He was transfixed by Edwards' gun.

'*Wah-hair! Pearl* handles! This is a *real* black man's gun!' Rich said excitedly. Rodgers turned around and saw the film producer virtually drooling over Edwards' black automatic and its mother-of-pearl grips, feeling its heft and damn well caressing the thing with the tip of his index finger, all the while filling the car with his curdled moan, lost in his own space. Edwards watched Rich in his rear-view mirror, his brow creasing with incredulity and hilarity.

'If you're gonna stereotype, you might as well get it right,' Edwards

said through his laugh. 'Niggers and spics love their guns shiny –
chrome, nickel and silver-plated. You get that down in you book now.
Word for word.'

Rich said nothing, didn't seem to hear, so transfixed was he with
Edwards' gun and whatever fantasies it was transporting him into.

They got on to Dade Boulevard and made for the Venetian
Causeway, heading back towards downtown Miami.

The dead guy on the boat had been a disco fan – and a big one. He'd
called his forty-foot-long yacht *Studio 54* and the vast downstairs
lounge area they found him in was a like a personal nightclub. There
was a mirrorball hanging from the ceiling, banks of coloured lights
in the corners, close to the speakers, a small DJ booth at the far end,
complete with two turntables and microphone.

Taking pride of place over a faux fireplace next to a fully stocked
bar was a picture of the person they took to be the victim and John
Travolta, with their arms around each other's shoulders. They were
almost indistinguishable – both with those chiselled features,
dimpled chins, bouffant black hair and sparkling blue eyes. Rodgers
wondered whether the dead guy hadn't had surgery to look more like
Travolta.

The corpse was face down in the middle of the room, his left hand
wrapped tight around a woman's turquoise shoe with a stiletto heel.
He was barefoot, but wearing white duck pants and a blue-and-white
striped shirt. There was an open bottle of champagne and a half-
empty glass on a coffee table, next to some lines of coke and a gold
straw on a chain, which spelled confirmed user. There was an open
billfold next to the drugs. Rodgers checked it. No cash or cards save a
Tucson driver's licence and gun permit.

'Don Tubbs.' Rodgers read out the name.

Edwards told Rich to hang back, out of the way, so as to not disturb
the scene. Admiring the surgical gloves Edwards had given him to
wear, Rich went off and stood close to the stairs leading below deck.

Rodgers crouched down over the body and rolled his jacket sleeves up to the elbow.

'What do you think?' Edwards asked.

Rodgers felt the corpse's right hand and tried to move its arm. The flesh was stiff and cold, the joints frozen in place.

'Dead twelve. Rigor mortis.'

The body had the slight smell of death about it.

He raised the shirt up and pointed to the dark red tinge of the skin.

'PM lividity here,' Rodgers pointed out.

'What's that?' Rich asked.

'Means he went to disco heaven last night,' Rodgers said impatiently. He wanted to get this shit over and done with.

Edwards explained that the colour came about because the heart was no longer beating and mixing the blood up, so the heavier red blood cells sank through the serum and settled.

Rich scribbled all of this down, emitting a constant low groan-moan as he wrote.

Rodgers felt Tubbs's head for wounds then turned him over. There was a smashed champagne flute under the body. He checked the neck for signs of bruising consistent with strangulation, and prised open his closed eye sockets to check the eyeballs for burst capillaries. Edwards gave a running commentary on what he was doing and why for Rich's benefit.

Rodgers spotted a white crust of cocaine residue at the edge of the corpse's nostrils.

'Who called it in?' he asked Edwards.

'Cleaner, came in this morning, found the body,' Edwards said. He'd talked to the two uniformed cops who'd been waiting for them on the jetty.

Rodgers looked at the body.

'No sign of external trauma. I think what happened was he was partying with some girl – probably a hooker – did some coke, had a heart attack. Bye-bye. Girl takes off. Doesn't want to hang around for questions because she's probably got a record,' Rodgers said.

Rich moaned more loudly, wrote furiously.

Rodgers carefully turned the body over back on its front.

'Guess that about wraps it up in here,' Edwards said.

'You haven't finished here, guys,' Rich piped up. 'You gotta go check below deck too. In fact, one of you should've checked the whole boat out while the other one looked at the body.'

Rodgers and Edwards exchanged a 'what the *fuck*?' look. Rich was, of course, right, but Rodgers wasn't going to take that kind of shit from him.

'You tellin' us how to do our jobs?' he said angrily.

'You don't seem to be following procedure is all I'm saying. I'd hate you guys to get into trouble.'

'Man's right,' Edwards said, making a calm-down gesture to Rodgers, as if he were patting the back of a large fearsome dog. But Rodgers wasn't having it.

'You wanna look below deck?' he said to Rich, just about holding his anger in. 'You go down and check it out and come back here and make a full report.'

'*Really*?' Rich gasped excitedly, looking at the two of them.

'Our gift to you,' Rodgers said sarcastically. 'You can do some real police work, help with your show.'

'Sure, OK. *Neeet*!' Rich said keenly.

He started to go down the stairs.

When he was out of sight, Rodgers bared his teeth and flipped him the finger. Edwards guffawed.

Then, suddenly, from downstairs, they heard a piercing –

'*JEEEEZUSSSS* CHRIST!'

– and saw Rich scrambling back up the stairs, glasses askew, panic stricken.

'What's wrong?' Edwards asked

Then he saw.

'FUCK ME!' Edwards yelled.

Then Rodgers saw.

He couldn't quite believe it.

A gator!

A nine-to-ten-foot-long set of deadly, grinning jaws on tiny legs, encased in solid brownish-green hide, sprinting up the stairs after Rich.

Rich ran behind Edwards. Edwards reached for his gun, but he was too late.

The gator sprang up at him, jaws open.

Rodgers pulled out his ankle piece and shot the animal four times in the centre of its body.

The gator flipped and landed on its side with an almighty crash, which shook the whole boat, toppling speakers and lights and bringing down the mirrorball, which shattered into a hundred shiny pieces.

'Fuck me!' Edwards repeated.

'Where the *fuck* did that come from?' Rodgers asked Rich, who just pointed at the stairs.

'How many more down there?'

'I just saw that one.'

Two uniformed cops, who'd been standing outside the boat, rushed in, guns drawn.

'Call your people in,' Rodgers told them. 'Plus gator handlers.' Then he turned to Rich. 'Show's over. We're outta here.'

'*Wah-hair*! That was just so *awesome*! The way you shot that gator, man! That move you made – that ankle piece! That was so damn *neat*! Neat! Neat!! *Neat*!!!' Rich squealed when they were leaving the Marina. He was scribbling away like crazy. 'God, this material is just sooooo *neat*! How come you didn't tell me about your ankle gun?'

Rodgers didn't answer. He was doing the driving now and Rich was *really* pissing him off. He decided not to talk to the jerk at all for the rest of the day, so he could at least avoid telling him what he really thought of him. He wished that ten-foot luggage set had taken a bite out of the fuck. That would have solved having to spend the rest of the day with him.

'Man gotta have some secrets,' Edwards said before the silence became too awkward. Edwards was pretty shook up by what had happened. He'd turned a shade of grey.

'What kind of gun was that?'

'Detonics Combat Master,' Edwards answered, still in tourist-guide mode. 'It's like a cut-down version of my Colt. Same bang to it.'

'*Oh*! *Neeeet*!' Rich gushed. 'Can I see it?'

'You already did,' Rodgers said. Jesus – not even a thank you for saving his arsehole life.

They toured Liberty City's desolate streets, Edwards explaining the history of the ghetto and telling war stories. He tried to put the crime into context, to explain how the city's other ghetto – Overtown – had once been an affluent place, a kind of Dixie Harlem, before city officials had decided to build I-95 right through the middle of it, as good as driving a stake into the heart of the place. Business had collapsed and people had moved to the Liberty Square projects – the first of their kind in Miami. Rich wasn't interested. He kept on prompting Edwards for more black-on-black crime stats, more horror. He wanted to hear about the recent riots during which a black mob had dragged a white driver from his car and killed him. Edwards grudgingly complied and the producer scratched away at his pad, moaning very pleasurably.

'You got any actors in mind for your show?' Edwards asked, changing the subject.

'A few for the leads, yeah,' Rich replied. 'I don't know whether to make one of the cops white and one black, or have a white guy and a Latino – maybe get a black Latino, cover both demographics. And we're talking to Pam Grier about a part.'

Rodgers couldn't help himself.

'You know Pam Grier?' he asked.

'Met her a couple of times, yeah.' Rich nodded.

'What was she like?'

'To be honest, I couldn't get past her tits.'

Rodgers smiled.

'Do you like Pam Grier?' Rich asked him.

Like her? Rodgers thought. I fucken *love* her. That passion had started way back in 1972 when he'd gone to see *Hit Man* at the drive-in with a girlfriend. He'd seen that movie all five nights it had played, just for her. He'd felt like a pervert, but what the hell? He'd seen pretty much every film she'd made in the '70s.

'I seen a couple of her films on TV, yeah. She's OK, I guess.'

'Have you seen *Fort Apache, The Bronx*? Paul Newman flick just opened. She's in that.'

'What as?'

'A prostitute.'

'*Yeah* ...?' Rodgers said, thinking he could take his fiancée then deciding maybe it'd be best if he went alone.

'She's a psycho junkie, too. Kills her clients. And she keeps her clothes on – for once.'

'Oh...' Rodgers said. Maybe he'd skip that one.

Rodgers took North West 71st Avenue.

'And I'm thinking of getting some famous musicians to play cameo roles,' Rich continued.

'Like who?' Rodgers asked.

'Talking to Frank Zappa. You know his stuff?'

'No.'

'And I'm also considering Willie Nelson, Jerry Garcia, Johnny Cash, Miles Davis...'

'Miles, huh?' Rodgers smiled. Maybe this guy wasn't such an arsehole after all. He loved Miles Davis.

'Yeah, maybe.' Rich looked out of the window and locked eyes with a guy standing with a group on the sidewalk, talking and smoking. The guy mouthed something in his direction. Rich waved. The guy flicked him the bird. Rich did the same back.

'You met him?'

'Not personally, but my people are talking to his people.'

'What kind of role would you have him play?' Rodgers asked.

'Thinking of him as a real cool pimp.'

Rodgers suddenly hit the brakes. Rich flew forward, hit the back of the front seats and bounced back, glasses askew.

'A *PIMP*!' Rodgers turned around and roared. 'The finest fucken musician this country has ever produced and the *best* thing you can fucken think of is gettin' him to play a *PIMP* on your bullshit cop show!'

'B–bu–but—' Rich stammered, scrabbling for his pen and notebook.

'Al—' Edwards said.

'Keep out of it!' Rodgers snapped at him.

'*Kind of Blue! Sketches of Spain! In A Silent Way! Bitches Brew! Porgy and fucken BESS!* … All that groundbreakin' fucken music he made and you want him to play a fucken' *PIMP* on *PRIMETIME TV*! Who the *FUCK* do you think you are?'

'But – but—' A confused look crossed Rich's face. 'Wait a minute,' he said to Edwards. 'Didn't you just call him *Al*? I thought you—'

'Get the fuck outta my car!' Rodgers yelled at Rich. 'NOW!'

'Wh–what – *here*?' Rich looked out of the back window at the group of men, all of whom were looking at the car.

'Yeah, *HERE*, you cocksucker! You wanted to "capture the ethnicky beat of the streets"? You can start right here – with an ethnicky *beat down*! Now fuck off!'

'Listen, please – I – I – it isn't safe here.'

'*FUCK! OFF!!*' Rodgers yelled.

Rich scrambled out of the car.

Rodgers floored the pedal and sped off.

'Al...?' Edwards said.

'*WHADDAYAWANT*?'

'Miles *was* a pimp,' Edwards said quietly. 'That's what you tole me.'

'I knew *THAT*!' Rodgers shouted, seething.

'So – why the fuck d'you kick him out for?'

'That little prick was pissin' me off! Had enough of that cocksucker!'

Edwards laughed loudly and shook his head.

'The guy *was* an arsehole,' Edwards said. 'But... Hartman's gonna be pissed.'

'Fuck Hartman! I'll take responsibility.'

They drove on in silence for a few minutes.

'What did that arsehole say his series was called again?' Rodgers asked.

'*Miami Homicide*,' Edwards said. 'And it ain't a series, it's a *pilot*.'

'Yeah? Well, it won't fly.'

The Queen Is Dead

Jeff Noon

Here lies Old Blighty, devoured by feedback. The song spins off from the incident in 1982 when an intruder broke into the Queen's bedroom for a bit of a chat. At the same time the lyrics admit to the difficulty of finding a real love. I pictured a punk romance in which England struggles to dream. Advice to young royals of any stripe: beware not the enemy without, but those who love you the most.

Several young punks were strolling along, talking of the night to come. To look at them you would think they were kings of the town. In truth, they hardly knew their next step, while acting as though they knew every step and swearing life was theirs and theirs alone. Presently, they stopped beneath a neon sign to light up a round of cigarettes and one of them said to another, 'William, I can't help but brood over the fact that one day you'll have a great desire to leave this behind, friends and all.' Now William of course denied this, he swore his loyalty both to the gang and to Johnny Boy especially, Johnny being the speaker and the leader thereof.

The two men stared at each other.

And then Johnny smiled at William and at his underlings one by one, as smoke fluttered in the red-and-yellow halo above their heads, above their sculpted hair. He said, 'I'm just warning you, that's all. Do you hear me?' William did. And with that, they set off once more on their adventures, if such they might be called.

The gang. Johnny, aforementioned. William, the same. And then Brick, and Danny, and Doug. In age they ranged from almost nineteen to just gone twenty-four. William was the youngest of them, the most handsome, but the weakest, and despite what he had just claimed, the least loyal. Certainly, he had a need to be among the others that these others would hardly understand, and yet Johnny spoke the truth in part, that another force entirely tempted William away, out of orbit. It was a subject not to be mentioned.

All this took place on a Tuesday night in the winter of 1979. The promenade was more or less deserted of life, with only a few tramps huddled in a bus shelter, and a dog or two, shivering. The sea was bitter, grey-washed at the wave-edge, black otherwise. No moon. The small drab town was sleeping. The gang walked on until they reached the pier with its lacklustre parade of light. Only the penny arcade was open during the cold months. Here they stood, Johnny combing back his hair to its correct tangle of spikes. Resplendent in his brand-new second-hand suede jacket, he said, 'God would wear this, if he could find one.' Indeed, the others longed for one of similar cut and colour. William's eyes sparkled.

On the afternoon previous to the night in question, he'd been sitting around cutting up his father's *Daily Mail*, making haphazard poetry out of the fragments. He was that kind of person, filled with such desires, such crazy dreams, but with no real clue as to how to bring them alive. He had a plan that maybe he would move to London one day, dressed up like a character in a play. He could see himself clearly, wearing a pork-pie hat and a black raincoat and a thin, perfectly ironed tie held in place by a pin of gold. Thus wise, he would recreate himself. Oh, you'd swear then that he could go along easy, dodging around the dog shit of life, no problem. Instead, he stayed put, signing

on the dole, scribbling his verses, singing melodies. Once or twice he
wrote something that he could call halfway decent; most times he went
down to the sea alone and tore up the papers, letting go the words, so
many windblown tatters. Only the gang gave him any fixed purpose.
He'd said exactly this to Johnny once, receiving in answer: 'Don't get
all sloppy on me, boy. Or else I'll slice you, good and proper.' That was
as much as they got from each other. It passed for love.

Being now suitably natty and spruced, the five young men entered
the arcade. They were the only punks in town, and proud with it. Proud
of the bruises, the scars, the bitter remarks flung their way, proud even
of the glimpse of a knife brandished by way of warning. England was
theirs, if only they could find it among the dirt, the puddles, the dust,
the damp and the rain, the cracked windows, the grey skies, the litter
and the boarded-up shops. And so they passed along between the
machines, uncaring of the staring. They lived and breathed and played
that evening amid artificial songs of bleep and spark and one by one lost
their way in the games, being zapped or losing energy, or running out
of cash. Until only Doug was left. He was the fairest of them all when
it came to shoot-'em-ups. A small crowd gathered around the Zombie
Squad box as streaks of light flew across the screen and rectangular
flesh exploded into smaller rectangles. He was a surly wreck of a boy
most times, was Douglas, his face a broken mask, but at moments like
these his skin was painted hot by life and the blood jolted through his
veins, electrified. His eyes were more than halfway closed, and yet his
hands moved with unguided confidence on the buttons.

Zap! Zap! Zap!

His friends watched from the sidelines, gathered together, and
Johnny leaned in close to William's ear, whispering, 'I'd like to take a
knife to the milk-white body of the sleeping world, slit its little throat
wide open.' William would swear he had never been happier than at
that moment. But then Johnny led him out on to the pier itself and
they watched the sea broiling against the pillars below. Salt crusted
the handrail where their hands almost touched. William could hardly
speak. Johnny said, 'We can talk about things both curious and divine,

if so you wish.' His eyes held his friend's nervous gaze within them. 'Or we can kiss.'

The wind blew ragged flecks of the sea against their faces as their lips met.

Tingle at the brief contact, then full.

Warmth. Softness.

Ghostly shimmers of the blue and still midnight air, flashes of light from the arcade doorway.

This moment. A chance to write a sonnet made of flesh, of speed and cigarette smoke, of blood and sex, of love, of death, a chance to write your own name and that of your lover, the two names entangled in street code, unreadable but to those in the know, to scrawl it seven feet tall on the side of a building, a real production number, multicoloured.

Johnny Boy. William.

The night wore on. Brick and Doug had chanced upon two local girls and the whole throng of them went round to Brick's house, empty at this time on account of his mum and dad being half cut in a gutter somewhere, clinging on to each other for fear of falling off the world completely. The boys raided the drinks cabinet and started to bang out Bowie on a cheap acoustic. The girls joined in on perfume and harmonies. Brick was strumming with careful fingers the six dull, yellowing, rusted strings. Johnny sat alone meanwhile, ruffling through his hair, worrying at the slight recede, even at such a tender age. A mere human being, after all.

Around Brick's bed hung a string of little coloured lights. The two girls looked beautiful in the soft glow. One was Abigail, the other Denise. Abigail in particular was a thing to gaze upon, a new girl in town. Short black hair, black eyes shaded by mystery. The brief smile, her face turning towards William. He had to look away. Meanwhile, Danny was wiping down the grooves of the first Velvet Underground album with a sponge and a spray of mist from a can. He was seeking to hold back the pop and crackle.

William glanced across at Johnny.

It was all he could manage to keep his eyes dry, shocked out on bliss as he was at the sheer beauty of the scene before him, and then he took hold of the guitar himself and he started up a new song, there was no choice but to sing and his voice the sweetest of them all, the most precise, the most golden, and the songs melted into each other as the sweet smell of dope circled the room, until the players were making up the lyrics as they went along, happy enough to let the music dissolve to their being.

By the time they walked out again, the air was drifting in from the sea colder and blacker still, caressed by clouds. Danny announced to all and sundry who cared to listen: 'Life is a bad and lonely drug. One that gives just enough pleasure, but not enough to really get you high.' But young William was too far gone to care about such talk. He was dwelling on the memories of a kiss. He was wondering how far it would go with Johnny, and whether the others would care to know, whether they would react with violence, or with friendship. There was no way of knowing for sure.

They dropped in for a pint at the Boar Between Arches. Here they sat, making light of their situation, celebrating the conditions of being here, in this time, in this place. But William was feeling out on a limb. He got Johnny in a corner over by the cigarette machine and he pulled up close to him, saying, 'I'm getting the sense of being all hemmed in, Johnny. It's like I wanna feel all the shame of the world, and pass it on to you, and you alone.' Johnny said nothing. William glanced over at the table where his friends sat. He went on: 'What I'm saying is, we don't need the others so much. It's changing, see. Can't you feel that? We can make our own way forward.' Johnny smiled back in reply and said, 'You think that can happen, really?' William said it could. Johnny said, 'It can't happen. Not yet.'

William clung to those two last words desperately, but it was hardly enough to lull his troubles asleep.

He needed release.

He needed to wrench the rusty spanner around his screwed-down life. Only then would he sing, really let his voice go wild, only then, letting slip the Cheap Lager Blues, as he called them, the Queen of Dirt and Forgiveness Blues, the Blues of Lost Love, the Bone-White Lonesome Moon Piano Blues, as he called them. The One-Way Bus Ticket Blues, the Late-Night Going Nowhere Blues, the Black Tie Blues, the My Daddy's Done Up and Gone and Got Himself a New Woman Blues. As he called them. He got to thinking of all the towns and cities of England as a string of broken pearls that he would never get to breathe upon, never get to see glisten in his palm.

So long, my Liverpool, with your music of sadness and dreams, your various escapades. So long, my Birmingham with your sleepy eyes forever closed in the midst of prayer. Farewell to Leeds and Manchester, curtained by the rain falling in silver lines and sparkles.

And farewell most of all to old London Town, where the ghost of a man that William could one day have become still wanders, a shadow cast on a wall and forgotten.

All of these places alive in his heart, but never yet witnessed for real, ungraspable.

The group left the pub behind them and walked along the coast road towards the Palace Ballroom. They slipped down the side, to the back of the building. The place was quiet, dark, long closed up since the summer's glitter and shine. Now they stood in the alleyway, contemplating a window some few feet above their heads. There was a slight gap visible, between frame and ledge. The two girls urged the young men to action, so Douglas bent down and made a cradle of his hands, into which William stepped, to feel himself being lifted aloft. From this vantage he worked the window open fully, and crawled through into the gentlemen's loo. The others followed, making their way towards the ballroom. Here the floor was dust-covered, scuffed and marked by countless heels, by the twists and turns of dancers' shoes over the years gone by, making these ghost tracks.

Brick found the box of light switches and he brought the room up just enough to add a reddish tinge to people's faces. At this cue, Danny set off waltzing across the parquet, moving his legs in a most peculiar manner and nodding his head to the music that only he could hear.

William looked nervous in the shadows.

His eyes darted hither and back. He could not see Johnny anywhere, so he set off walking, climbing the stairs to the upper gallery. There he found his target, but not alone. Abigail pressed herself forward, and her lips met Johnny's in the dim light.

A hand folded itself around William's heart as he watched this.

The hand tightened.

Some ten minutes later he was rushing along the beach path, hardly knowing which circuit to follow. His mind reeled and he felt himself alone, some distant relative to the sliver of moon now visible, hanging low over a church made of purple clouds. And there amid the stench of seaweed, he thought about certain precious subjects: about reading Melville's *Billy Budd, Midshipman* and finding himself in the pages; about taking a long shot, kicking the tin bucket over, cranking out the music loud; about snatching at love like stealing a penny, or is that stealing love like snatching at a penny? Best of all: the trick Johnny had taught him, about putting some grease in your hair, and then talcum powder. Spiking it high against the rain. And he thought about that time he had read aloud from *Johnny Panic and the Bible of Dreams,* and Johnny saying, 'That's me. That is me! Johnny Panic!'

For sure: precious things.

Johnny's mouth, for instance. That one sweet time when they had kissed, that one time alone; liking the taste of it. Thinking about how that taste might change, according to his mood. And now never to be known. William was pouring salt on the wound of his own heart, because it was all that he could do. Terrible images flickered in his mind.

His two hands tearing a bridal veil to shreds.

Stopping at the archway that led beneath the promenade, he cried out his despair in a wordless voice. Then he turned, hearing an echo, or more than an echo, an answer of some kind. There was but a faint light in the tunnel, the shadows heavy with the smell of damp and rust and human sweat. Here the Anytime Anywhere Boys hung out, boasting of their prowess, their lucid desires, and their eyes filled with lust when they spotted William. One of them began to recite in a gentle but mocking tone.

Sweet Cupid drew back his bow
To let fly his poisoned dart,
Which did wend its wicked way
Straight forth into my heart.

The lads moved towards William. He let them come.

Whatever happened from now on, it seemed cut off from what he was or wanted to be. He was putting the sleepers on himself, a stone soul loser serenaded by the quarter-dead screech of a broken guitar.

The blows came in.

A seabird flew low over the beach, gliding along the silence it made for itself in the cold dark air.

William looked up from the concrete floor.

He saw graffiti on the wall, a boy's name and a scrawled heart, and then a girl's name beneath. Here was love. Here was love encoded by a low-down but boisterous specimen, laughing her dear old Blighty soul out that one day this beau, this boy known only as Brian in red felt tip, might be hers.

Here was love, Sweet Cupid...

William wiped the blood away. His fingers ached, his wrist also, and one or two ribs. He opened his eyes to see that he was alone once more, voices echoing down the tunnel like car alarms howling to each other from a distance.

He got to his feet and walked on, dragging himself.

Then Johnny appeared above, hanging over the railing. He called down, quoting one of William's fragment poems back at him:

'O silken sleep! Come to me with your powders now and lull me into darkness, faraway and gone.'

William could not respond, until he felt Johnny's arms around him, and then, 'Put me on the music machine,' he whispered. 'Give me the noises of the town.' Johnny dried William's mouth and tested his limbs, deeming him in fit shape, if only just, and they went out together, the two of them alone, farther along the promenade, away from the lights. Johnny said, 'You can only fall so far, William, before I miss my catch. Do you follow?' William did. He nodded so. Yes. They walked down to the sea's edge. Here the moon was clearly seen, or what little of it the Earth's shadow allowed into view, ghostlike.

The clouds hung as mist over the world.

They found Johnny's body three days later, washed up in a dirty salt-river basin, his cold rotten hands clinging to an old discarded boat spar as though to climb free even now, free of the icy clutch, the claws of the sea, the terrible drag of the moon.

The funeral followed. What could William do? He thought of turning the key of his tongue deftly if he only could, opening the mouth to let the words out, the most perfect words. *Hush now, hush!* Check the casket. Closed lid. There he sleeps, well hidden. Johnny Panic, the one and only. The smell of wax and incense, perfume to hide decay. A soul flickering in the candle flame. In truth, here lies a man who never really broke the seal of himself, holding all inside.

But what could William do, really? He was waiting for the last amen to finish the hymn.

It never came.

After the ceremony, Brick, Danny, Doug and William went down to the riverside, to the place where the body was dragged from the water, and there they stood bowed, whispering, praying to whatever god was on duty that day that Johnny Boy would be taken up pale and weak into the care of strangers with wings. That he would yield to the darkness softly, without voice, without tears.

All good boys and girls come home to a world at the end of time, but this was the day the sour rain fell on the new young queen divine, and William's fingers changed, they changed their shape that evening when he picked up Brick's old battered acoustic. He could feel his hands seeking new patterns on the strings, finding new harmonies, new ways of moving from each to each, from chord to chord along the neck and back again, minor key, then major, then falling away once more, soft and sad, drifting like dust to a song's fade-out.

A week later, William walked alone towards the station.

He felt he was the fallen descendant of some slut of a bedraggled princess, hooked on living through pain. His head was all gnarled up and tender. But he was done with crying. Rather, he was the one true embalmer of Johnny's blood, Johnny's fingerprints on skin, Johnny's breath. Johnny's words: 'You can't play guitar as though you're sitting in some woodland fucking bower. You have to plug yourself in, baby, hit the switch, feel yourself like stripped wire singing and trembling for darkness, cutting the sky six ways crazy. You need to be scraped against the limits, skin raw and open. That's it.'

Indeed, that was it.

William climbed aboard the train, London bound, dallying on a new title for his life to come: *Billy Budd, Rock-and-Roll Star*. He began to sing under his breath, in perfect time to the train's motion.

The pub can go fuck itself. Work can go fuck itself. Love. Love can go fuck itself. Tenderness also. Go fuck yourself. Hatred, go fuck yourself. Bosses. Lessons. Men and women and all that praises one and not the other. Go fuck yourself. Parents, sisters, brothers, go fuck yourself. Machinery, old brown shoes, grey shirts, flared trousers, bus stops in the fog, go fuck yourself. Broken windows, unbroken windows, go fuck yourself. Friends, lovers and enemies, go fuck yourself. Tower blocks and bungalows, fast food, slow movies, sports cars, cheap imitation guitars, the moon and the sun and the stars, go fuck yourself.

To sing. To sing on.

His hands tapped out rhythms for himself, for his litany. These two same hands, frozen around the wrists as they might be, holding a body beneath cold accepting waves, as they might be, waiting for the moment to end, the struggle.

Stretch Out and Wait

Chris Killen

Discovering The Smiths when I was seventeen was the same as discovering Richard Brautigan or Knut Hamsun or J. D. Salinger: I just wanted to devour it all. I ran out and scoured the charity shop LP bins. I wanted to somehow play all the albums simultaneously. I hadn't thought bands could be so witty and literate and slightly sarcastic. I think I learned something important about writing, listening to the lyrics; something that went in at the deepest level and took root and shifted my perspective very slightly. If someone sat me down right now and forced me to write a list of my 'influences', I think Morrissey would be somewhere near the top of that list.

Emma arrives twenty minutes late, dressed like someone from 1935. She has a scarf wrapped around half her face, covering her mouth. Craig wishes she wasn't wearing the scarf. He'd like to be able to see whether she's smiling as she walks towards him. Her eyes look like she's smiling. She has a kind face.

There's a strange bird in the sky.

Today is cold and overcast, some time in autumn.

'I really need a piss,' Emma says. 'Sorry, but I do.'

She pulls down her scarf and her mouth isn't smiling and she kisses Craig quickly, just a peck, on the cheek.

'Let's go in,' Craig says. He rubs his hands together and blows on them to demonstrate how cold he's become while waiting. He feels as if he does it too obviously, though. She narrows her eyes at him. He feels awkward. 'They probably have toilets somewhere,' he says.

Craig isn't sure whether they do, whether cemeteries have toilets.

They hold hands automatically and walk down the path. Emma's fingers feel like wet, icy-cold twigs.

The bird lands in a tree. It watches them. Craig thinks about pointing it out but doesn't know quite what to say.

At the bottom of the first path is a church.

'They probably have toilets in there,' he says.

They go round and look at the doors. It's closed up. A sign says the opening times and right now isn't any of the opening times.

'I'm just gonna go behind here,' Emma says, pointing at a bench in a memorial garden for dead babies. 'Keep a lookout.'

Craig turns his back. He listens to her rustle behind the bench and shuffle up her skirt and start to piss. There's a jogger in the distance, he notices, but jogging away from them. Squirrels run up and down the trees. Someone's left half a Swiss roll in a plastic packet next to the church. A lot of the graves look untended and forlorn. Nobody is coming and leaving flowers. Emma taps him on the shoulder and he jumps.

'That was quick.'

'What can I say? I'm startlingly efficient.'

A few months ago, Craig stopped finding things funny. The only thing he ever finds funny now is the overhead melodramatic vision he sometimes gets of himself; a kind of strange conceptual art piece called *My Life Is Not Turning Out How I Imagined.*

(Emma has an American ex-boyfriend who she's probably still in love with.)

'I love you,' Craig says.

It's a test.

She pretends not to hear.

'This way,' she says, grabbing his hand and leading him towards some older, more elaborate graves. 'I think Tony Wilson's buried in this bit somewhere, too.'

They're not here to look at Tony Wilson's grave.

They walk along some more paths made mostly of grey dust and tiny brown leaves. They are not speaking and holding hands limply, as above them a few dark clouds start to shuffle up together in the sky.

'It's that one over there,' says Emma.

She points at a grave obscured by another couple. The couple are dressed like goths. The couple are holding hands. The couple are wearing chunky New Rock boots and lots of eye make-up. The boy is waving a bunch of roses around. The girl is twirling and singing something.

'Let's go for a walk and come back,' Emma says.

So they go back the way they came but somehow end up in a different part of the cemetery, in a kind of clearing between some large tombs, with dried-up trees overhead and home-made wind chimes dangling off one of the branches, rattling unmusically. They stop walking and look at each other.

Emma has a strange face. It's the face she does when she looks at herself in the mirror; a sort of sour pout.

'Give me your hand,' she says.

Craig wants to lie on the floor and roll around and stuff some pine leaves and bits of dirt into his mouth. Then he wants to run away and scream 'FUCK AMERICA' and kick down some of the headstones and disappear into the sky.

He holds out his hand obediently and she puts it on her boob. The boob is soft. Her nipple tries to press itself against his palm.

'There's no one around,' she says.

A squirrel is frozen halfway up one of the trees, watching them nervously with its tail twitching.

'Lie down,' she says. She puts a hand up her skirt, steps out of her knickers, and stuffs them into her bag, all in one practised, economical movement.

Craig lies down obediently.

He feels worried about getting caught.

He feels like a nervous squirrel halfway up a tree.

Emma's knees crack as she climbs over him and fumbles around with his belt buckle. There's something hard sticking into his back. He reaches around and digs it out – a broken piece of plastic, half a plug socket – and throws it over his shoulder. It hits the trunk of the tree and the squirrel runs away.

We don't have normal sex any more, Craig thinks. This isn't normal sex. This is almost not sex at all. My life is not turning out how I imagined.

Craig starts laughing. He can't help it.

'What?' says Emma. She has his belt unbuckled and about two buttons undone on his jeans. He's not helping her out. His penis is flaccid and hiding in his boxer shorts. 'What is it?'

'Nothing,' Craig says. He wants to be in a warm bath by himself. He wants to start smoking again. He wants to look over his shoulder and see a zombie lolloping towards them. This is not the start of a film.

'I give up,' Emma says, standing and taking the knickers back out of her bag. They look like a small white flag or a handkerchief. A small white flag made out of a handkerchief.

'Sorry,' Craig says. 'I wasn't laughing at you. I just thought of something funny.'

'Good for you,' Emma says.

She touches the tree, running her hand up and down it, her back to him.

'Someone should tell those wind chimes to shut the fuck up,' she says.

'I'm sorry,' Craig says. 'I love you.'

He sounds like a greeting card. Maybe everything he says from now on should be a rhyme. He could wear a T-shirt with a wide-eyed pink kitten on the front, and go round Piccadilly Gardens saying things like

'Hope your day is filled with wonder and cheer / You make me happy whenever you're near'. He'd probably get chased around by lads. Beaten up outside the Burger King.

She doesn't say it back. She says, 'Let's go.'

Craig is unsure whether she means 'Let's go home' or 'Let's go and look at the grave'.

'Look, I'm sorry,' he says. I hope your day is filled with wonder and cheer. 'My life isn't working out how I imagined,' he says.

She sighs.

'I'm getting a bit sick of your melodrama,' she says.

'Fuck's sake,' he says.

You make me happy whenever you're near.

Later on they will go to Craig's room and lie on a bed and hammer the final coffin nails into their relationship and then start to cry and say irreversible things and look on the Internet for the number of a local taxi firm.

But first Emma starts to walk back towards the grave and Craig follows her. The goth couple have left their bunch of flowers and gone home. It's about to rain. They go up and have a look. Emma's seen it before. It's Craig's first time. He doesn't know what he was expecting, but this isn't it. This is just a grave. An average-looking grey headstone, with carved white lettering. There's no quote or lyrics. Craig was at least expecting lyrics or something. And it has his first name on it, too; he feels strange, he wasn't expecting that.

'I can't imagine he's actually buried here,' Craig says.

He stands on the bit of grass that's still newer looking than the rest. Six feet below his feet, apparently, is a coffin with Morrissey's body in it.

'All those people, all those lives, where are they now?' Emma says.

'What was that?'

'Nothing.'

Contributors

Jenn Ashworth was born in Preston, studied in Cambridge and Manchester, and divides her time between her job as a prison librarian and her writing. Her blog www.jennashworth.blogspot.com won the 2008 Manchester Blog Awards, and her first novel – *A Kind of Intimacy* – is out with Arcadia.

Matt Beaumont has written six novels. His favourite Smiths song is 'Asleep'. His favourite vegetable is peas.

Rhonda Carrier has always felt Mancunian but only became so, in an honorary capacity, three years ago, when she moved there with her husband, the novelist Conrad Williams, and her young sons. Although she works mainly as a travel writer, Rhonda, who was born in the Midlands in 1968, has had her short fiction appear in a wide variety of publications, including *Neonlit: the Time Out Book of New Writing II*, the *Time Out Book of London Short Stories*, *Image* magazine, the *French Literary Review* and *'68, New Stories from Children of the Revolution*.

James Flint (www.jamesflint.net) is the author of the novels *Habitus*, *52 Ways to Magic America* which won the Amazon.co.uk Bursary Award for the year 2000; and *The Book of Ash*, winner of a 2003 Arts Council Writers' Award. He has also published a short story collection, *Soft Apocalypse – Twelve Tales from the Turn of the Millennium*. His short fiction has appeared in collections published by Penguin Books, the New English Library and the ICA. When it was published in France in 1992, *Habitus* was judged among the top five foreign novels of that year's Rentrée Littéraire. In 2002 one of Flint's stories ('The Nuclear Train') was filmed for Channel 4 by the director Dan Saul. Flint also scripted the film installation *Little Earth* (www.londonfieldworks.com/little/main.html). In December 2006, Flint took a full-time position as Arts and Features Editor (Digital) at the Telegraph Media Group. In 2007 he oversaw the set-up and launch of Telegraph Earth. He is currently General Manager of Telegraph TV.

David Gaffney is the author of two collections of short stories, *Sawn-off Tales* and *Aromabingo*, and the novel, *Never, Never*. He lives in Manchester. See www.davidgaffney.co.uk.

Mike Gayle is the author of a whole bunch of books including the novels: *My Legendary Girlfriend, Mr Commitment, Turning Thirty, Dinner For Two, His 'n' Hers, Brand New Friend, Wish You Were Here, The Life and Soul of the Party* and one non-fiction work entitled *The To Do List* based around the year in his life that he spent attempting to tackle a 1,277 item long to-do list. His journalism has appeared in the *Guardian, The Times* and the *Daily Telegraph* as well as *FHM*, and *Girl Talk* (the number one read for eight-year-old girls). Google him at your peril.

James Hopkin has lived in Manchester (the blue side), Berlin and Kraków, not to mention a few other towns, ports and dosshouses across Europe. His first novel, *Winter under Water*, is now out in paperback, as is a small book of two stories, *Even the Crows Say Kraków*. His new novel, *Say Goodbye to Breakfast*, is coming soon.

Nic Kelman is a novelist and non-fiction writer living in New York City. His first novel, *girls*, was an international bestseller published in the UK by Serpent's Tail. His second book, *Video Game Art*, the first art history of video games, is available worldwide. He writes short stories and essays for a variety of publications and anthologies.

Chris Killen was born in 1981 and is currently living in Manchester. His first novel, *The Bird Room*, was published in early 2009. He also writes a blog: www.dayofmoustaches.blogspot.com.

Alison MacLeod grew up in Canada and has lived in England since 1987. She has published two novels, *The Changeling* and *The Wave Theory of Angels*. Her short fiction has been published in a variety of magazines and collections, and her story collection, *Fifteen Modern Tales of Attraction*, was released in 2007. She is the recipient of the 2008 Olive Cook Award for Short Fiction, and teaches English and Creative Writing at the University of Chichester. She lives in Brighton. For more information about her work, see www.alison-macleod.com.

Mil Millington is an English author with vaguely girlish wrists. He was named by the *Guardian* as one of the Top Five Debut Novelists of 2002 and has now written four books, the latest being *Instructions for Living Someone Else's Life*. He is also the founder of the cult website thingsmygirlfriendandihavearguedabout.com and co-founder of the even cultier theweekly.co.uk. He writes for various newspapers and magazines and he is not remotely above appearing on radio or television to mouth off on subjects he knows nothing about. Mil lives in the West Midlands with his girlfriend and their two children.

Jeff Noon was born in Manchester. He was trained in the visual arts, and was musically active in the punk scene before starting to write plays for the theatre. His first novel, *Vurt*, was published in 1993 and went on to win the Arthur C. Clarke Award. His other books include *Automated Alice*, *Pixel Juice*, *Needle in the Groove* and *Falling Out of Cars*. His plays include *Woundings*, *The Modernists* and *Dead Code*.

Gina Ochsner is the author of a book of stories, *People I Wanted to Be* and a novel, *The Russian Dreambook of Colour and Flight*. She is now writing a novel set in Latvia.

Catherine O'Flynn's first novel, *What Was Lost*, won the Costa First Novel Award 2007. She lives and writes in the middle of England. She very much hopes The Smiths never reform.

Kate Pullinger's books include *The Mistress of Nothing* and *A Little Stranger* (both published by Serpent's Tail), *Weird Sister* and *The Last Time I Saw Jane* and the short story collections *My Life as a Girl in a Men's Prison* and *Tiny Lies*. Her current digital fiction projects include her multiple award-winning collaboration with Chris Joseph on *Inanimate Alice*, a multimedia episodic digital fiction – www.inanimatealice.com – and *Flight Paths* – www.flightpaths. net – a networked novel, created on and through the Internet. Kate Pullinger is Reader in Creative Writing and New Media at De Montfort University. Find her online at www.katepullinger.com.

Graham Rae, originally from Falkirk in Scotland, is now resident in the Chicago suburbs. He lives there with his lovely wife Ellen, their beautiful toddler daughter Fiona Leah, and their dignified old man cat Bailey. First published in America at the age of eighteen in the horror film magazine *Deep Red*. Graham has also written for *Cinefantastique* and *American Cinematographer*, though how he managed this from Falkirk without a cinematic background he is still not entirely sure. The thirty-nine-year-old has also written for the English literary journal *Pen Pusher* and www.laurahird.com, among others. 'Back to the Old House' is his first published short story. He has also just finished his first novel.

Jeremy Sheldon is the author of two works of fiction, *The Comfort Zone* and *The Smiling Affair*.

Nick Stone is the author of *Mr Clarinet* and *King of Swords*. His favourite Smiths album is *Strangeways, Here We Come*.

Scarlett Thomas was born in London in 1972. Her novels include *Bright Young Things, Going Out, PopCo* and *The End of Mr Y*, which has been translated into twenty-two languages, and was longlisted for the Orange Prize. In 2001 she was included in the *Independent on Sunday*'s list of the UK's 20 best young writers. She currently teaches English Literature and Creative Writing at the University of Kent.

Born and raised in Reno, Nevada, **Willy Vlautin** has published two novels, *The Motel Life* and *Northline*. Vlautin founded the band Richmond Fontaine in 1994. The band has produced seven studio albums to date, plus a handful of live recordings and EPs. Vlautin currently resides in Scappoose, Oregon, and is working on Richmond Fontaine's eighth album and his third novel. An avid fan of horse racing, Vlautin can often be found writing behind a closed circuit monitor at Portland Meadows racetrack.

Helen Walsh is the author of two novels, *Brass* and *Once Upon a Time in England*. She lives on Merseyside.

Peter Wild is the co-author of *Before the Rain*, and the editor of *The Flash*, *Perverted by Language: Fiction inspired by The Fall* and *The Empty Page: Fiction inspired by Sonic Youth* (published by Social Disease and Serpent's Tail, respectively).

Charlie Williams's novels *Deadfolk, Fags and Lager, King of the Road* and *Stairway to Hell* are published by Serpent's Tail. He has had many short stories published across various genres and has lately branched out into screenplays, his first short film *ARK* getting some attention on the festival circuit. He lives in Worcester with his wife and two children. Read more at www.charliewilliams.net.

John Williams lives and works in his hometown of Cardiff. His latest book is a biography of Michael X. He is currently at work on a book about the early years of Shirley Basset, of which he suspects Morrissey might approve.

Acknowledgements

The editor would like to thanks: The Smiths, John Williams, Pete Ayrton, Anna-Marie Fitzgerald, Niamh Murray, Ruthie Petrie, Janine Bullman, Simon Trewin, David Gaffney, Sarah Hymas and all at Litfest, Richard Evans, Nick Johnstone, Conrad Williams, Dave Swann, Matthew David Scott, Hannah Westland, Alex Holroyd, Jessica Axe, Angela Robertson, Anna Frame, Nicola Barker, Lil Gary, Pam Ribbeck, Merck Mercuriadis, Alison MacLeod, Matt Thorne, Laura Hird, Jess Walters, Jeanette Perez, Alberto Rojas and all at HarperCollins, Chris Killen, Sally Cook and all at No Point in Not Being Friends and, as always, Louisa, Harriet, Samuel & Martha.

ALSO BY
PETER WILD

NOISE

Fiction Inspired by Sonic Youth

**With an Introduction by
Lee Ranaldo of Sonic Youth**

ISBN 978-0-06-166929-3 (paperback)

**NOISE
FICTION INSPIRED
BY SONIC YOUTH**
EDITED BY PETER WILD
WITH AN INTRODUCTION BY LEE RANALDO OF SONIC YOUTH

For more than twenty-five years, the antimelodic "noise" of Sonic Youth has assaulted us, exhilarated us, inspired us. Why? Katherine Dunn says it's because they operate in the foggy world between the real and the surreal. Mary Gaitskill says that Sonic Youth caught her, years ago, when she was falling. J. Robert Lennon says it's because Sonic Youth rip it apart. Emily Maguire was hooked because once she was in love with chaos. Their sound is caustic, elemental, nihilistic—and quite unlike any other cult band ever to achieve rock godhood. In *Noise*, twenty-one great literary voices offer short fiction based on or inspired by songs from Sonic Youth—a raucous coupling of music and literature featuring marrow-colored goo, severed hands and abandoned babies, Patty Hearst watching the apocalypse on TV, and other unruly images of the Zeitgeist.

Contributors

Hiag Akmakjian • Christopher Coake • Katherine Dunn • Mary Gaitskill • Rebecca Godfrey • Laird Hunt • Shelley Jackson • J. Robert Lennon • Samuel Ligon • Emily Maguire • Tom McCarthy • Scott Mebus • Eileen Myles • Catherine O'Flynn • Emily Carter Roiphe • Kevin Sampsell • Steven Sherrill • Matt Thorne • Rachel Trezise • Jess Walter • Peter Wild